SUBURBAN

A Novel

Roy A. Teel Jr.

The Iron Eagle Series: Book Twenty-Two

NARROWAY PRESS

An Imprint of Narroway Publishing LLC.

Narroway Publishing LLC.
Imprint: Narroway Press
P.O. Box 1431
Lake Arrowhead, California 92352

First Edition

Hardcover: ISBN: 978-1-943107-33-9

Teel, Roy A., 1965-
    Suburban: A Novel, The Iron Eagle Series: Book Twenty-Two /
Roy A. Teel Jr. – 1st ed.– Lake Arrowhead, Calif.: Narroway Press
c2019. p.; cm. ISBN: 978-1-943107-33-9 (Hardcover)

1. Hard-Boiled – Fiction. 2. Police, FBI – Fiction 3. Murder – Fiction 4. Serial Killers – Fiction
5. Mystery – Fiction 6. Suspense – Fiction. 7. Graphic Violence – Fiction. 8. Graphic-sex – Fiction
9. Thriller- Fiction
I. Title.

Book Editing: Finesse Writing and Editing LLC
Cover and Book Design: Priceless Digital Media
Author Photo: Z

For those fortunate enough to have survived.

Also by Roy A. Teel Jr.

Nonfiction:

The Way, The Truth, and The Lies: How the Gospels
Mislead Christians about Jesus' True Message
Against the Grain: The American Mega-church
and its Culture of Control

Fiction:

The Light of Darkness: Dialogues in Death: Collected Short Stories
And God Laughed, A Novel

The Iron Eagle Novel Series:

Rise of The Iron Eagle: Book One
Evil and the Details: Book Two
Rome Is Burning: Book Three
Operation Red Alert: Book Four
A Model for Murder: Book Five
Devil's Chair: Book Six
Death's Valley: Book Seven
Cleansing: Book Eight
Rampage: Book Nine
Dark Canyon: Book Ten
Deliverance: Book Eleven
Phoenix: Book Twelve
Pray: Book Thirteen
Equality of Mercy: Book Fourteen
Metro: Book Fifteen
Reaper: Book Sixteen

"Poverty, to be picturesque, should be rural. Suburban misery is as hideous as it is pitiable."

— Anthony Trollope

"I grew up in the suburbs of Los Angeles with neat little houses all in a row, depicting a scene of serenity and happiness. Nothing could be further from the truth for the suburbs are the perfect breeding ground for savagery and unimaginable horror, wrapped in an illusion of happiness."

— Roy A. Teel Jr.

SEAL OF THE IRON EAGLE™

Table of Contents

CHAPTER ONE

"That's exactly why he's so popular."

John and Sara landed at Santa Monica Airport after two weeks on vacation. Sara took a deep breath and said, "Oh, fuck this. I'm going back to St. Lucia."

John started laughing as the pilots pulled their bags, and their driver put them into the waiting limo. "Come on, honey. We had two weeks of uninterrupted time. No cellphones, no internet. Just the two of us." Sara nodded as she got into the car that whisked them back to their home in Malibu.

Sam was sitting on the smoker's bench outside her office and staring off into space. Jade and Jim were watching her from his office window, and Jade said, "I had to come, Jim. I just couldn't hold up the report."

"I know, I know. Sam's taking Maria's death hard. She feels responsible."

"She didn't put the booze in Maria's mouth and force her to swallow it. She didn't drive the car at ninety miles an hour onto a well-marked closed freeway offramp into the back of a dump truck."

"You don't know any of the back story about that night, do you?" Jade shook her head. "Then don't pass judgment. While Maria's death was tragic, it was serendipitous in ways that you will most likely never know. Sam is feeling tremendously conflicted and has been since she got the call from you the night of the accident. She loved Maria with all her heart. She's broken, and I don't know that her heart will ever be right again."

"Jesus, Jim. I've never heard you speak like this."

"Well, there are times for sarcasm and humor to break the tension, but this isn't one of them. Sam is broken, and with John and Sara coming back today I don't know how she is going to react to seeing everyone again."

"I called her once the LAPD identified Maria's car. Sam was on scene in less than ten minutes. Maria was still inside; the scene was horrific, but Sam stood strong asking for her own investigators and took the case away from the LAPD and CHP."

"Sam is a strong woman, but this is one of those situations that no matter how you look at it, it's just a plain waste of love and life."

Mark Bench held his weeping daughter Judy as two detectives from the West Valley division of the LAPD questioned her about her attack. Judy was doing her best to hold it together as was Mark. Her younger sister Tabitha had been sent out of the room, so she wouldn't hear the details.

"So, you were drugged and assaulted by Sally Owen, one of your school friends, at a party?" one of the detectives asked.

"Yes."

"And the attack was videotaped?"

"That's what I was told."

"Did you see the video?"

"No. I was heavily drugged. Sally kept bringing me drinks, and the next thing I remember I was coming to, and she and this monster of a man were telling me that Sally and I had had sex and that if I told anyone he would rape and kill my sister."

"The rape kit is in for processing."

Mark frowned. "I'm the head of pathology at Northridge Hospital. I have already processed all of the evidence. The DNA on my daughter's body is positively identified as that of Sally Owen."

One of the detectives asked, "Are you and Sally close, Judy?"

"I suppose. We've been friends since preschool and have been in the same school all our lives."

"And do you usually go to parties with Sally?"

"I have been to a few pool parties at her house. We sleep over at each other's homes a couple of times a month. We've been friends our whole lives."

"Have you and Sally ever played together sexually before this?"

Mark got red-faced. "What the hell kind of question is that?"

"Mr. Bench, your daughter is making very, very serious accusations against a lifelong friend. Now, we are going to investigate this, and we take this very seriously, but I have been a detective for twenty years, sir, and I have had many experiences where a young man or woman got into a consensual sexual situation and suddenly changed their story. I take my job seriously, sir, and I'm going to ask some hard questions that you and your daughter aren't going to like, but that is to make sure that we don't send a case to the DA that could ruin a young girl's life. Now, Judy, have you ever talked about sex with Sally or experimented when you were at one of your sleepovers? There's nothing wrong with any of those things."

"Detective, I'm a virgin. I have never had sex. I'm not attracted to girls. I have never fooled around or experimented with Sally or any other girls. Sally is the one who is always shooting off her mouth and saying that she makes all this money and that she has sex with people.

I only went to the party because I was tired of hearing what I thought were lies."

"And at this party you were paid for sex?"

Judy pulled out her purse and handed the detective twenty-five-hundred dollars that Sally had given her. "This is what she gave me after I came to. She said, 'Not bad for an hour's work, huh?' I didn't remember anything. I thought that I was having a dream or nightmare, but it was real."

"Look, detective, my daughters don't lie. I told you I tested the samples, and the DNA belongs to Sally Owen. I understand your concern, and there's no one more shocked than me at all that Judy has shared. I have known Sally and her family since before Sally and her sister were born. Mary Owen and I are very, very close friends, and we are both widowed single parents who lost our spouses in the great fire. My wife and Mary's husband were firefighters for the City of Los Angeles and died trying to save lives. I have called Mary, but she hasn't returned my call yet. Now, I don't know how all of this started, but Judy says there was a man there who threatened her sister if Judy didn't go to another party next week and have sex with him. What about that?"

"We had Judy work with our sketch artists, but she really doesn't recall much about the man outside of his smell, so there isn't a lot we can do with that. And your daughter doesn't remember where the party was. She claims it was at a house she has never been to before, yet she has no other information. No address, no phone number. She doesn't know who owned the home."

"I'm telling the truth!" Judy shouted.

"We have spoken to Sally, and she tells a much different story about what happened."

"What is she telling you?"

"I can't disclose that information right now, but it isn't anything close to the story you are telling."

"My daughter is the goddamn victim not the perp. You're going to take the word of the alleged perp over the victim?"

"No, sir, that's not what I'm saying. What I'm saying is there are two different stories here, and we have to take both into account."

Mark stood up and said, "Get out of my house. You're sitting here making my daughter feel like this was her fault when she was the victim. You're trying to twist facts, and I'm not going to tolerate it. I will get to the bottom of this myself."

Both men stood, and the lead detective said, "These are children, Mr. Bench. Teenage girls with differing stories. Don't try to take the law into your own hands, sir. All that is going to do is land you in prison and your children in foster care. I do understand your frustration. My own daughter was brutally raped several years ago by a stranger, and he has never been found. I had to hand the investigation off to a fellow officer as I knew if I got the perp I would kill him. So, I do understand the feelings you're going through as a parent, but level heads are what will prevail here. I'm sorry for your loss. I know many, many people who lost loved ones in the great fire. I'm grateful to your wife and others who paid the ultimate price to protect lives. I will get this report written up, and I will send it over to the DA for review."

The two men left. Once they were gone, Mark sat Judy down and asked, "Honey, you were drugged with Ecstasy?"

"That's what Sally told me she gave me."

"I checked your blood, and you had pretty high levels of the drug in your body. Have you ever used that drug before?"

"No, Daddy. I have never done any drugs."

"You also had pretty high levels of alcohol in your blood. Was this the first time you ever had alcohol?" Judy looked away, and Mark asked softly, "Honey, have you had alcohol before?" Judy nodded. "With Sally?"

"No. I had some at summer parties, pool parties, but never any drugs, Daddy. I have never done any drugs."

Mark was seated with his hands clasped in front of him and asked, "Do you remember our talk about taking open beverages from friends or strangers?"

"Daddy, I never thought Sally would do something like that to me."

"What have I told you about parties and drinks?"

"Never take a beverage that isn't sealed from anyone."

"You broke the first rule of going out. Now, I'm going to speak to Mary and even Sally if I can, but I have to agree with the officers that we don't want to ruin Sally's life over things that happened while you were drunk and drugged. Ecstasy is a powerful drug, and it lowers inhibitions and can even put you in such a suggestable state that you could have had sex with Sally and at the same time hallucinated some of the events."

"Are you saying I could have been talked into sex with Sally and that the man was a figment of my imagination?"

"It's possible, sweetheart. It's possible."

Sally Owen was sitting on the couch in the family room as her mother paced while talking on the phone. "Look, Mark, Sally and Judy have been friends their whole lives. I don't know what would have possessed them to fool around, but you and I know it's a part of young adulthood."

Mark was in the backyard of his home. Judy had gone to her room to lie down, and Tabitha was playing with dolls inside. "Mary, Judy is really shook up. My daughter is not a lesbian."

"Have you ever had sex with another man, Mark?"

"I fooled around a little as a teenager and in college."

"So, you tested your sexuality. I did the same thing in high school and college. Shit, for a short time I thought I was bi."

"What does this have to do with Sally and Judy?"

"I wasn't home when Sally had the party, but I knew about it. I have encouraged both of my girls to experiment from a young age. Sally is sexually adventurous, and I'm not going to apologize for that."

"She raped my daughter."

"That's not how Sally tells it. She says that Judy showed up at the house for the party. Sally had spiked some punch with vodka. There were several dozen kids here from school who saw Judy come in and watched her walk around with Sally. Sally admits that she offered Judy some Ecstasy, which Judy accepted and took herself, which I have strongly punished Sally for doing. I am sorry about that."

"Where the hell did she get the drug?"

"My stash. I like to use it when having sex or just to relax. Anyway, Judy started to get physical with Sally, and they started making out, and other kids were laughing and making fun of them, and they went into the sitting room off my bedroom and had sex. This was not a rape. It was consensual sex between two young girls."

"And the twenty-five hundred dollars that Sally gave to Judy?"

"It was a joke. Sally has been telling other kids at school that she makes money having sex, and Judy has been calling her a liar for years. She just didn't want to look like a liar, that's all."

"Where the hell would Sally get that kind of money?"

"She got into my safe and took some of my emergency cash."

Mark's shoulders slumped. "Jesus, Mary! Sally stole money from you to validate herself to Judy?"

"That's the long and short of it, Mark."

"What about the man that Judy says threatened her and her sister?"

"There was no man at the house, Mark. I don't know where that came from. Perhaps a reaction to the drug or the alcohol. There was no man here at the house, and there were, as I stated, dozens of kids who were here who can attest to that."

"Why would Sally be telling kids at school she makes money having sex?"

"It's a fantasy. Sally's in treatment with a therapist and has been for a few years. The theory is that she's watched one too many cop shows and movies that have dramatized the sex trade in a way that makes it seem attractive to young people."

"What have the cops told you?"

"Not much. They interviewed Sally and, from what I understand, several kids who were at the party. Sally maintains that Judy took the drug on her own and that she did not slip it to her. I did have to do some explaining about how Sally got the drug, which could end up with me being charged with child endangerment. Sally has been duly chastised, and I suppose we'll just have to wait and see what happens."

"Shit, Mary. I don't want this to turn into a damn federal case. Judy has never lied to me before, and I trust her."

"Hold onto that thought, Mark. I used to think the same of Sally, but she has told me her fair share of tall tales. However, she is not a predator or sexual deviant. She stays out after curfew now and then and drinks at parties, most of which are held here at the house. And if she does drink when she is out, she always calls home, and I make sure she is picked up if I'm not home. To me, this was just a case of kids being kids and exploring their bodies. Unfortunately, Judy had a bad experience."

"Okay, Mary. I'm going to leave this alone for now. Judy said the man threatened to hurt her little sister if she didn't show up for sex next week."

"Well, I don't believe that there was a man, so I don't think that there is any threat to Tabitha." Mark was nodding as he sat on the patio. He was about to end the conversation when Mary asked, "Are you seeing anyone?"

"No. I've been working a lot of hours, and the only people I see are either my lab techs, doctors who are either married or gay, and the occasional patient, and I can't go down that road. You?"

"Not right now. Same story. Busy with work. I opened two new offices in the Inland Empire, and now I'm looking at opening offices in San Diego and Oceanside. So, I'm not home a lot. Marina takes care of the kids."

"Well...I'm off tonight. How about dinner?"

"Oh, Mark, you know I love you, but we tried that after the fires. We are oil and water in so many ways."

"Not between the sheets. As I recall, you said I was the best lover you had ever had."

Mary laughed and said, "That's true."

"We have been running in crazy directions. Why don't we try a friends with benefits deal?"

Mary smiled big and said, "I think that could be worked out."

"Great! I'll pick you up at seven."

"Okay…but no more about the girls."

"Agreed. How about Sergio's?" She agreed, and Mark said, "Great! I will see you at seven."

Mary hung up the phone, looked at Sally, and asked, "Judy? Of all the people to try and recruit, you tried to get Judy?"

"I'm sorry, Mom."

"You're sorry? Look, Sally, I started this business from the ground up. I am well respected in the community. If you want to draw in other girls and boys to augment your own income and, of course, save your own body from being banged into oblivion, I get it, but keep your closest friends out of it. We now have the cops looking into our shit, and you know that it only takes one wrong move to throw years of work down the drain and send you, me, and others to prison for years. And don't kid yourself about being tried as a minor. You'll be tried as an adult and branded as a sex offender for the rest of your life. I'll call Pierce and tell him to get his boys to back off. He doesn't know the cops are involved."

"What about Al?"

"That's where you made your biggest mistake. Al Fleece is a fuckin' whack job. He's a physically repulsive raging alcoholic that sits in that damn film room beating off to the kiddie films and forcing himself onto the young ones. The fact that Pierce allowed Al to get that close to Judy is really, really bad. I don't think that Pierce knows what was said. It's not like him to have threats made after a first visit. He's too charming for that. Al must have really liked Judy and that in and of itself is a problem."

"You don't think Al would hurt Tabitha, do you?"

"You've seen what he can do. He's Pierce's enforcer, so to speak. If the property gets out of line, he puts them back in line, and he loves doing it, especially before they go to Hugh." Sally had a look of concern on her face, and Mary said, "I'll call Pierce. He'll deal with Al. Just stay away from Judy for a while. I'm going to fuck Mark, which always works to keep him happy. Hopefully, we can sweep this whole situation under the rug."

Sally nodded, and Mary called out for Marina who entered the room. "I know I asked for steak for dinner, but I'm going out, so make the girls what they want."

"Yes, Ms. Mary."

Marina turned to walk away, but Mary stopped her and asked, "How are your boys doing?"

"Good, Ms. Mary, very good. They are healthy and happy."

"That's good to hear, Marina. And your husband?"

"Paco is doing well."

"I heard that there was an altercation with his employer."

"Oh no, Ms. Mary. It was a misunderstanding. Paco doesn't speak English as well as me."

"You speak good English because I've had you since you were five."

"Yes, Ms. Mary, and I am so happy."

"So, Paco got beat pretty good, I hear."

Marina's face dropped a bit, and her eyes filled with tears. "He was beaten badly. That is why I was home last night…to put salve on the whip marks on the back of his body."

"I hope he learned a lesson."

"Oh, he did, Ms. Mary. He will be much more deliberate when he speaks to the master."

"I understand Pedro is starting work at the factory this week?"

"Yes. He is looking forward to it."

"He's a hard worker. I think he will do well. How old is he now?"

"Eighteen and just graduated from high school."

"And your youngest?"

"Salvador is doing well in school."

"I hear he is also very popular with our gay clients."

"Salvador likes the gay sex very much. He has since he was seven. He has really embraced the lifestyle and hopes to stay working in the brothel and not have to go to the factory."

"Well, he is well liked and a bit in demand, so I don't see any reason for him to leave the brothel when he graduates. I have seen him in the dungeon. He is a really good whipping boy."

"He really loves it, Ms. Mary. I don't understand it because it hurts, but he likes doing whatever the master wants, and no is not in his vocabulary."

"That's exactly why he's so popular." Marina nodded, and Mary excused her. She looked at Sally and said, "Do you see what we are trying to do here?"

Sally nodded. "Create a thrifty class of slaves?"

"Yes, look at Marina. I have had had her since before your father died. He used her for sex in her younger years because he had the urge for children but didn't want to do anything to you. I was pregnant with Casey when he died, but for those first five years that we had Marina she was a great outlet for your father and a few of his friends. Now, look at her! She works freely here at the house, comes and goes without any issues, as do her husband and children. That's what we are trying to build. A class of slaves that are well rounded and can serve multiple purposes for our customers. So, keep your recruiting to the unwashed masses, early and mid-teens, and steer clear of your close classmates. If there will be a chance for our undoing, that will be it."

CHAPTER TWO

"How do you know so much?"

It was just after seven, and Chris and Karen were having dinner when the phone rang. Karen placed her fork down gently on her plate and said, "For two weeks it has been nearly silent in this house, and it hasn't even been twelve hours, and you and I both know who's calling."

Chris answered the phone. "Hello? Uh…I see. Really? Well, that's just great. I'm in total shock. How did this happen? Really? Well, I'm sure my wife will be as flabbergasted as I am." Chris hung up the phone and said, "We won the Nigerian lottery and need to collect our fifteen-million-dollar prize." Karen burst out in laughter and picked up her fork and started eating again.

John and Sara were having a light meal with a glass of wine and chatting when Jim walked into the dining room. "Two weeks without a word from you."

"That's right, Jim. Two whole weeks by my order," Sara said as she put a piece of food in her mouth.

John nodded and invited Jim to sit. "The world didn't come to an end in my absence, I see."

"Only one…but you knew about that before you left."

"How is Sam holding up?"

"She's not."

"I read over Jade's report on Maria's death. It was tragic. It's one of the reasons we don't drink and drive."

"Well, Maria was in drunken hysterics when Sam last saw her. She'd narrowed down the identity of the Eagle to you or me, and she learned that Sam not only knew his identity but had even helped him." John continued eating, and Jim shook his head. "Aren't you the least bit concerned about Sam? Do you have any remorse over Maria's death?"

"Why would I have remorse?"

"Wrong word. Don't you feel a tad bit guilty over Maria's death?"

"I didn't kill her. She killed herself. She went off on a tangent and ended up careening into the back of a dump truck and decapitating herself."

Jim walked over to the wet bar, poured himself a scotch, and said after taking several sips, "I don't think Sam is going to recover."

Sara interrupted and said, "Sam will be just fine. This was a tragic accident caused by trauma and Maria's own recklessness. Sam just has to have time to mourn, Jim. You know this. Everyone mourns differently. It's been barely two weeks. You don't get over a death that fast."

Jim nodded. "You're right. When you're right, you're mother fuckin' right. Actually, I think that you're both WRONG and that Sam is at the least a suicide threat."

"If you feel she's a threat to herself or others, have her committed for seventy-two-hours on a psych hold."

"I'm not there yet, but I'm close. Have you spoken to Chris since you got home?"

"No. I'll see him in the office in the morning. Let him have one more night of peace before he jumps back in the fire with me." Jim nodded. John said, "So...I have looked over the new cases in my office in the past two weeks. Anything new in your department?"

"A couple of homicides, some drug arrests. The usual stuff. Nothing needing the Eagle's attention."

"Sweet. Perhaps we're entering a quiet season going into the middle of April. That would be nice for a change."

Jim swigged down his drink then stood up and said, "Well, I'm going home to Cindy. She's creating something new for dinner, and you know what that means?"

Sara laughed and said, "You'll be eating at Santiago's?"

Jim nodded and laughed. "I'm starting to think that she's making bad meals on purpose just so I will take her out."

John had his mouth full of food as he spoke, "Yes, but the only place she gets to go to eat is Santiago's."

"Hey, she likes what she likes."

Jim left, and Sara asked, "Do you feel anything over Maria's death?"

John sipped his wine and said, "Relief. Happy that I didn't have to deal with her like Jill Makin."

"You put Jill out of her misery. She killed herself...right?"

"Yes, much like what happened to Maria. Jill tried to kill me after revealing she knew I was the Eagle."

"Jill's death was an accident."

"Indeed. She shot at me. I hid, and she fell down the side of a hill on a construction site and was barely able to breathe. I knew there was no way to save her, so I put her out of her misery."

"But she also knew what her grandfather and his friend had done. What was his name?"

"Roskowski. A brutal man who died badly at the Eagle's hands. Yes, Jill knew Roskowski's secret as well as her grandfather's, so I would have killed her eventually for her own deeds."

"And Maria? Had she lived, she was a threat to your identity. What would you have done with her?"

"That's really asking for speculation."

"Would you have killed her?"

"Of course not."

"Then how would you keep your secret?"

"In the worst-case scenario, I would have grabbed her, and we would have used your secret cocktail to wipe her memory clean like we have others."

Sara nodded slowly and said, "I hadn't thought about that, but you're right. We could have taken part of her memory." She put her fork down, took a sip of her wine, and said, "I wish we could have gotten to her before the accident."

"You can wish all you like, Sara. We can't undo what has been done, and Maria Martinez has been cremated and is in an urn on Sam's bookcase in her bedroom, from what I understand. Sam is a strong woman. She will get a grasp on this and realize that the only person to blame for this is Maria."

Mark kissed the girls and told Judy to have Tabitha in bed by nine. Judy nodded and as soon as Mark was gone Tabitha said, "So do you want to play house?"

Judy smiled and said, "Let's eat our dinner, and you can watch one of your videos then bed."

The two girls were seated at the table, and Tabitha asked, "Why is Dad going out with Mary Owen if Sally was so mean to you?"

"I didn't know he was going out with Mary. How do you know?"

"I heard him on the phone with her while you were napping. They are going to be friends with benefits. What does that mean?"

"Not now, Tabby. Eat your dinner. You only have a little over two hours before bed." Judy had a look of anger on her face as she ate and asked Tabitha, "Did Dad say he would be home late?"

"No…but if he has sex with Mary he'll be home really late." Judy nodded and ate while looking up information on rape on her tablet.

Pierce Tallon was in a rage with Al Fleece. "You threatened to rape her sister after our first photo shoot with Judy?"

"Hey, I like that girl, and she's a hot, young virgin. Why are you so up in arms? It's why you keep me around…to make sure that the talent works and keeps working, right?"

"Al, you're an animal. I keep you around because your sheer presence is so menacing it keeps the boys and girls in line. You have never killed anyone that I know of, and it's going to stay that way."

"Look, Pierce, you pay me to keep the people in line, and that's what I do. I have a rap sheet as you know for molestation. As for killing, that's none of your damn business. I went a little over the top with the Bench kid. I'm sorry."

"Well, your 'over the top' made Bench call the cops." Al looked panicked, and Pierce said, "Relax. There's no harm. Mary is taking care of it with Sally, and the cops are treating this as two young girls fooling around and nothing more."

Al was still distraught and asked, "We live in one of Mary's rentals in Woodland Hills. What if Judy can lead the cops back to the house?"

"She can't. Sally wiped the phone and GPS. Everything is covered. Mary placed the party at her house, and the kids are all corroborating the story, so we're safe."

"You mean the operation is safe. I know I can be an ass at times, but we have a great thing going here, and I don't want anything fucking it up."

"Nothing is going to fuck it up as long as you control yourself. How many do we have in the porno rooms?"

"We have six in the kiddie porn rooms, five in the teenage porn rooms."

"Are the teens streaming?"

"Yeah. Several of the boys are doing bareback, and that's our second most popular channel next to the kiddies."

"How are the ratings on the teen live chat and stream?"

"A little weak. We need some new blood. Several of the girls have been on the stream for a couple of years, and the channel is getting stale."

"I'll talk to Mary about that. How about domestic operations?"

"Really good. Mary has had both Sally and Marina recruiting. Marina's youngest is a hot commodity for our gay pedophile feeds. He's doing bareback scenes now. I have to tell you that kid is really good, and he loves his boys. He has brought in dozens of other kids to the gay life, and we are making bank off of him. His older brother has been working to recruit his friends, and we have ten boys and fifteen girls at the house in Van Nuys who are about ready to go into domestic service."

"The boys are going to the fields?"

"Yeah, and the girls are going into private homes as domestic slaves."

"And our biggest customer? Is she taking the girls?"

"Every one of them. She has buyers for all of them."

"Tonya already has buyers for all of them?"

"Slave labor, Pierce. It's in major demand here in LA. From the upper to the middle-class, as long as they can get the labor cheap and control them, we will always be in business."

Tonya Hart was finishing up a quick meal before heading to her next showing. She had swallowed her last bite of sushi when she received a text and pressed the call back button. "Hi Mary. How are you doing?"

"I'm getting ready to meet Mark Bench for dinner."

Tonya laughed. "Reviving old flames?"

"Hardly. My daughter tried recruiting his bitch of a daughter, and I'm trying to placate the situation and keep the cops out of my life."

"You better protect this thing. I have a shit load of money on the line, as do you. Al called me on the kids, and I have placed them all in the auction for next week. I have them with Hugh Masters for the final breaking, and then all I need is one final inspection with the buyers, and we will have a sale."

"You're talking like this on the phone?"

"Relax. It's encrypted. So, tell me more about you and Mark."

"There's nothing to tell. I'd rather him fuck me than the cops."

"The cops will literally fuck you if you get the right ones, you know."

"Thanks, Tonya. I'd rather not have a cop learn the truth and blackmail me."

"Good point. I have to get to a showing in Hidden Hills. A twenty-five-million-dollar estate."

"The buyer hot on it?"

"Oh, I think he is going to be all over it…if you know what I mean."

"I do. You use that sweet little body to sell real estate, and you do it so well."

"What did you think of the nudes I sent you?"

"Beautiful. Your plastic surgeon does incredible work. I would swear you were twenty and not thirty-five."

"I'm still a little unhappy with the boob job, but he took care of everything else so well."

"You look damn hot, but I didn't see everything. Have you had some changes?"

"No. I am still thinking about that. After all, if it ain't broke, don't fix it."

Tabitha had gone to bed, and Judy was sitting alone in her room reading up on rape. She'd bookmarked multiple helplines and written a note to herself. *'Do you really want to get anyone else involved?'* There was one rape hotline that did have her attention, and it was a child exploitation line. It was nearing midnight, and her father wasn't home. She read over the information on the site again and then dialed the number.

"Exploitation Hotline. This is Andrea. How can I help?" There was dead air as Judy held the phone tight between her fingers. Andrea's voice was soothing on the other end of the line. "I know you're there. It's okay. You don't have to give your real name."

"What do you people do?"

"Well, we're here to help young women and men who might be in an unsafe environment."

"I'm safe."

"I see. If you're safe, why are you calling?"

"I'm curious about your services."

"If you're safe, then why are you curious about what we do?"

"I might know someone who isn't."

"I see, so you've read over the signs to look for in those who might be in human servitude?"

"Yes, but this can't be real."

"It's quite real."

"People are trafficked as slaves?"

"Yes, they are."

"Your site says that many people actually go into it voluntarily."

"It happens all the time."

"I don't understand. If someone is going to make you a slave, don't they kidnap or buy you?"

"That's part of the trade, but a lot of people, through no fault of their own, end up victims in these trafficking rings."

"Your site has a list of the things they do to get people in and then keep them, like using fear and threats as well as abuse and physical harm."

"That's true, so do you want to tell me about your friend?"

"She seems very, very happy, and she is making a lot of money."

"I see, and how do you know her?"

"We go to school together. I've known her my whole life."

"How old are you?"

"Seventeen."

"And how old is your friend?"

"The same age."

"So, what happened?" Judy told her about the party and the rape and how no one believed her. She told Andrea about the creepy man and the threats he made, and when she was done Andrea asked, "And you reported this to the police and your parents?" Judy said she did. "And they aren't taking it seriously?"

"No, not really. There was alcohol and drugs. I didn't know I was being drugged at the time. I trusted my friend, and she bragged and bragged, and I thought she was lying, but, Andrea, she wasn't. When I came to she gave me twenty-five-hundred dollars for an hour of lesbian sex that to be honest, and I will never tell another soul this, I liked."

Andrea was quiet for a moment then said, "It's normal for you to want to explore your sexuality, and there is nothing wrong with it. However, when that exploration is brought out by someone else using drugs and alcohol that's really not exploration, that's rape. You need to stay away from this friend."

"Why would I do that? She pisses me off a lot, but deep down I love her. We've been through so much together. We both lost parents in the fires. Her mother and my father are good friends. I need to talk to her. I need to understand."

"What's your name?"

"Jill."

"Is that your real name?"

"You said names don't matter."

"Okay, Jill. Your friend sounds like she might have gotten into one of these rings and is being used as a recruiter for a child sex ring. These groups lure you in with the promise of easy money and no hassles. You agree to let them take some pictures of you naked, then they want you to have sex with a boy or girl your own age, even older or younger, and they will film it. They pay very, very well as the relationship starts and then one day…boom…you're a prostitute or a high-priced escort or worse."

"Worse?"

"Yes. You could end up as a domestic sex slave."

"How do you know so much about this stuff?"

"I'm one of the lucky ones. I got out but not before losing five years of my life to bad people."

"So, what do I do? I go to school with my friend. I will see her tomorrow. My father and the police don't believe me. How do I protect myself and my sister?"

"You keep your distance from your friend. If she invites you to another party, refuse. Keep track of your conversations and record them, so that you have something to share with your family or police."

"That isn't going to help me if no one believes me. What if that man comes after my sister? He wants to have sex with me next week, and if I don't show up he said he will hunt down and rape my sister."

"If you saw him, would you recognize him?"

"I don't know. The room was dark, and I could only make out shadows. If I could smell his breath again or hear his voice, I would know him."

"He got that close to you?"

"Yes. He was right in my face and stank of liquor, cigarettes, and bad teeth."

"You can report it to the FBI. They have a tip line and agents who can help you and or your friend, if indeed she is in a human trafficking situation." Andrea gave Judy the phone number and web address to the Los Angeles field office of the FBI and said, "You can call twenty-four seven. If you are afraid for your sister, call them. They can help."

Judy told Andrea she would do it then hung up the phone. She looked over at the clock on her nightstand, and it was ten after one. "Well, Dad isn't coming home tonight that much is for sure." She turned off the light and tried to go to sleep.

CHAPTER THREE

"It's not early if you want to be there."

"So, are we good?" Mary asked Mark as she tried to catch her breath.

"Well, you have one hell of a way of discussing these things."

"They're young girls exploring their bodies. Nothing more."

"I'm not going to argue that with you. If it hadn't been for the booze and the drugs, I would take this much more seriously. Sally and Judy have been friends all their lives. I just can't imagine that Sally would do anything to hurt Judy."

"She wouldn't, Mark. You know that."

"What about this man that Judy said threatened her and her sister?"

"The imagination of an adolescent under the influence. Come on, Mark. You're a pathologist. You know how the human body and mind work. Judy can't come to grips with what she did, so her imagination went wild."

Mark rolled off the bed and walked into Mary's bathroom and said while peeing, "It's three a.m. I don't want to drive home after a night of dinner, drinks, and great sex."

"I don't want that either. I also think it might be a good thing if you were here in the morning, so you can hear it straight from Sally's lips."

"Oh no. I think that is a really bad idea. Let's just let this run its course."

"And if Judy comes out as a lesbian?"

"She's my daughter. I'll love her no matter her lifestyle choices."

Sam was asleep at her desk when Jim arrived. He could smell liquor and cigarette smoke hanging in the air. He checked for a pulse to find she was unconscious. Her left-hand drawer was open, and there was a half-consumed bottle of The Glenlivet Scotch and a pack of cigarettes in the drawer. He gently closed the drawer and then the door to her office and locked it. He walked into her private bathroom, wet a rag, and came back into the room and put it on the back of her neck.

"What the fuck are you doing, O'Brian?"

"One, keeping your career from going down the toilet, and two, hoping that I can prevent the dry heaves that are no doubt going to come soon."

"I'm fuckin' fine!"

"Yeah, I see that. When was the last time you had something to eat?"

"Oh, fuck. I don't know. Jesus! I don't need food. Cigarettes and booze work fine for me."

"You can't stay drunk all the time, Sam."

"I can if I don't sober up!" She pulled the bottle from the drawer, took a few swigs off it, then staggered to her bathroom and promptly threw up.

"The only thing you're going to do is drive yourself into an early grave."

"It's not early if you want to be there."

"Maria's dead, Sam."

"Don't you think I know that? I read the news. *'Dike Lawyer Dead After Crashing Car While Drunk.'* One of my favorite lines."

"Don't read the tabloids."

"I don't. That was a quote from some CalTrans asshole in the *Los Angeles Times* this morning. Jesus Christ! Can't they show a little compassion?"

Jim capped the bottle and put it back in her desk and said, "That's not their strong suit, Sam. You know how the liberal media works. They can find the cloud in the silver lining any day. If they can't get the facts, they make them up and cite 'anonymous sources' or 'people close to the situation.'"

"Yeah, well, fuck 'em, I have a good mind to swear out a search warrant for the *Times* offices."

"On what grounds?"

"You just said it, Jimmy. Anonymous sources and people close to the situation. I'll just make some shit up, and we can storm their goddamn offices."

"That sounds good in theory, but it's probably not the best idea in practice."

Sam sat back in her chair. Her uniform was rumpled and dirty, and her badge was hanging off. "I'm not going to remain Sheriff, Jim."

"Look, Sam, I understand you've been through a lot of shit, but you're a good cop. You're good for the department, and the men and women need you. Morale is at an all-time low; officers and deputies are being targeted by psychos, and we're all that stands between some semblance of peace and anarchy."

"Well, fuck them all. Fuck you, fuck the department, and fuck the Eagle."

Jim sat down just as there was a light rap on Sam's door. He walked over and saw John's face on the other side of the frosted glass. He shook his head, stepped out, and said, "She's hammered."

"Got it."

Jim walked back to his own office, and John stepped in and shut and locked the door. Sam's head was down on her desk, but she started to smell the air in the room and asked, "So, how was your goddamned vacation?"

"Good, good. I can smell that you're trying to drink yourself into an early grave. You know that suicide is slow with liquor, right? You would be better off putting a gun in your mouth."

"That's great advice, John. Thanks. Are you here to cheer me on?"

"No. I just want to know when you're going to get over your pity party, speak to Jade, and get the facts and move on with your life."

Sam lifted her head off the desk and said, "How fuckin' dare you. The love of my life is dead because of you and me."

"Really?"

"Yes, really."

"I don't recall killing her. Do you have some deep dark secret you want to confess?"

"Go fuck yourself, Swenson. You, Sara, the whole lot of you."

"Have you read the goddamned report?" John's voice was stern and angry.

Sam pulled out her tablet and said, "Fine…you sadistic mother fucker. I'll read the damn report." She squinted a bit as she tried to focus on her tablet. Her eyes opened wider as she read, and she swiped her hand across the screen several more times then looked at John and then back at the tablet and asked, "A BAC of .45? There is no way that Maria had that much alcohol in her body. I was there when she left the condo. She was lit but .45 at only one hundred and twenty pounds? Maria would have been dead long before she ever tried to leave the condo let alone get to her car."

"Yeah, well, it seemed a bit high to me, too. There was a half-consumed fifth of vodka in the car at the accident scene but that still would not have given Maria that level of alcohol in her blood stream. The other very strange thing is that Maria had no food or alcohol in her stomach or small intestines on autopsy. The large majority of the alcohol was in her blood stream. Her liver and other organs actually had very, very low traces of alcohol in their tissues."

Sam shook her head hard and asked, "She had some type of resistance to the alcohol that kept it in her blood and brain, but it wasn't being removed from the body?"

"Based on Jade's findings, and, as you see in the toxicology reports, Maria had a genetic condition that made it difficult for her body to clear alcohol from her bloodstream. The average person's liver can process about an ounce of alcohol an hour. Some heavy drinkers, like Jim, process faster, but Jim also eats heavy meals and has a lifetime of alcohol abuse. Hell, that's what's going to kill him." Sam laughed in spite of herself. "The problem for Maria is that she didn't know she had this genetic disorder. She had only half of the enzymes that the liver uses to break down alcohol."

"But she drank."

"Yes, she did, but she also got drunk faster on less alcohol, didn't she?"

Sam got a thoughtful look on her face. "You're right. It didn't take much to knock her out."

"That was her body's way of protecting her. Rather than letting her BAC rise to lethal levels, she would pass out, allowing her body to process the alcohol at a snail's pace."

"But that night she had been drinking before I even got home."

"And you don't know how much Maria had to drink before you arrived, only after. She drank too much, and her body couldn't process it. In reality, Maria was dead and didn't even know it. She could have gone to bed with you that night and died due to alcohol poisoning. Maybe, in some way, the accident was a blessing."

Sam sat back in her chair, tears running down her face. "I should have kept her out of the whole damn thing. I should have slapped a wig on Jim instead of putting her in the situation that led to her death."

"Sam, no amount of wishing is going to change what happened. Sooner or later, Maria was going to learn my secret. I know she suspected I was the Eagle when I saved her from Barstow." He stood and looked her in the eye. "I'm sorry for your loss. I liked Maria a lot, and I know how much you loved her. Neither one of us killed her; her genes did. So, you have two choices: throw away a career and drown yourself in alcohol, or pick yourself up, mourn her loss, and do the job that the people of Los Angeles elected you to do. There are no other options."

"You look like hell, Judy. Did you sleep?" Mark asked while fixing Tabitha's breakfast.

"Nightmares, Dad. How was your date?"

"It wasn't a date."

"So, did you and Mary talk about me and Sally?" Mark nodded. "And you still believe Sally over me?"

"No."

"So now what?"

"We let the police do their jobs, and you decide if you want to talk to Sally anymore."

"That's not going to be easy. We go to the same school and have the same classes and extracurricular activities." He asked if she wanted to change schools, and she said, "God no! I'm nearly ready to graduate. It's the only school I've known."

"Then my suggestion is to speak to Sally and see if you two can put this behind you."

Judy poured herself a cup of coffee then sat down and asked, "Dad, what do you know about human trafficking?"

Mark started choking on his food. After a moment he asked, "Human what?"

"Trafficking. Human slavery."

"What the hell brought that up?"

"I'm just asking. What do you know about it?"

"Only what I read in the papers or see on the news. It's not an issue here, Judy; it's a Third World problem."

"You can't really believe that."

"What the hell is going on, Judy? One minute you're telling me you were raped, and now you're asking about human trafficking."

"I've been doing some research. I'm writing a paper for my sociology class, and we were given ten subjects, and I picked this one."

Mark shook his head and said, "Now, I'm beginning to see what might be going on here. My beautiful and brilliant daughter with the very active imagination has gotten engrossed in a school project."

"Um…are you saying that I got raped because of my school project?"

"Stop it, Judy. Enough. You're scaring your sister, and you scared the hell out of Sally, Mary, me…and you have the police department investigating something that I am beginning to think you manufactured in order to draw attention away from drug and alcohol use."

"Dad!"

"Don't dad me. I have known the Owen family since before you were born. I realize that the past several years since the loss of your mother have had a huge impact on you. It has me, too. Tabitha didn't know her mother since she had just been born. I don't know what is going on with you, but I'm going to talk to Doctor Karen Mantel at the hospital when I get in, and I'm going to make you an appointment."

"Who is this Doctor Mantel?"

"She's a psychiatrist."

"So now you think I'm crazy?"

"No. I think you need someone to talk to. I'm going to make the appointment, and you WILL go. Am I clear?" Judy nodded with tears in her eyes. "I have to get to work now, and you and your sister need to get to school."

Mark left, and Judy went upstairs to his bathroom, opened his shaving drawer, and took a straight razor from it and stood looking at her reflection in the mirror. "My father thinks I'm nuts. I don't even know what's real anymore." She opened the blade and accidentally cut her finger. "Jesus! That's sharp." She filled the tub with hot water and was about to undress when Tabitha walked in.

"What are you doing?"

Judy quickly hid the blade in her pocket and said, "Nothing, Tabby, now get down to the car. We need to get to school."

CHAPTER FOUR

*"What can I say? I don't
have a lot of hobbies."*

Sally was in home room talking to several of her fellow classmates when Judy came in. No one said anything to her, and Judy took her seat and opened her tablet. The small group broke up, and Sally took her seat next to Judy, wrote something on a slip of paper, and passed it to her. Judy ignored it at first then took it, read it, and slipped it into her pocket.

"Did I buy broken-in domestic workers or fuckin' newbies?" Tonya said while looking over the girls and boys that Mary had delivered. The girls all made eye contact, but the boys did not. The oldest was nineteen, the youngest ten.

Al was standing in the room as Tonya looked over the kids and said, "This is what I was instructed to deliver, Ms. Hart. Mr. Tallon said this was your order."

"It was my order six months ago when they came into the system. What the fuck has been going on with them? Pierce is really dropping the ball on his training."

"I worked with all of these kids myself, Ms. Hart."

Tonya turned on her heels and said, "You worked with these people? You? A sick, smelly, disgusting bastard who drinks like a fish and doesn't even bathe?"

"I bathe every day, Ms. Hart. I have a genetic condition that causes my breakouts, and the odor that comes from my mouth and skin is not something that I can control. I don't appreciate you insulting me."

"I'm sorry. I didn't know. Just what am I supposed to do with this group? They aren't ready to be domestic servants. Jesus, I might just as well put them into one of my brothels. At least a john could use them." Tonya pulled out her cellphone and called Pierce, and after yelling at him for five minutes told Al to leave.

The house was quiet, and the children stood at attention. Some had scars on their faces. The girls were all in shorts and half T-shirts; some had belly piercings. "Strip!" The children did as directed, and Tonya had each child walk in front of her for inspection. She was looking the second child over when Mary walked in.

"So, how's this batch?"

"A joke, Mary. A goddamned joke. Pierce is really dropping the ball." Tonya shooed the last of the kids away.

"Well, their skin is clear."

"Several young ladies and boys have belly piercings, Mary. What the fuck is up with that?"

"Most came to us like that. They're all clean, and they are all clear skinned. We have our refund policy. Do you want your money back, Tonya?"

She shook her head. "No. I have already had the final walk through with my clients who bought this group. They are willing to take in some of the rougher ones. They feel their staff can break them in with little trouble."

"Then what's with all the bitching?"

Tonya laughed and said, "Mary, if I showed satisfaction with every product your people delivered to me I would really get the dregs, wouldn't I? My bitching keeps Pierce and his people on their toes."

"So, the sale is final?"

Tonya nodded and called Al back into the room. "Get them all restrained to the wall." He smiled and took each of the children and chained their arms and legs spread eagle against a far wall in the room. Tonya walked by each child with a marker in one hand and a list in the other and marked a letter on each of the children's right buttocks. Al was stoking a hot fire in a fireplace in the room where three long steel rods were sitting in the flames. On the end of each rod was a symbol, and he had his own list with the initials of the buyer and their mark.

Mary had stepped back and said, "I can't be here for this. It's nauseating."

"Well, you might not like it, but the buyers want their property branded, so there is no confusion when delivered." Tonya nodded at Al, who pulled the first branding iron out of the fire and pressed it into the buttocks of a ten-year-old boy. The child let out a blood curdling scream, and the others began to resist their restraints as Al slowly and methodically moved from child to child branding them in the exact same spots stopping only to replace the iron in his hand with another for another buyer. After ten minutes, the room was filled with smoke and the smell of burning flesh as well as the weeping and screaming of the slaves. Tonya smiled as Mary stood in the hallway outside of the room. "Thank you, Al. Cool off their brands and then bag them and deliver them…in perfect condition to the buyers." She walked out of the room as Al started to douse each child with ice water.

Mary looked at Tonya and asked, "You really get off on that, don't you?"

"What can I say? I don't have a lot of hobbies."

It was three p.m., and Judy was standing toe-to-toe with Sally under the bleachers of the football stadium. "You're sorry? You're sorry? Do you have any idea how much your actions and the actions of others have hurt me?"

"I thought you'd get off on it, Judy. You're not a prude. I had no idea you were still a virgin."

"That has nothing to do with it, Sally. You drugged me. You raped me, and men took pictures of us." Judy reached into her purse and pulled the cash out of it and said, "This isn't Monopoly money, Sally. You handed me this and told me there was more if I wanted it."

Sally sat down on a concrete pillar. "Look, it's complicated."

"No, it's not. You're involved in a human trafficking ring, or you're the victim of one."

Sally looked startled. "What the hell are you talking about? There's no trafficking going on. I engage in sex with men for hire. I give full consent and have been doing it for several years."

"So, you're a prostitute?"

"Hardly. Prostitutes don't make money like I make money. I'm not a street walker. I'm a high-priced escort."

"How the fuck can you be an escort? You're fuckin' seventeen."

"Do I look seventeen?"

"How old you are and how old you look are two different things. Who is your pimp?"

"I don't have a damn pimp."

"Then how do you get these high paying jobs? How do people know about you and your services?" Judy saw the look of realization in Sally's eyes. "Did I just ask an 'Oh shit' question?"

"Look, Judy, just forget about it. You're not the type for this work."

"Forget about it? How the hell am I supposed to do that? You drugged and raped me, and if I had my way I would kill you for it, but I can't because the second your body turns up all eyes will be on me. I know you're into some bad shit, and I'm going to get to the bottom of it…and when I do, I'm going to take you and all those involved down."

Sally was really trying to back pedal. "You're hysterical, Judy. You liked the sex, and you know it. You just can't live with the fact that you're into me. You're into women."

"I'm not into you, and I'm not into women." Judy started to walk away but stopped and looked at Sally and said, "You just keep in mind that when the smoke clears, you invited me into this sick world of yours. And right now…I'm really glad that you did."

Judy walked away, and Sally immediately called her mom and said, "Mom, we have a problem."

Al had finished delivering the last of the kids to their new homes when his cellphone rang. "What's up, Pierce?"

"That little slut you threatened the other day."

"What about her?"

"She's onto us. She's onto Sally and will sooner or later get to Mary and Tonya."

"I don't understand. I thought that the situation had been rectified."

"Yeah, well, it was rectified with the father, but Judy thinks that Sally is into human trafficking."

"Huh? Well, she's not wrong."

"Not funny, Al. You threatened the kid. You threatened to rape and kill her little sister, and now she is on the war path."

Al laughed. "She's a seventeen-year-old kid. How much war path could she have?"

"She went to the cops."

"You told me they didn't believe her."

"She went to her father."

"And you said he doesn't believe her."

"And she just confronted Sally at school and accused her of being into human trafficking."

"What do you want me to do?"

"Kill her."

"What?"

"Kill her and get rid of the body."

"So, put her through a wood chipper?"

"I don't care how you get rid of her, just do it."

"I'm not a murderer, Pierce. A rapist, a pedophile, but not a child killer."

"Do you remember how well your pedophile ass did in prison? Do you want to be face first into a wall while guys take turns fucking you up the ass and shoving their cocks down your throat again while the guards look the other way? Do you want to be raped and killed in prison back in the protected unit? You made the mess, now you fix it. Have I made myself clear?"

"Crystal." Pierce hung up, and Al sat in his truck looking at the clock on the dashboard. "Seven thirty. I'll drive by Bench's home. Who knows? I might get lucky and maybe she'll be outside."

Judy had been researching child predators and human trafficking. She picked up her home phone and blocked the caller ID on the line and called the FBI's tip line.

Karen was locking her office door when Mark Bench appeared out of nowhere and asked if she had a minute to talk. "Oh, hey Mark. I'm just getting ready to head out to dinner with my husband."

"This will only take a minute."

She unlocked her office door and invited Mark in. "What's going on? You seem upset."

"I am. It's my oldest daughter, Judy. She's having some issues."

"What kind of issues?"

"It's really complicated. She seems to have some sexual things going on. You know, teenage angst, exploring her sexuality. Anyway, she ended up in a sexual relationship with one of her female childhood friends, and there were drugs and alcohol involved." He paused for a moment then said, "I think she needs someone to talk to, and I thought who better than someone near her own age."

"I'm twenty-two, Mark."

"My daughter is seventeen and reminds me a lot of you. She's smart, pretty, engaged with the world. She's just lost, and I think that you might be able to help her."

"Of course, Mark. Let me look at my calendar. When did you want me to get her in?"

"The sooner the better."

Karen thumbed through her calendar. "I'll have to move a few patients around, but I can see her tomorrow at four-thirty."

Mark smiled and said, "Thank you, Karen. I really appreciate it. I will make sure she's here tomorrow."

He went to leave, and Karen asked, "I need her name and age, Mark."

"Sorry, sorry. Judy Bench. She's seventeen and a student at Barenwood Preparatory Academy."

"Wow! That's a big money school. You make that much money running our laboratory?"

"No. The money comes from a life insurance policy that my late wife had. After her death in the fires, she left me and the children well off, and it was our dream for our children to get the best possible education."

"So, she is probably more adult than child."

"Very much so. Most people who meet her when she is with me think she's my wife."

"I'm not sure how to respond to that."

"She's mature, Karen, physically and mentally. Emotionally, she has her issues and that's what I need your help with."

"Okay. I will see her tomorrow afternoon."

Judy had finished making dinner, and she and Tabitha ate and talked about school. Tabitha did most of the talking as Judy scrolled through her tablet speaking every now and then. Tabitha noticed the concentration on Judy's face and asked, "Are you okay?"

"I'm fine."

"What are you reading?"

"Just some stuff for school. How did it go with your math test?"

"I aced it. One hundred percent."

"That's great. Are you finished with dinner?"

"Yep. What's for dessert?"

"Chocolate cake, but only if you take a shower without making a fuss." Tabitha jumped up from her chair and ran upstairs to the bathroom.

All the lights were on in the Bench home. Al walked around the side of the house looking in the windows. He couldn't see anyone, but he could hear two female voices. He spotted Tabitha and licked his lips as he watched her run up the stairs in a pair of underwear and a T-shirt. "Now, that's what I'm talking about. Fresh meat." He had no sooner said it to himself when he saw Judy enter the living room. She was dressed in a sheer robe, bra, and panties. He patted his crotch and said, "Down boy. We will get us some of that, but we have to lure her out first." He'd gotten Judy's cellphone number by way of Pierce from Sally's mother. He called the number and watched as Judy looked at it but didn't answer. Tabitha came running back down the stairs nude, grabbed one of her dolls, and ran back up. He could hear Judy yelling at her but couldn't understand what she was saying. He called the phone again, but she still didn't answer. Since he didn't see her father, he sent her a text message.

"Hey, Judy, what are you doing?"

Judy read the message and responded, *"I'm home. Who is this?"*

"An admirer."

"Who R U?"

"I've been watching you at school, and I know you've been watching me."

"I don't know who U R."

"Think about it. Who do you like that only a few people know about?"

"David? Is this U?"

"I want to talk to you."

"Text isn't talking. Talk 2 me @ school."

"You will just make fun of me."

"No, I won't."

"Yes, you will. You're so beautiful, and I'm ugly and unpopular."

Judy paused for a moment before responding. *"Where R U?"*

"Bill's Ice Cream Parlor around the corner from your house."

"What R U doing there?"

"I'm here with my family, but I drove. Would you meet me?"

"I'm babysitting 'til my dad gets home."

"When will he be home?"

"9."

"It's 8:50, so he will be there any minute, and my family is leaving, and I will have to follow them. Please. Just five minutes."

"OK. Where R U parked?"

"In the back near the dumpsters."

"It's dark there."

"I know, but I want to ask you something."

"What?"

"I would rather do it in person."

"Why?"

Al paused to think then texted, *"Sally and others say you're a lesbian and that you had sex with Sally the other day. I don't want to believe it."* Al watched as Judy threw the phone across the room and said to himself, "I might have just fucked this up." He watched as Judy walked back across the room and picked up the phone. She stared at it for several minutes, and Al was about to leave when he heard a car pull into the driveway on the other side of the house. He peeked around the corner and saw Mark walk in. He headed out as fast as he could, and by the time he made it back to his car a block away he had a text from Judy saying she would meet him at the parlor in ten minutes. He smiled and rushed to the ice cream parlor, but there were already two cars parked near the dumpster. There was a bench under a set of lights, and he parked a few blocks down and sat in his car for a few seconds then texted back that he would meet Judy under the lights on the bench.

CHAPTER FIVE

"What are you burning?"

Judy parked in front of Bill's and went in. Bill Patron was standing behind the counter cleaning up and saw her come in and said, "Let me guess. A double thick chocolate malt, extra malt?"

"That would be great, Bill. Thank you." Bill started scooping the ice cream into a mixing cup, and Judy leaned on the counter with her purse over her arm and asked, "Where's David?"

"David? David who?"

"David Franks. He just texted me and said that he was here with his family."

"Not tonight, honey." Bill started making the malt, and Judy got an uneasy look on her face. He turned around and saw it and asked, "Are you okay, kid?"

"I think so. Can I use the side exit?" Bill handed her the malt, and she tried to pay him, but he refused and unlocked the door for her. "Are you sure you're okay, Judy? Do you want me to call your father?"

"No. I'm fine. Thanks." Bill let her out and then locked the door and went back to cleaning.

Judy knew the area very, very well. She followed a long sidewalk back behind the shop and then into some deep shrubbery. She made her way quietly to the back of the lighted bench and stayed out of sight as she texted back to David that she would be there soon. Al was so excited by the message that he jerked several times in the bushes behind the bench. Judy spotted him right away and shuddered. "You've come to hurt me and my sister, you son of a bitch," she said softly to herself as she pulled her father's straight razor from her purse. She could see the top of Al's head in the bushes bathed in shadow, and she moved quietly around the side until she was right behind him. She texted, *"David, where R U? I'm @ the bench."* She saw Al's head start moving rapidly from side to side in a searching motion. She crept up behind him, and as Al craned his neck to see, Judy brought the blade around his neck and ran it across it in one smooth stroke. Al didn't react at first, and arterial spray began shooting from the left side of his neck. He grabbed his throat with his left hand as Judy ran the blade across the right side and watched him collapse. She walked into the shadow and leaned down over the dying man and said, "Got'cha! You won't be hurting any more children, asshole." She pulled a scarf from her purse and rummaged around in Al's pockets, taking his wallet, cellphone, and car keys. She pressed the key fob and heard the chirp of an alarm and followed it a few streets down. She opened the driver's side door and rummaged through the front seat then the passenger side and the glove box, pulling all of the paperwork then locking the car.

Al's lifeless body lay in a pool of blood. Bill had locked up the shop and was long gone when Judy returned. It was even darker in the back of the shop, and a single car remained with two people in it. Judy didn't realize it, but she was covered in Al's blood, and she also didn't know that Bill's infrared security cameras had caught the whole murder on video.

Mark was eating his dinner when he heard the front door chime. "Judy, honey, is that you?"

"Hi, Dad."

"Did you get your malt?"

"I did."

"Well, come in and talk to me while I eat."

"Just a second. I need to go to the bathroom." Judy bolted up the stairs and into Mark's bathroom to put the blade away. She had pulled the bloody instrument from her purse and was running it under hot water when she saw her blood-covered reflection in the mirror and let out a light scream. She stripped and jumped into the shower and washed off.

She was about to grab the blade from the edge of the sink when Mark came in and said, "What the hell are you doing, Judy?"

"I needed a shower, and mine doesn't get as hot as yours."

"I thought you were going to be a minute?"

"I was. I was. I'm sorry, Daddy. Please don't be mad at me."

She started to tremble, and Mark grabbed her in his arms as she began to weep. "I'm not mad at you, sweetheart. I just didn't know where you were." He lifted Judy's trembling and teary face in his hand and asked, "What's going on, kiddo?"

"Nothing, Daddy. I'm just stressed out, that's all. I'm scared and stressed out." Mark nodded and took another towel from his rack and started to dry her hair. Judy had wrapped her arms around him with the edges of the towel that was covering her nude body, and when she let go, the towel fell to the floor.

Mark tried to avert his eyes, but he couldn't. He handed the towel to Judy and said, "I see why you're popular with the boys. You're physically mature."

She was standing nude and staring at her father when she spotted her bloodied clothes on the floor near the sink. She grabbed him tight and asked, "Can I sleep in your bed tonight?"

"Of course. Tabitha always ends up there at some point, too." Mark walked into the bedroom, and as he did Judy placed her clothes in the laundry chute. She hadn't covered up yet, and Mark asked, "Don't you think a nightgown or T-shirt would be appropriate?"

She got into his bed and said, "Please hold me, Daddy. All I want is to be held."

Mark was fully clothed and got under the covers and held her on his chest and stroked her hair until she fell asleep. As soon as Judy was asleep he went into the bathroom to clean up. He saw his straight razor on the edge of his sink, picked it up, and placed it back in its drawer. He washed his face and then turned on the shower. The shower doors were open as he undressed, and he looked down and saw a light crimson flow going down the drain from the middle of the shower. He looked back at Judy sleeping in his bed and then the shower floor and said to himself, "Great. My daughter is on her period and is laying nude on my sheets."

The 911 call came in at just after two a.m. LAPD detectives were working when Jade and Jessica showed up. Jade spotted Senior Homicide Detective Simon Bates standing over Al's body and said, "So, there really is still one good cop in the West Valley department."

Simon was six feet tall. His short grey hair and beard coupled with his pot belly made him look older than his forty-five-years. His black skin shone in the light of the street lights, and his smile looked almost neon through the darkness. He stepped into the light and asked, "Jade, do you know how to find a nigger in the dark?"

She laughed. "Yeah. Tell him to smile!" There was a round of laughter from several white officers, but two black officers and one Mexican weren't laughing.

Simon walked up and shook her hand then gave her a hug. He looked over at Jessica and said, "Jesus, girl! You have grown up. The last time I saw you was at the Hollywood Dam after the murder of your friend Ally."

"I remember."

"I know. Not a great memory but look at you now! You look great. I hear nothing but good things about the work you do with Jade. You're a success story, child." Jessica nodded slowly.

"So, what do we have here?" Jade asked.

"A very personal murder. Someone didn't like the victim very much and went to great lengths to make him suffer."

Jade's team put up several spot lights and once the scene was lit she looked down at Al's body lying on the ground in his own blood and said, "I see what you mean. In order to have slit his throat, the killer would have had to come up behind the victim. Do we have an ID?"

"The guy's name is Alan Fleece."

"Anything special about him?"

"Um…a low life sex offender. Did a couple of stints at Chino State Prison for child rape and porn charges."

"Is he registered?"

"Nope. Parole dropped the ball on this one. He's managed to stay off radar for several years."

"So, a pedophile?" Jessica asked.

"It looks that way."

Jessica laughed. "Well, it looks like he might have either gotten to the wrong victim or a parent or loved one found out and took him out."

Simon laughed. "The good thing about a dead pedophile is they won't reoffend." Both Jade and Jessica nodded, and one of Simon's officers asked if they could clear the scene. Simon nodded and released all but one street unit and had his CSI team back off so Jade and Jessica could work. Jessica jammed a thermometer into Al's liver as Simon watched and asked Jade, "Does the kid have a thing for pedophiles?"

"Oh yeah. In a huge way. She would rather be doing that to this perp while he was still alive." Simon nodded as his photographer shot pictures. Jade was walking the scene and recording with her tablet and talking.

Jessica looked around and said, "A family ice cream parlor. The perfect place for one of these pigs to molest or abduct." Simon nodded as Jessica measured the wounds. The women worked the scene until nearly four a.m. before allowing the body to be bagged for the morgue.

Judy was curled up against Mark's pajama clad body with Tabitha in between them. She noticed a bright light coming into the room from the balcony and slid out from her father's grasp allowing Tabitha to fall into her spot. She could see the ice cream parlor's roof from the house, and there were several bright lights in the area of Al's body. She looked over at her sleeping family and then the clock. It was ten after four. She went downstairs to the laundry room and found her clothes. They were heavily covered in Al's blood, and Judy took them to the living room and put them in the fireplace and set them ablaze. She sat nude staring into the flames while saying, "It was just a nightmare. I'm going to wake up any second. There's no way that I should know how to kill and then get rid of evidence. This has to be a nightmare."

She kept whispering it to herself until Tabitha showed up on the landing and asked, "What are you burning?"

Judy was startled and jumped. "Tabitha, you scared the hell out of me."

"Sorry. What are you burning?"

"Just some wood. I'm cold."

"Well, put some clothes on, and you won't be." She rubbed her eyes and walked back up the stairs, and Judy realized for the first time that she was indeed nude and that she had been sleeping with her father. She walked back up the stairs as the fire was dying down, got a nightgown, and climbed into her own bed. She tossed and turned until nearly five a.m. when she finally fell back to sleep.

Sam was asleep at her desk when her cellphone rang. "Sorry to bother you, Sam, but I have a murder scene out here in Woodland Hills that I think might interest you." Jade's voice was bright on the line, and Sam looked at her watch, and it was a quarter to five.

"Why would it interest me?"

"It's a pedophile with his throat slit in an interesting pattern."

"It's LAPD's jurisdiction. Let them deal with it."

"Well…it's kind of on the edge, and Simon Bates isn't a fan of line disputes."

"Simon is handling this case?"

"For the moment. I really think you should come out. We've bagged the body, but it's quite the scene out here."

Sam stood up and stretched her arms. "Okay, I'll bite, but I wouldn't want to have Jim miss any of the fun."

Jade started laughing. "I didn't think so."

She was still laughing when she hung up, and Jessica said, "That was just mean."

"Hey, Sam needs to get back on the horse, and Jim…well, you're right. I was just being mean."

Jim was in pair of sweatpants and a sheriff's department sweatshirt when he walked on scene. He had a cigarette hanging out of his mouth, and his eyes were tired and blood shot. It was nearing six a.m., and the area was covered in crime scene tape. He spotted Jade standing near the gurney holding the body bag with Al Fleece in it. "Okay…who's the smart ass that thought it would be a good idea to get my ass out of bed at five a.m.? I was having a great dream, but it was fucked up by a text message from Sam." Jade shrugged as did Jessica. Sam came around a corner of the shop, and Jim said, "You, you, you bitch."

"Hey, if I have to be up, then so does my second in command."

"I'm fuckin' retired."

"Well, to look at you, you would think so, but you're not. You're my undersheriff, and we have an interesting murder here."

Jim stomped out his cigarette. "It better be the most goddamned interesting murder case in the history of murder cases, Sam, because if it's not…I will create one on this very spot."

CHAPTER SIX

"Nope… they died badly."

"Al's dead. He's been murdered."

"What? What the hell are you talking about?" Tonya said in a sleepy voice.

"I just saw it on the seven a.m. news," Mary said.

"Do you know anything about his death, how he died?"

"Well, murdered is pretty graphic, Tonya, so I would say it wasn't a nice death."

"Where?"

"An ice cream parlor on the edge of Woodland Hills."

"What the hell would he be doing in Woodland Hills?"

"I can give you three guesses, but you should only need one."

"The Bench kids?"

"Very good. Only a few blocks from there."

"Does Pierce know?"

"I haven't called him. I'll wait to see if he calls me."

"I don't like this, Mary. I just got a dozen kids sold off last night, and Al helped me with branding them for the buyers and delivering them. What would possess him to go to the Bench home?"

"I'm more worried about who killed Al. He had a long rap sheet as a sexual predator, but he wasn't in the database of sex offenders."

Tonya took a deep breath and said, "You dealt with that with probation. You worked that out with his probation officer, right?"

"I did, but his probation officer is going to learn of his murder, which shouldn't have an impact on me. I figure anyone who knew Al expected he was going back to prison or that someone would kill him."

"Just don't let it interfere in business. I have an auction next week. You do still have the fresh batch of girls and boys for me, right?"

"Of course. They're still in training but doing well. They'll be ready."

Tonya asked, "The Bench kid…do you think we should kill her?"

"Oh, hell no. I just got her father out of my house a few hours ago after a night of fucking. He's happy with the situation. We need to leave Judy alone. The last thing we need is a fuck up with her. This whole thing could come down."

Tonya laughed. "We're in good shape, Mary, and do you know why we are in good shape?"

"Yes. Because we aren't greedy. We are keeping the trail on the low down and moving a few dozen people a month."

"That's right. We aren't raking in millions, but we have a really, really nice base income from sales, the brothels, and the rentals. All we need to do is just keep our suburban clients happy, and we will never get caught. We'll make our millions from your real estate businesses and my human trafficking operations. Am I clear?"

"Of course."

"Good. Greed is the downfall of decent operations. I don't care if you have people trafficking drugs, booze, cars, people. If you keep a low profile and don't get on anyone's radar, you will do well. Get greedy or careless, as in the stunt that Sally pulled with Judy, and you'll get caught." Mary agreed, and the two hung up the phone, but it was only a matter of minutes before Pierce called in a panic.

Simon was leaning on his car while waiting for Jim. He watched as Jim walked the area and pointed at the cameras on Bill's shop then pulled out a cigarette, turned, and saw him. There was a light wind blowing, and Jim opened his Zippo, lit his cigarette, and then slowly walked toward him.

"So…you got me out here, fat ass."

"Not me, Jim. You've been putting out quiet APBs saying that Sam needs work to keep her mind off her girlfriend's death, and I have a case that's on the city limit line."

"The shop's in your jurisdiction."

"True, but the murder took place in LA County, that's where the body was found." Jim offered Simon a smoke, but he refused. "I gave that shit up. I don't want to be breathing on oxygen when I'm as old as you."

"What the shit? You're five fuckin' minutes younger than me, asshole."

"Maybe so, but I gave it up."

Jim took a deep hit off his smoke and asked, "So…what? You figure some victim took this asshole out? Maybe an angry parent?"

"Hard to say. The dude was disgusting, and his history speaks for itself. He liked boys more than girls, so I figure either he got the wrong boy or one of his victims from the old days found him and slit his throat."

"Makes sense. The only address on the guy was the LA Mission."

"I'd start there."

"So, you're dropping this in my lap?"

Simon smiled. "Don't think of it like that. Think of it as putting out a call to help Sam out. It'll be a distraction if only for a few days or weeks." Jim nodded, and Simon asked, "How are you doing, by the way?"

"What do you mean?"

"I heard about Barbara's death a few months back. She was a good woman. Tough as nails. How are you doing since her passing?"

"I'm doing what she told me to do. I'm moving on with life. Do you remember Cindy Bartlett?"

"Your old girlfriend from high school? The one you knocked up?" Jim nodded. "Sure. She was hot."

"She still is. We're together now."

"That's great. How old is her kid?"

"He's dead, Simon."

"I'm sorry, Jim. I didn't know."

"You need to keep up with the news. Do you remember that encryption application last year?"

"Sure. Your boy was involved?"

"It got him killed."

"And the killers?"

"They died badly."

Simon laughed and said, "I bet they did."

Judy was dressed for school and sitting at the table with Mark and Tabitha. The radio was playing, and a breaking news story came over about the murder at Bill's. The reporter ran down the story, and Mark looked at Judy and said, "You were at Bill's for ice cream last night, weren't you?" She nodded. "Did you see anything out of the ordinary?"

"Nope."

Mark shook his newspaper and said, "Well, stay away from there or don't go alone. Jesus! This used to be a nice neighborhood."

Pierce was sitting in his living room as two scantily dressed young women cleaned. They were working quickly but seemed unfazed at their near nudity or Pierce's. He was scanning his tablet and as he swiped his hand over the screen he said to himself, "It was only a matter of time before Al was going to end up dead." Just then, his cellphone rang. He looked at the caller ID then answered, saying, "I wondered when you would call."

Andrew Haas was on the other end of the line, and his thick British accent was both soothing and unsettling. "So, Al went and got himself murdered?"

"Is this a surprise to you, Andy?"

"Hardly. I'm surprised he lived as long as he did, but I am now low one assistant for the porn and video feeds."

"You have to have someone you can call on."

"I do, but that would mean asking Mary to allow me to pull Sally in full-time, taking her out of rotation in the outcall service as well as the pornos."

Pierce was shaking his head. He rang a small bell next to the chair, and two nude girls entered the living room. He didn't have to say a word. They removed his robe, and one massaged his legs while the other massaged his back and shoulders. The two other maids continued cleaning unaffected. "Look, Sally has all but graduated from high school from what I understand. Mary wants her to start taking over operations for her anyway. The girl recruits so many kids and young adults, and she is in such high demand for outcall. I don't know that Mary is going to want her older daughter going full-time in porn right now."

"I can use her for everything that you just spoke of. Tonya has an auction next week, and I have two dozen boys and girls that I have had in obedience and house training for a year. All but one of them is broken, and the one girl still fighting her captivity has been with Hugh Masters for nearly a year."

Pierce was quiet for a moment and then asked, "I thought you had stopped using Hugh's services?"

"Not at all. Why would I? He's a great handler and trainer, and I like his style."

"He's cruel and savage."

"Not so. I admit that some of his techniques for breaking these people can be a bit rough, but sometimes there's no way to get people in line as slaves without a person like Hugh. Do you have the time and the expertise to break the human spirit and humble another human being into servitude? That's the side of the business that you don't want to talk about. You just want to live in a fantasy world that all those well-behaved girls that you bought were just born that way. Those girls eat, sleep, work, and can leave your home, and you never have to worry that they are going to give you an ounce of trouble. You want to know why you have that type of loyalty?"

"I know why. I treat my girls well and in return they treat me well." Pierce smiled at one of the girls working on his legs, and she smiled back as she ran her hands up his thighs and started to caress his penis.

Pierce groaned, and Andrew said, "So, I hear you have the girls working on you. Do you think that they were born like that? Get a hold of yourself, man. Every one of those girls was with Hugh before they ever came up for sale and eventually got to you. Do you think they suck your cock and swallow your cum and let you do anything you want to them sexually and allow you to take out your fetish desires on them naturally?" Pierce didn't respond. "Of course not, and you know it. You can be as kind or cruel to them as you like, and they would respond the exact same way and that is due to Hugh's training." Andrew could hear Pierce breathing deeply, and he could also hear the sound of a woman gagging. "Am I on speakerphone?"

"Yes. Just give me a moment."

"Well, at least put it on camera mode, so I can watch."

Pierce lifted his cellphone and turned on the camera while he was pushing the young girl down on his penis. Andrew recognized her. She was holding her ankles while Pierce was pressing his penis down her throat. Her mascara was running from being choked, but she offered no resistance, and Pierce held her head firmly to his groin as he orgasmed, then pulled his penis slowly forward keeping it in her mouth until all of the semen had been swallowed. He released the girl's head, kissed her forehead, and said, "Good girl. You are such a good girl. You don't have to do chores today. Go to my bedroom and be on your knees nude in the middle of my bed. Your duty is to sexually please me today."

The girl smiled, and Pierce had the phone directed in the girls' direction. Andrew said, "Hi Tammy. How is Master Pierce treating you?"

"Oh, hello Master Andrew. Master is taking very, very good care of me and all of us girls. I have pleased him, and now I get to have sex and don't have to work today."

Andrew nodded, and Tammy ran upstairs to Pierce's bedroom. Andrew laughed. "Pierce, when you're fucking her this morning, remember that none of this would be possible without Hugh."

CHAPTER SEVEN

*"...her rebellious spirit in sexual
servitude for the rest of her life."*

"Why...must...you...disobey...my...orders?" Hugh was winded, and Lori Fleming was screaming on the cross she was hanging from. Hugh dropped the whip to the floor while small trickles of blood fell on plastic sheeting beneath Lori's suspended body. She was chained with her arms outspread as well as her legs. Her body was beet red, and her breasts and vagina were purple and bleeding. Her brown hair and hazel eyes were cast down at the floor, and she was breathing heavily with a ball gag in her mouth. Hugh stood before her nude. His five-foot ten body glistening with sweat, and the muscles in her arms and legs bulging from the beating he had given the girl. At sixty, Hugh Masters was in great physical condition. He was classically handsome with a neat appearance and well-groomed short hair. He was well-endowed, and his flaccid penis hung down near his thigh and moved with his movements. "So, Lori, do you want another go at my cock, or would you prefer another beating?"

Lori weakly lifted her beautiful, young, tear-stained face and said, "Fuck you!" and promptly passed out.

"Fuck me? Fuck me? Oh, no child. I'm going to fuck you." There were two young men standing on both sides of the room during the beating, and Hugh ordered them to remove her from the cross and to chain her spread eagle to her bed. "Don't hurt her. I will be in to fuck her in about an hour. Make sure that the rest of the girls are ready to finish up training. We have a week."

The men did as ordered. At one point, Lori woke up as she was being chained for further rape and said, "Help me. Please help me."

One of the men just shook his head. "Just do what the master wants, and this will end."

"I want to be free."

"And you will be at the auction next week if you just give in. You will get a home, and this nightmare will end."

"That's not a home. It's a life as a slave. I'd rather be dead."

"If you keep resisting, your wish will come true. If Master Hugh can't break you, he will kill you. And believe me, the way he kills is even more savage than the way he breaks people." Lori passed out as the two men left the room.

Sam and Jim were watching the security video from Bill's. Sam was squinting and asked, "What the fuck is this? You can't see shit."

"Yeah. I wonder if Bill knows his cameras are outdated and so filthy that we can't see anything." Sam had watched up to Al's death, and all she saw was Al's head lurch to the left and then right and then his body fall to the ground. The bushes around where he was killed were so thick that the killer couldn't be seen. Jim turned off the video and said, "We have to take this to John. His AV department is so much better than ours. Perhaps he can enhance this and make out the killer." Sam nodded, and

Jim called John and told him he and Sam were bringing some murder footage over that they needed enhanced.

Sally was crying off alone when Judy got to school. She asked the other girls what was going on, but none of them knew. She put her bag down next to her desk, and David Franks smiled at her and waved, and Judy waved back. She walked over to Sally and put her hand on her shoulder and asked, "Are you okay?"

"No, I'm not okay."

"What's going on?"

"A friend of mine was murdered last night."

"A friend? Anyone that I know?"

"No. He was an adult friend of my mother."

"I'm so sorry, Sally. What happened?"

"We don't have the details. All we know is he was found dead next to Bill's Ice Cream Parlor early this morning."

"Oh, wow. I'm so sorry. What was your friend's name?"

"Alan Fleece, but he went by Al."

"How's your mother holding up?"

"Better than me."

"You must have been really close to Al."

Sally dried her eyes and said, "We were."

The bell rang, and the two girls sat down in their seats, and Judy asked, "Will you teach me more about what you do?"

Sally got a stunned look on her face and whispered, "What I do to make money?" Judy nodded. "Um…sure…if you want."

"When is the next party?"

"Well, with Al's death I don't know, but once I do I will text you." Judy nodded and went back to paying attention to the teacher as Sally looked on sadly, clearly holding back tears.

John and Chris took Sam and Jim to their AV department and ran the film through several different units, but the killer was still not recognizable. The glint of the razor could be seen as it slit Al's throat, and there was a hint of a hand but nothing else. John blew up the image several times, but it just got grainy, and Chris said, "I don't see any way to ID the perp."

Sam was staring hard at the screen and asked John to play back the video of the slashing. He ran it several times as Sam stared on. "What do you see, Sam?" John asked.

"Small hands."

All four of them stared at the split-second video image, and Jim said, "I don't know what you guys think, but that looks like a female hand." John called in two of his AV techs and had them work more magic, and in a matter of minutes there on the screen were the glowing red eyes and a dark dressed image of a young woman. She could be seen moving behind Al and then slitting his throat.

Sam looked on and said, "She slit his throat from the left and then the right, and she used a straight razor."

"She looks like she knows what she's doing," said Chris.

"No, she doesn't," John said and pointed at the screen. "Look at her movements. She's hesitant at first, then as she moves closer to Fleece, she draws back for a moment then reaches out slowly and flicks her wrist on the side of Fleece's neck, catching part of the carotid artery. She got lucky. Had she missed, he would have been cut but not mortally, and he would most likely have gotten her."

"Do you think we're dealing with one of Fleece's victims?" Chris asked.

"That's the million-dollar question. We need to know who was in that shop last night."

"So, let's talk to the owner. He was the person working that night. The LAPD took his statement, but they didn't get into the deep investigative work like asking who was in the shop," Chris said.

"The only good cop on that scene was Simon Bates," Jim said.

John cocked his head and said, "I thought Bates retired."

"Oh, hell no. He likes police work too much. I have all of his notes and photos from the scene. He was glad to dump this off on Sam and me, so let's go get some ice cream."

"We might have a problem," Sally told her mother over the phone.

"Okay. What type of problem?"

"Judy Bench has asked me to introduce her to my work."

"Really? After all the drama of the past few days, she's interested in the very thing that she called rape?"

"Well…she wants to understand what I do. Pierce texted me at school asking me to meet him at his house, and I don't know what that's about either."

"Al's murder."

"What does Al's murder have to do with me?"

"I was going to talk to you at his house this afternoon, but with Al out and only Hugh Masters to deal with recruit training, we need you to get more involved in overall operations."

"Are you saying you want me to oversee Pierce, Hugh, and the others?"

"Yes."

"Mom, I like being a high-priced escort. I enjoy sex and role playing. It pays well, and I have a great stable of johns. You want me to give that up to run your business?"

"Sally, there are brothels that need oversight. There's the porn business, slave trade for domestic servants and sex and labor, as well as the people we put out on lease to our clients."

"I don't know anything about those operations, Mom. I'm a porn star, escort, online entertainer, and recruiter. Once I get the people through the door, you take it from there. I have only met Hugh twice, and while he's a nice man, I have also heard some really disturbing things about him."

"And they are all true. He deals with slave breaking and training with an iron fist in a velvet glove. He is, however, pivotal to our services in the slave trade. Pierce and you have the porn taken care of, and I agree you do great at all of the things that you do, but Tonya is my biggest client. She moves slaves monthly at auction and works out leases and placement when the people fall out of use or favor with her clients."

Sally shook her head. "Mom, we both know that no matter who they are, men or women, when they are washed up they are sold into servitude for sex. What happens to them after that, I don't want to know."

"Well, grow up, baby. This isn't a game. Al's been murdered, and while I think I have Mark satisfied, Judy's wanting to get into business concerns me."

"That was the whole purpose of this call. How do you want me to handle it?"

Mary was typing on her laptop and looking at several sites that she ran on the deep web. "When does Judy turn eighteen?"

"In a few weeks. Why?"

"She will be legal then. If you refuse to bring her in, it is going to raise red flags."

"If I bring her in, I have a feeling it will bring the police right to our door."

"I don't think so. Let her do some soft porn with you. Keep Pierce in the background. Just the man behind the camera. If we get enough film and photos of Judy, we can use them to blackmail her. Mark would protect her, but he would also lose his mind if he saw his little girl sucking and fucking for dollars."

"I'll do it, but I think it's a bad idea."

"It's the only option we have. You made the mistake when you decided to drug and rape Judy on video. You made the mess, now you have to control it."

Everyone rode to Bill's in John's truck. There were kids everywhere. They looked around the shop with its fifties soda fountain and décor, and Jim said, "It's like going back in time." Sam nodded, and John asked one of the soda jerks behind the counter for the owner. Soon, a portly man all of five feet walked out from a storage room and introduced himself.

"Bill Caster. How can I help you?" IDs came flying at him, and he laughed and asked, "FBI? Sheriff's Department? So, who do I talk to?"

John smiled. "Mr. Caster, we're here about a homicide that occurred last night."

"Well, I would hope so. You four don't look like hamburger and ice cream eaters." Bill looked Jim up and down. "Well, Mr. O'Brian there probably eats my food." Everyone laughed, including Jim, who ordered a burger, fries, and a chocolate shake. "I turned over everything that the police wanted. I know my cameras aren't state-of-the-art, but you should have gotten something out of them."

John shook his head. "They were too grainy, Mr. Caster. We want to know who was in your restaurant last night."

"Every customer, Agent Swenson? Look around. I know every one of these kids and their parents by name. Most of them are regulars and live in the area. I can pretty much recite what they are going to order and can basically set my inventory on their regular patronage of my shop."

"Do you recall anything unusual? Anyone who stood out?"

Bill put his fingers to his chin and tapped. "Not really. I had a large lunch and dinner crowd and then my regulars who come in at closing."

"Do you recall anyone in your shop at closing time that would not have usually been there?"

"Nope. My last three customers were all regulars. Judy Bench was the last to get her malt, but that's normal for her. She's always here Monday, Wednesday, and Friday at closing for her malt. Double chocolate, double malt. Then, she comes in on Saturday nights with her father Mark and her little sister Tabitha for dinner."

"So, all of that was normal?" John asked.

"Yes, sir. I don't recall any strangers about. We have the occasional homeless person who strides in. Most are locals who have fallen on hard times, but none leave my shop hungry." Bill paused and said, "Please don't advertise that. I lend a helping hand to the few who come in, but if word got out I was serving free food I would be out of businesses."

John nodded. "So, no strange behavior. The Bench girl was the last one you served?"

"Yes, but she's far from a little girl. She's seventeen going on twenty-five. Looks way more mature for her age, a curse to her father, who is ultra-protective of both his daughters."

"And why is that?"

"Mark lost his wife, a firefighter, several years ago in the great fires. Becoming a widower changed his life and the life of his children forever. He works as a pathologist at Northridge Hospital, and when he's not working, he's spending time with the girls. They're a close-knit family."

"Okay. Thank you for your assistance, Mr. Caster. We'll be in touch if we need further information."

Bill nodded then said, "I heard that the guy who was murdered last night was a sex offender. Is that correct?" John nodded. Bill laughed, and John asked what was so funny. "Oh, you know how they say what goes around comes around?"

"Yes."

"Well, it looks like a bad guy got what was coming to him. Makes the world a safer place if you ask me."

"And the person that murdered the man doesn't worry you?"

"Not at all. The guy got what was coming to him. I bet one of his victims found him and killed him. I doubt that person is a threat to the general public."

Jim had gotten his food and said, "Mr. Caster, anyone willing to murder another person is a threat to public safety, even if the dead guy was a pedophile." Jim was drinking his shake as they left the shop, and Sam took a few of his fries, and the four sat down at a table across from the murder scene. Jim was eating his lunch and looking around when he said, "You know, the girl would have had to have snuck around the building using the cover of the shrubbery and trees to get the drop on Fleece."

Sam nodded and walked around the back of the building. There was a small dirt path that had been created by local kids and animals that curved around the back of the shop ending where Fleece's body had been found. Sam said, "She came around the side of the shop then followed this small path, which would have led her behind Fleece." She looked at the blood spatter and said, "The killer got arterial spray on her."

"How the hell do you know that?" Chris asked.

"The spray pattern is interrupted. It was clearly coming out at full speed, but the kid's arm was in the way during the second cut, so she got covered in blood." Sam looked around some more and pulled out her tablet and started recording as she walked away from the scene in the direction of the street. Blood had been dripping off the killer's clothing, which ended abruptly in the street where a car would be parked. Sam asked Jim, "Where was Fleece's car found?"

"Where you're standing."

"Where is it now?"

"LAPD has it waiting for us to pick up for processing."

"Well, get an OPG tow truck over there and get the car moved to our impound. The car had been ransacked, right?" Jim nodded. "The victim had no ID or keys on him either, did he?" Jim nodded once more. "Our killer cleaned out our victim and the car before she left the scene."

Jim walked to where Sam was standing, looked around, and said, "You're right. Look at that, John. She's getting the Eagle eye for crime." Sam frowned and hit him in the stomach, knocking the wind out of him. Jim was doubled over laughing and trying to get his breath back as the four climbed inside John's truck.

Judy arrived at Karen's office at three thirty and took a seat in the empty waiting room. Karen came out and asked, "Judy Bench?"

"Yes, ma'am. Doctor Mantel?"

"That's me. Won't you come into my office?" Judy entered, and Karen invited her to sit. After they exchanged formalities, Karen said, "Your father tells me that you had a scary experience?"

"If by scary you mean being drugged and raped, then yes. I do, however, have a very important meeting to get to by four-thirty, so can we make this a quick session?"

"As you wish. Would you like to talk about what happened?"

"Why not. It's not like I haven't told the story twenty times over already." Karen recorded the session as Judy told her the harrowing story.

"Fleming won't break, Tonya."

"Are you telling me that the all-powerful Masters can't break a fifteen-year-old girl?"

"If I keep her for myself, she'll be fine. I will just put her in one of my dungeons and let the members of my private club enjoy her. She will never be broken enough for sale. She's just too strong-willed."

"You'll put her in one of your dungeons, and let your 'members' fuck and beat her to death?"

"Yes."

"It's such a waste of prime grade meat. She's so beautiful, and I have already had several buyers getting their bids ready for her."

"I'm sorry, Tonya, but it is just not meant to be. Either I take her into my dungeon or just take her out to the wood chipper. Those are the options."

"Either way, she will end up in the chipper. I know you, though. You'll make a few bucks on her before you grind her into pulp."

"What can I say? You see right through me."

"I'm going to come to your place and talk to the girl."

"Fine. I have her chained to her bed, and she isn't getting released anytime soon. When you come, just make sure that you don't release her. She will tear you to pieces, no joke."

"Have you shot any porn with her?"

"BDSM. Mostly S&M. She likes pain. I think that is part of the problem. She needs a man or woman who is going to take charge."

"So, it sounds like she is breakable after all."

"Everyone is breakable. I just can't have her ready for your auction. Set her up as part of another lot in a few months and maybe then she'll be ready. Until then, you'll have to pull her off the site and accept the reality that she might never be more than what she is…a person who will live as long as I am satisfied with her rebellious spirit in sexual servitude to me for the rest of her life."

Sally was sitting at home with her sister; it was four forty-five when Judy showed up. She invited her in, and the two went off to Sally's room to talk. "Where is your mom?"

"Working. So, you want to get into the business?"

"After careful consideration, I do."

"Uh… huh."

"What? Now you don't want me?"

"You can understand my reticence, can't you Judy? I mean, one minute you're running to the cops screaming rape and the next you're sitting with me on my bed in my bedroom talking sex trade." Judy nodded. "So, what are your ambitions in this world?"

"I want to make the kind of money you make. We've both graduated high school; it's just the formality of walking in graduation. We don't even need to go to school if we don't want to."

"So, you're looking out for your future?"

"Well, yeah. If I can bank the kind of money that you have told me about and shown me, I could work at this for a few years and then go on to college without having to worry about student loan debt or living expenses."

"Doesn't your father have a college fund for you?"

"There isn't enough to pay the tuition for four years, let alone expenses, and I want to go all the way and get my PhD in Engineering. It's been one of my dreams. I have the skills, but the best schools in the country don't come cheap."

"Where do you want to go to school?"

"My first choice is MIT; second, Stanford; and third, if I have to, UC Berkeley."

"What's wrong with Berkeley?"

"Liberals are what's wrong with Berkeley."

Sally started laughing. "You're a conservative who wants into my game? Now, I've heard everything."

"No...I'm just a free thinker, and Berkeley is a nut job school."

"Have you applied to any yet?"

"I have applications in for MIT and Stanford."

"But not Berkeley?"

"No."

"Well, if you really want to do this, I need you to pass one little test."

"And what test would that be?"

"Have sex with me right here right now. Straight. No drugs, no alcohol, and with explicit consent."

Judy didn't skip a beat. She stripped off her clothes, leaned in and kissed Sally deeply, and asked, "Is this explicit enough for you?"

"How did your talk with Judy go?" Mark asked Karen as she passed his lab.

"Good. She has a good head on her shoulders. She gets that from her you. We had an hour-long session, and we're going to meet again next week."

"Did she open up?"

"You know I can't talk to you about it."

"But she's my daughter."

"She's also protected by HIPAA. Unless she is willing to give you a release, I can speak generally about our conversations but can't go into detail."

"I understand. I know you will take good care of her." Karen nodded, and Mark said, "I know you can't talk about the things that she says, but I hope she will talk to you about the rape. It's really bothering me. She has changed since the incident. Last night, she was pretty unhinged. I found her in my shower, and when she got out, she hugged me and wouldn't let go, then she insisted on lying in bed with me nude."

Karen's head tilted. "She was nude?"

"I wasn't. She just curled up into the fetal position and wanted me to wrap my arms around her. You've met my daughter. She might be seventeen, but she has the body of a much older woman. She kept putting my hands around her breasts and pressing her rear against me. It was a very unsettling night."

"Has she ever done anything like that before?"

"When my wife was alive and out on shift, Judy would come to my room and jump into bed with me. She never liked wearing clothes, and we have always been an open house when it comes to nudity. After her mother's death, and as Judy approached puberty, she got a little more private but still walked around the house in thong underwear and a bra. I guess in all of the turmoil of work and raising a family I stopped paying attention, and last night when I first walked into the bathroom and saw Judy nude under the water and then out of the shower it was as if I was seeing her for the first time. Like the girl was gone and was replaced by a woman. For a fraction of a second I was aroused."

Karen laughed. "So, you're worried that you're going to try something with your daughter?"

"No, no. It was upsetting, but no."

"It's normal to have those feelings, Mark. First, there's the shock of seeing your nude daughter in your bathroom. The fact that she is now a well-endowed young woman who caught your attention in a shocking way set those emotions in motion. Don't lose sleep, Mark. It will be fine." She started to walk away but stopped to say, "With all that said, if Judy makes an advance toward you, I want to know about it."

"I don't understand. What type of advance?"

"Sexual."

"Sexual? You think my daughter might try to get me to have sex with her?"

"It's not unheard of. It's known as the Electra complex. Sometimes a child who didn't get the love they needed from their mother and or father in their young life feels a devotion to the parent, and it can have devastating consequences. The trauma that has befallen Judy is real, and she might seek your protection and love, and that could end up misplaced if she feels connected to you to a point where she doesn't see you as her father but her lover."

"Okay, Karen. You're starting to make me sick. I will tell you right away if I get any advances from my daughter, but I don't see that happening."

"That's why I brought it up, Mark. In these types of cases, the parent rarely sees it coming until it happens...and then there is hell to pay on the other side of that darkness."

CHAPTER EIGHT

*"I've seen tougher cases
than you go down...in agony."*

Judy dressed after she and Sally showered together. Sally had taken photos of the two using her selfie stick while having sex and uploaded them to Pierce via a secure server. Judy was sitting in an arm chair in Sally's bedroom and asked, "So...when do I meet the people behind this porn?"

"Um...tomorrow after school. We'll meet here at my house."

"So, more sex with you?"

"Yeah, unless you want a guy in with us. We can do a threesome."

"Like I told you, I'm a virgin...at least to the male anatomy."

"You don't have to. It can just be you and me. There will be a man filming as we have sex. That's part of the deal."

"And what does it pay?"

"The same. Twenty-five-hundred."

"Is that the going rate?"

"No...you will have to branch out. If you want to come out as lesbian, then I will introduce you to other girls, and you will have different types of sex with them. The more adventurous you are, the bigger the money."

"And if I'm bi?"

"Even better. It opens all of the doors in porn to you. If you want to keep your virgin status, you do oral and anal with men and women."

"How can I do anal with a woman?"

Sally laughed. "You really don't have a clue, do you? Have you ever heard of a strap-on?"

"You mean a dildo on a belt?"

"Basically. You wear it to use on your partner, or your partner wears it, and you do each other up the ass or the pussy. My suggestion to you is to give up the virgin thing and go all in. The more you do, the more you make."

"And this is just in porn?"

Sally sat silent for several seconds. "No...there are a lot of other ways to make big money, Judy. Again, it's just how adventurous you're willing to be."

"I don't understand."

"You can work for an escort service where you are hired out to men and women for sex. We're called 'accommodating escorts,' so while we can be eye candy for our clients for functions or events, we can also fulfill their carnal desires."

"You're an escort? But you're only seventeen."

Sally whispered, "I've been an escort since I was fourteen. That's where I make the big bucks."

"And who runs all of this?"

"That's a secret and will remain one until such time as the powers that be feel you should know."

"I see. Do you know who they are?" Sally nodded. "But I have to wait?" Sally nodded again. "The man who was murdered...did you know him from this business?"

Sally teared up. "Yes. He was a nice man."

"Is he the one who talked to me after you drugged me at the party? He was an unforgettable person."

"He didn't have a lot of tact when it came to dealing with people, but he was a good person deep down."

"Obviously not if someone killed him."

"He had a history. In some cases, a history of hurting people."

Judy smiled and said, "Not anymore."

Lori was chained to the bed in the small room that had been her cage for almost a year. Tonya entered the dark room, turned on the lights, and then turned her head quickly after seeing Lori's brutalized body.

"What's wrong, Ms. Hart? Can't handle the results of your slavery?" Tonya turned quickly and then sat down on a small steel chair. The smell of urine and feces were heavy in the room, and she looked around and saw a small steel bucket with a round piece of wood on it and a wash basin. "It stinks in here, doesn't it?" Tonya didn't respond. "That's because I have been dehumanized, Ms. Hart, or I should say that Hugh has tried to dehumanize me. I piss and shit in that bucket over there, and once a day I am given water and some food, mostly gruel. Just enough to keep me weak but alive, and I get hosed off once a week with a fire hose. Nice, right?"

"If you will just submit, I can get you to auction this weekend. I have three bidders who have been fighting over you."

"How can they fight over what they have never seen?"

"Oh, they have seen you. Lots and lots of you during sex."

"You mean rape."

"They have seen your BDSM and S&M sessions."

"Torture, Ms. Hart. Involuntary torture. Release these restraints, and I will give you a taste of what I have been going through."

"Look how far you have come since Sally first recruited you."

"You are well aware that recruited is not at all accurate. I was also slipped a mickey and then raped several times. Your precious Sally lulled me in with the promise of money and freedom, but that's not what happened, is it Tonya? No. You moved me from brothel to brothel, allowing men and women to rape me morning, noon, and night. You kept me in a cage between rapes, and then when I would not submit, you handed me off to that monster Masters. Not exactly the most motivating person."

"You have a choice to make, Lori, and I'm going to put it as bluntly as possible. You will either submit to your master's will and get out of this hell hole and into a life that, believe it or not, you will grow to enjoy as the slave of a loving owner who will treat you well, or I will have no choice but to remove you from the auction and sell you to Hugh, and this will be your reality for the rest of your life."

"There is a third option."

"And what's that?"

"I off myself and end this pain now."

"Why would you want to do something like that? You're young and beautiful; you have your whole life ahead of you."

"This is no life. Even if I am sold to the best person in the world, I would only be trading this cage for another."

"I agree, but wouldn't you prefer a gilded cage to this dark and savage one?"

"You have lied to me from day one. You caught me up in your web of lies, and here I am beaten and dehumanized but not broken. I would rather die than to submit to the will of anyone. I'm my own person, and no one can take that from me."

Tonya stood up, opened the door, and turned off the lights. "Hold onto that thought, Lori. I've seen tougher cases than you go down, and when they did, they went down in agony."

"How did it go with Judy?"

"The sex was great, and she asked good questions, but I feel that she will need special attention if we are going to break her into doing this work."

Mary was fixing dinner as the two spoke. "Are you thinking of sending her to Hugh?"

"Not right away, but in short order, she and I will be having sex tomorrow while Pierce films, and I would like you to have Hugh present but not in our line of sight."

Marina walked into the kitchen and said, "Mistress Owen, I was going to fix you and the girls dinner."

"No, thank you, Marina. I'm making it for the girls, and I want you to finish the laundry and make my bed. I want to play with you in the dungeon after dinner. So, strip and put on the leather wrist and ankle restraints and wait for me, okay?"

"Yes, Mistress. Will Ms. Sally be joining us?"

Mary looked at Sally who said, "Sure. Sex is on the table, right?"

"Of course. Marina would much rather play with us in my dungeon than in the dungeons of some of my clients. Right, Marina?"

"Yes, Mistress Mary. You're kind to me and not hurt me like many of the others have."

"Very well. Run along. We'll be up in an hour."

Marina left the room, and Sally asked, "Does the fact that you and I have sex ever creep you out?"

Mary shook her head. "Why? Does it creep you out?"

"No. I mean, you and Dad introduced me to sex young, and after his death you introduced me to the lesbian lifestyle, and I like it. You then introduced me to the straight lifestyle, and I like it, too, so now I'm bi. It's actually been a cool experience and worked out well for my escort status."

"You're ready to dive into running more of the operations. Who knows? You might have an understudy in Judy but indoctrinate her slowly. She is interconnected to too many people. If anything happens to her, it will be our undoing."

CHAPTER NINE

*"Someone trying to do
what the Eagle does?"*

Jim was drinking a beer at Santiago's with Sam. The two had said little
to each other as they stared out the large windows. Karen spotted
them as she entered and asked if she could have a seat. Jim patted the
one next to him, and she sat down.

"It's good to see you out and about Sam."

"There's no sense in wallowing in self-pity, and now that I have the
facts surrounding Maria's death, I understand more of her own actions."
Karen nodded as Javier brought her a glass of wine.

"So, what brings you in here?" Jim asked.

"Chris and I are having dinner. We need a night out. How about you
two?"

"I'm waiting for Cindy, and Sam is going to have dinner with us."

Karen was about to speak when her cellphone rang. It was Mark
Bench. She listened intently then said, "Mark, I told you I can't talk
about my patients. You need to give Judy time to work through this in
therapy." She listened some more then hung up.

"What was that all about?" Sam asked.

"One of my patients' parents is trying to delve a little too deep into her therapy."

"It's her parent. Why can't you talk to him?"

"HIPAA laws. Even children have rights. His daughter is nearly an adult, but in order to keep her trust I must keep her secrets. Unless, of course, she's a threat to herself or others, then it's a different story."

Sara popped her head around the corner and smiled. "Is this a private party?" Sam shook her head as Karen kept speaking. Sara sat down, and Javier brought her a glass of wine, and they all made small talk until John and Chris showed up.

Javier hobbled over to the table and asked, "So, you eat alone or all together?"

Cindy had arrived and heard Javier's question and said, "Let's make it a party. Wine for everyone, Javier, on me."

The old man laughed. "It's on me. Sit and I will send an order taker over."

Cindy leaned down and kissed Sam on the cheek. "I'm sorry for your loss." Sam nodded. Cindy sat next to Jim, who had just lit up, and grabbed a cigarette out of the pack on the table, and asked, "So, what are we talking about?"

"Karen was just telling us why she couldn't share patient information with a parent."

Sara nodded. "HIPAA. The patient would have to give consent."

"Well, I don't know who this Mark guy is, but I would think if he is concerned enough about his child to be calling you at seven o'clock at night, he has a right to know."

"Mark who?" Jim asked.

"Doctor Mark Bench. He's the head of our pathology department, and his daughter went through a traumatic experience, and he asked me to see her."

John looked up. "What type of trauma?"

Karen shrugged then said, "Well, the reason she is seeing me is public record, so I can talk about that. Her name is Judy Bench. She's Mark's oldest daughter, and she claims to have been raped a couple of days ago."

"Claims?"

"There are discrepancies in her story, and I am working with her to try and uncover all that happened."

John, Jim, Sam, and Chris had their tablets out, and Karen looked around the table and asked, "What have I started?"

Jim looked up at her, "I think… the first step to answers to a whole lot of questions."

Dinner in the Bench home was quiet. Judy made fried chicken, and Tabitha helped. Mark had gotten home late, and the three ate, and then Judy sent Tabitha up to take a shower. Mark helped Judy with the dishes and when they were finished he asked, "So, how was your first meeting with Doctor Mantel?"

"Good. Really good. I like her a lot."

"That's great. I like her, too. She is very savvy."

When the dishes were done, Judy went up to shower, and Mark did the same. Tabitha was drying off when Judy entered the bathroom, and she helped her put on her nightgown. "Why were you asleep in Dad's bed naked last night?"

Judy was surprised by the question. "I took a shower and was scared, so I slept with Dad. You sleep with him almost every night. What's the big deal?"

"I don't sleep with him naked, and Dad usually sleeps naked, but last night he had pajamas on."

"So?"

"It just seemed weird."

"Well, it's not. I get scared, too, you know, and Dad comforts me as much as he comforts you." Tabitha shrugged and went off to her bedroom. Judy showered and shaved her legs and pubic hair then stood for several minutes allowing the hot water to run over her body. She ran her hands down her breasts to her vagina and fingered herself until she orgasmed. Her whole body shuddered, and she got out of the shower, dried off, and went to bed.

Mark had gone back downstairs after his shower and poured himself a glass of bourbon and was sitting in the living room thumbing through a magazine. The girls had their own magazines. Tabitha's were preteen mags whereas Judy's were young adult, mostly makeup and beauty magazines as well as modeling magazines. He grabbed a couple of Judy's magazines and looked through them and was surprised by the content. One magazine had a whole article on anal sex and the pros and cons of the act. He was surprised by the graphic nature of the article and by others that talked about sex, pregnancy, and other subjects that made him both curious and disturbed.

It was ten after twelve as he finished his bourbon when Judy came down the stairs dressed in nothing but a sheer robe. "Aren't you a little old to be walking around the house nearly nude?"

"No more than you. You walk around naked all the time, Dad. What's the big deal?" She opened her robe wide to Mark's face. "It's nothing you haven't seen before." She noticed the magazine in his hand and asked, "Are you catching up on my reading?"

"To be honest, I hadn't been paying attention to what you girls read, but your magazines have some pretty graphic subject matter."

"Like what?"

"A whole article on anal sex!"

"Yeah, that's a good article. I had no idea that the anus had so many nerve endings and that you can have deep orgasms from anal penetration."

Mark put the magazine down, poured another bourbon, and asked, "Outside of the experience with Sally, are you sexually active?"

Judy grinned. "Why do you ask? Are you jealous?"

"Hardly. I'm your father. I know that growing up without your mother has been hard on you and your sister. I know I've never had the birds and bees talk with you."

Judy sat down on the edge of his chair and said, "Dad, you have done great by me and Tabitha. You've been a rock for us since Mom died. I'm not having sex with anyone. The experience with Sally was a strange one, but we talked it over, and I may have overreacted, which is one of the things I spoke with Karen about yesterday. All I came down here for was a glass of milk, not to have a birds and bees talk." Mark smiled, and Judy leaned down and kissed him gently on the lips then got up and went into the kitchen. She reappeared with a glass of milk in her hands and stood drinking it as he looked on.

"And just like that my little girl is back in the room."

"What do you mean?"

"Drinking a glass of milk, like when you were little. Sometimes I forget that there is still that little girl inside of you. You're growing into a beautiful young woman, and I don't always stop and take in the moments of innocence in you." She finished the milk, washed her glass, and put it on the drying rack. Mark had followed her into the kitchen with the bourbon in his hand, and she looked at him and asked, "Can I have drink of that?"

"Have you ever had it before?" Judy shook her head. "It probably won't go over well after milk."

"Well, let me try it."

He handed her the glass. She smelled it and made a face then took a large sip. She coughed and gagged, and Mark took the glass from her while laughing and said, "Stick to milk, kiddo."

"It burns, but I'm starting to feel warm and tingly."

"Well, you weigh what? Ninety pounds?"

"A hundred and five. I look thinner because of my height."

Mark took the last sip of his drink. "You're five feet four inches, honey. The same as your mother."

"Ah, but you have to admit I carry my weight well."

Mark nodded. "Go to bed. You have school in the morning."

"About school."

"What about it?"

"Well, I have all the credits I need to graduate, so I was thinking of taking a job for the rest of the spring then walking in graduation."

"What kind of job?"

"Mary has her real estate company, and Sally has been helping out there, you know, learning the family business, and they offered me a position if I want it."

"So, you and Sally are best friends again?"

"We're good. What do you think?"

"I think that I paid thirty thousand dollars for your last year, and you should use the time to prepare for college."

"I'm thinking of taking a year off after I graduate. You did it, so did Mom. A little break from school would do me a world of good."

"I don't know, Judy. You've worked so hard. I can tell you that it was hell for me and your mother to get back into the discipline of school after our time off."

"You were high school sweethearts, Dad. You took the time together and from what I recall you two used to say it was the best year of your lives."

"It was, but we weren't working. We were traveling the world. We wanted to experience different cultures and places before we settled down into our lives. If you recall, before your mother became a firefighter she graduated from college and was going on to medical school but changed her mind."

"It was the car accident that changed her mind, wasn't it?"

"Yes…we were both in the car, and if it had not been for the quick work of firefighters we would have both died that night. Just a few more seconds and the whole thing would have been engulfed in flames with us inside it."

"Well, it's not as safe these days, but I guess I could talk to Sally about taking a trip around the world instead of working."

"Oh, no you don't. We will talk more about this in the morning. Now, get to bed." Judy went on up to her room, and Mark shook his head. "Travel the world. If you want to do something with your life, do it here. The world is a dangerous place."

John and Sara were sitting on the deck enjoying a glass of wine at a little past midnight. Both were nude and spent from making love, and John was out of breath from swimming laps. Sara asked, "So, what did you find out about Mark's daughter?"

"She filed a rape complaint with West Valley LAPD that isn't being taken seriously."

"I don't understand. Rape is a serious crime. What makes this rape different from any other?"

"The victim is seventeen, and the sex was with a childhood friend who claims it was consensual."

"I don't care if the guy was her friend from birth. Rape is rape."

John laughed. "You hear rape and just assume it was male on female."

"It wasn't?"

"No. It was female on female. The Bench girl claims she was drugged and raped, but the girl she had sex with, Sally Owen, says that the sex was consensual. She admitted to giving Bench Ecstasy beforehand but says that she offered it and Judy accepted."

"Owen? Sally Owen? The daughter of real estate tycoon Mary Owen?"

"Do you know them?"

"Mary has sold some property for me, and she helped us find this lot of land to build our compound on."

"Did I meet her?"

"In passing. You were in the middle of a heavy case load, and it was back when we learned that Steve had ALS."

"How well do you know her?"

"Pretty well. She donates to the hospital and sits on our board of directors. She has a great reputation in the community, and I have never heard anyone say a cross word about her."

"Do you know her daughter?"

"Daughters. She has two. Sally is seventeen and Casey's ten. I know that Sally has a birthday coming up and high school graduation. Can you get involved in what's going on?"

"Jim and Sam are going to interview Sally tomorrow, then Judy Bench."

Sara sipped her wine and asked, "What are you sensing?"

"Jim has an unsolved pedophile murder in Woodland Hills. It might be just a random crime, or it could be that the perp's past caught up with him and someone took him out."

"So, if the guy was a pedophile, and we know that pedophiles can't be cured, I would think that his death would make you happy."

"One dead pedophile is a good thing. The person who took him out worries me."

"Why?"

"Because I think this was an impulse murder, and I also think that there is something a whole lot bigger going on, and this killer is young and impetuous."

"You don't think this was a victim. You think it might be someone trying to do what the Eagle does?"

"I sure as hell hope not."

Sally was standing near her car in the school parking lot when Judy drove in and parked. "So…how was your night?" Sally asked.

"Fine. Why?"

"I got us out of class for the day. Are you ready to make some money?"

"Sure."

"Follow me back to my house, and we'll get started."

The two girls got back in their cars, and Judy followed Sally to her house where two black vans were parked on the street. The girls parked in the driveway, and Judy asked, "What's this?"

"This, my bisexual friend, is your formal introduction to underage pornography."

"Are you talking child porn?"

"There are different levels of that. These people shoot films of young people between thirteen and eighteen."

"And who do they shoot the films for?"

"All in good time, Judy." She looked her up and down and said, "That's a cute dress. I like the cleavage and the leg."

"Thanks. You look great, too." The girls walked into the house and found seven boys and girls wandering around the family room, some half nude, others fully nude. There were young women and boys dancing in front of seated boys and girls, and some were fondling them. Judy looked around the room and asked, "What's going on?"

"We have a big shoot today, so the people acting in the pornos need to be kept aroused in order to perform. Those girls and boys dancing and playing with the performers are called fluffers."

"Fluffers? I thought that was a myth."

"Hardly. We need them a lot in underage porn. It's too dangerous to give the actors erectile drugs. They use those a lot in adult porn, but in kid porn it's too risky. Besides, boys have an endless reservoir of hormones, especially those in puberty."

"And the girls?"

"We don't hit our stride until we get into our late twenties, so fluffers don't have the same impact. Girl on girl porn is easy, and so is guy on girl. I mean, in the end, we're just receptacles for the guy's cum. A good actress who can turn it on when the camera is running makes the big bucks."

"How did you get into this?"

"I'll explain more after our shoot. Are you ready to play?"

"Do you have some Ecstasy?"

Sally pulled a bottle from her purse and took Judy's hand and poured several pills out. "Take two and you will be relaxed." Sally walked away, and Judy put the pills in a small empty case in her own purse and waited for her to return.

Mary had just finished with Marina, and the two were in the shower. Mary was gently wiping the light blood streaks off of Marina's back. "You beat me good, Mistress Mary."

"You enjoyed it?"

"Very much." Mary smiled, and the two stepped out of the shower and dried off. The music from downstairs was loud, and Marina put on a loose-fitting top and short shorts and was brushing her long black hair as Mary looked over her tablet. "It sounds like a real party downstairs."

"No. Sally is conducting her first porn shoot, and she is doing it with Judy Bench."

"Judy is lesbian?"

"I don't think so, but Sally is working with her. She wants to learn the business."

Marina was still brushing her hair. "You think Mr. Mark like it if he know what she doing?"

"I know for a fact he would not, so no talk of it if you see Mark." Mary left the bathroom and read over the text from Tonya on the situation with Lori. She went to her office and called her.

"I have to pull this girl out of the auction because Hugh can't break a fuckin' kid?"

"Look. I tried to talk to her and got nowhere. The girl will die before being broken."

"Oh no, she won't. You call Hugh and let him know I'm coming over to talk to her unrestrained."

"She will kill you if not restrained."

"You let me worry about that. Just have her ready this afternoon around two."

John and Chris were going over the Fleece crime scene photos once more. "So, who do we talk to first?" Chris asked.

"We don't talk to anyone. Jim and Sam will. They're going to talk to the Owen girl."

"I thought you wanted Bench?"

"I want Owen's side of the story, and I want it at the sheriff's station."

"All that's going to do is bring in lawyers."

"That's exactly what I'm hoping for."

Chris shook his head. "You want lawyers? What the hell for?"

"It's not just lawyers but the type of law they practice."

"Did you fall on your head while in St. Lucia? Lawyers are the enemy."

"No…they're a window into their client's behavior. They let me know just where their client's priorities lie. Mary Owen is a real estate mogul, so her lawyers should run in that vein. If they have other parts to their practice that Ms. Owen uses, that will give us more information."

"What the hell are you looking for, John?"

"Looking for? Oh, I'm not looking, Chris. I've found it. All I need is for a few pieces to fall into place and then I will have proof."

"Of what?"

"A darkness, a plague, an even deeper layer of human cruelty than we have seen in a long time."

Sally and Judy were dressing after their sex and shower scene. Sally asked, "Do you think you're ready to do it with a guy?"

"I do, and I'm going to share my body with him tonight."

"So, you're going to lose your virginity?" Judy nodded. "Well, let's shoot it now. You can make twenty grand for a cherry popper shoot."

"No. This has to be intimate and romantic. I am enjoying the money and the sex with you, Sally, and I am getting really interested in more work." She looked around the room and asked, "What's up with all the mirrors?"

"They help when shooting. The cameraman can use mirrors to trick the eye, and he can also catch scenes and closeups that they will use in editing before posting the videos."

"Where do they get posted? We are under age?"

"We have a huge clientele who subscribes to our porn channels. Come with me. Let's talk to my mother. She'll explain."

Pierce was sitting in a director's chair behind the two-way mirror. There were several sex scenes being shot, and there was more screaming and crying than there was pleasure. Young children between three and ten were being raped and sodomized by adults on live streams. Clive Baxter and Andrew Haas were standing in the film room with Pierce.

"I have to admit that Judy girl is hot stuff. Is she going to be part of our mission?" Andrew asked.

"In time. Mary is meeting with her now, and if all goes as planned, we will do a few more shoots with her and then send her on to Hugh."

"Why would you send her to Hugh? He will only destroy her."

"Not for breaking. I think Mary can handle Judy based on what I have seen and heard. She will go to Hugh for the last step of desensitization to the industry. She will make the perfect addition to our stable of handlers, and she is very suggestable. Sally told me before the shoot Judy asked for Ecstasy, and she gave her six to eight pills. I don't know how many she took, but it worked wonders. We'll use that along with some LSD and deep training, and she will be the perfect foil to Sally. Not only will she be a porn sensation, but she'll make a great assistant in the pornography side of the business."

Clive spoke up. "The pornography side? What the hell are you talking about? Pornography is the side."

"No, it's not. We haven't been getting a fair shake on the profits."

Clive sat and said, "I don't understand, Pierce. You're talking in riddles."

Andrew laughed as Pierce continued. "We introduce the kids to the industry, the trade, if you will. Once they are ready, they are taken from us, and then they are brought into the trade."

"Trade? What bloody trade?"

"The slave trade, Clive. The very profitable human slave trade."

CHAPTER TEN

*"How did the Eagle miss
killing this asshole?"*

Judy and Sally were sitting in Mary's office chatting when she entered. "Judy, I'm impressed. You've also impressed some of my business partners."

"Business partners? I only met the cameraman, and his face was covered. Given his thick British accent, I hardly think his real name is John Smith." Sally laughed as did Mary.

"You catch on fast, but you would not recognize John in a crowd, would you?"

"Not unless I heard him speak. I have a thing with smells and voices. I never forget them."

Mary smiled a little more hesitantly. "So, Sally tells me you want in."

"Sure! Who wouldn't? Major paydays for doing something pleasurable? I would be a fool to turn that down."

"Indeed. Sally is going to be taking a more active role in the business side of things, and we could use someone we've known all her life to take over the pornography operations."

"I've only done it twice, so I'm hardly ready to run something like this."

"Of course, you're not, silly. We have an extensive training program, and I would like you to jump into it right away."

"What does that entail?"

"Well, leaving school then working here at the house and a few properties that I own where we shoot porno plus a week's training."

"Training? Where?"

"With my master trainer. He'll bring you up to speed on operations, and you can see step by step how the process works."

"Your industry is child pornography and exploitation."

The smiles left Mary and Sally's faces. "What makes you say that?"

"Oh, I don't know…common sense. Come on. You're shooting kiddie porn and underage porn and streaming it through the deep web to pedophiles. It doesn't take a rocket scientist to see that."

"How long have you known?"

"Since that creepy guy threatened to rape and murder my sister."

"I heard about that, and I'm sorry."

"I understand that you need to keep the kids in line. I have been doing a lot of research on the human trafficking business, and it is quite profitable, but if you get caught, it carries long prison sentences. And in the case of the bad breath guy, most likely the death penalty." Mary nodded slowly, but Sally sat motionless. "The way I see it, you've been doing this for a long time. I mean, Sally was able to discredit me with the cops on a child rape. That's impressive. Her whole story was brilliant. Now, here's the deal. My father is a loving, caring man, who I love deeply. I know that you got your talons into him after the rape and settled him down, and I'm fine with that. But I want you to stay away from him, Mary. I want in, but the first thing off the table is my father."

Mary nodded with her mouth hanging open. "I can't just cut him off. It will have to be done carefully."

"I understand, and I agree; however, he's mine, not yours. Don't touch. As for the business, all of my research has showed that you start off with kiddie porn but then move the victims up the ladder until you have them indentured to you, and they become slaves. Domestic. Sexual. There's not much of a difference, is there? If you're going to sell a human being into slavery, they're going to end up being abused and used for sex as well as other duties, right?" Mary didn't respond. "Then there are the auctions. You sell off the best of the lot to buyers in the slave trade, and the rest are either used in sex houses or for street prostitution, which in most cases takes care of itself when it comes to the usefulness of those girls and boys as they usually die badly at the hands of their johns, right?" No response. "So, here's my thinking. I have a great business head, Mary, and so obviously do you or you would not be as successful as you are. I don't know how much of your wealth is from the human trafficking trade, but I'm going to guess that it is substantial. I'm very persuasive myself. Hell, I have Sally convinced that I like lesbian sex." Judy looked over at her and said, "I don't like lesbian sex, Sally. I'm straight, but you opened the door and that, after some research, told me I better run with it. Make no mistake...I don't like it, and you said it yourself, if I can turn it on and off for the camera I will make big bucks. Well, I can. That said, I will keep having sex, and after I lose my virginity to my true love, then I will have sex with other men. I have no intention of doing anything to hurt this business; it's lucrative. I just want to lay my cards on the table here and now. I will go to great lengths to protect my interests here, and yours, so let's work out an agreement that will make us all happy and rich."

The women sat speechless. The only sound in the room was the ticking of a desk clock. Before Mary could respond, her cellphone rang, and she was informed that two sheriff's deputies were at the door seeking Sally.

Lori had been beaten and raped over the last several days. Hugh Masters had brought in a group of thirty servitude worker slaves he leased out to several farmers in the Ventura area to do some work on his property. When the work was done, he threw Lori to the men, so they could have their way with her, but he gave strict instructions not to kill her. She was beaten and bloodied. The man servant who had told her to submit had taken her after the men were through with her. She was on the toilet for over an hour, and he listened as she moaned and screamed. He walked into the bathroom and saw Lori standing over the bowl filled with semen and blood and watched as she passed it from her anus and vagina and then turned and threw up semen and repeated the event for nearly an hour. When she was finished, he took her into the shower and cleaned the weak girl then dried her and took her back to her bed. He chained her nude body and said, "He will have more men coming in you tonight and every day and night until you break or die."

"Fuck him. Do what you want to my body. My mind is my own." The young man shook his head. "You are just another girl I will have to bury on the back property." Lori didn't respond, and the boy looked down at her battered and still seeping body and said, "Hugh likes his final torment of those he can't break to be burial, but not the way you might think. He buries them alive, after he places them over a concrete parking block so their bodies arch in the middle leaving their asses up in the air and their shoulders and heads upward as well. The rest of their bodies are covered in dirt that is wetted down, and as they slowly die from brutal rapes and dehydration, he keeps watch over them because as the end grows near and the pain and suffering become unbearable, people like you always break in those last minutes or hours, and at that moment when you think he will save you, he won't. He will rape you himself then if he feels extra merciful he will put a gun to the back of your head and blow your brains out. I have only seen him do that once. No. He allows nature to take its course, and it is savage."

Judy hid in a closet when the deputies entered the office. Mary and Sally were seated, and the two men handed them an order for detaining Sally for questioning in the rape of Judy Bench. The deputies were surprised at the calm both women exhibited, and Mary instructed Sally to go with the officers then picked up the phone and called her attorney then followed the cruiser to the sheriff's downtown offices.

Parker Stone was shouting at the front desk of the sheriff's station and calling out for Sam and Jim. "I want to know why the sheriff's department is harassing my client in a case they have no jurisdiction in?" Sally was being escorted into the building and saw Parker, who walked up to her and said, "Say nothing." He looked at the deputies and asked, "Has she been read her Miranda Rights?"

"Ms. Owen isn't under arrest, Stone. She is being brought in for questioning."

"That's not what I asked you."

"No. We have not read her her Miranda Rights because she is not under arrest."

"Have you spoken to these deputies?"

"Um…they said come with us, and I said okay."

"That's it?"

"Yes, that's it."

"Don't say another word until I am in the room with you, do you understand?"

Sally nodded as Jim's voice boomed through the foyer. "Parker fuckin' Stone, the ambulance chaser turned corporate big wig lawyer. What are you doing in my police station?"

"I'm Ms. Owens attorney, and it's not 'your police station.' It's Sheriff Pritchard's. Where is she?"

Sam stepped out from behind Jim. "I'm right here, and you're right. This is my station, so are you going to give us trouble?"

"Have you ever known me to do anything but?"

Mary had entered and called out to Parker, "Stone, don't start a bunch of crap. The Sheriff wants to talk to Sally. Let them speak."

"Mary, as your lawyer, I am advising you and Sally to be quiet."

Jim took two cigarettes out of his top left pocket and handed one to Sam, who placed it behind her ear as did Jim. "We just want to have a simple on the record conversation with Ms. Owen, that's all Parker. If you want us to escalate this to an arrest, we can do that. We have a pending rape charge against the girl. Is that what you want?"

Mary was shaking her head, and the frustration on Parker's face was clear. "Where are you taking her?"

Jim smiled. "An interrogation room. Care to join us?" He waved his arm for the group to follow him, and as they walked several steps ahead of them, Jim leaned over to Sam and asked, "How did the Eagle miss killing this asshole in the Cohen case a few years ago?" Sam shrugged and laughed as they entered the interrogation room.

Pierce, Clive, and Andrew had hidden when the sheriff showed up on scene. All of the kids had been moved to another section of the house, and the men thought they were alone outside of Marina. Judy got out of the closet and walked down the hall after the group had left. She knew Sally's home as well as her own and went down a back stairwell that was off the family room and looked at the three men. Pierce's rugged good looks and British accent enthralled her as she looked the rather short but muscular man up and down. Andrew Haas was tall and lanky, unkempt, with a pair of board shorts on and a tank top. His long blonde hair was straight and oily looking, and his face was pock marked and covered in pimples. Clive, on the other hand, was handsome, young, and clean shaven with a shaved head. Judy pulled her cellphone from her pocket and started the video and recording option and set the phone, so she had the men in frame as they spoke.

"So, what now?" Andrew asked. "We have all the footage we need. The live streams are automated, and the kids know what to do, so I say we clear out of here and meet at Hugh's."

"Why the hell are we going to Hugh's house?"

"Mary has a girl there that she wants in the auction this weekend who Hugh can't break."

"So?"

"So, Mary is going to talk to the girl, but Hugh thought that you and I might like to get off and also get some video of her since he feels he is going to end up killing her."

Andrew shook his head. "Why does Hugh have to take these steps? Just throw her in a brothel. We'll all make a few bucks, and nature will take its course. Hell, a week in one of the dungeons, and the kid will be dead, and a lot of men and women will have had some fun."

"You know Hugh can't accept failure. If he can't break her, he will keep her for himself and then kill her in his time-honored tradition."

Andrew shuddered, and Judy noticed the hair on the back of her neck standing up and goosebumps appearing all over her arms. "I have only participated in his tradition once. Never again. We take kids off the streets, recruits that Sally brings us, as well as others from foster care, and we make a great living. I don't like the steppingstone approach that is used to enslave these kids and people."

"Who asked your opinion? Listen, Andrew, any time you want out just say the word. Clive was a homeless junkie a year ago when I found him, and what did I do? I cleaned him up, helped him get his GED, gave him a home to live in, and taught him a profession in photography and cinematography. I took a seventeen-year-old high school dropout from the street who was on a one-way trip to overdosing and made him a man. As for you, my brother, I gave you back your self-respect and protected you. Now, you make good money, you and Clive live very, very well." Andrew was looking at the floor as Pierce spoke. "Do I exaggerate on any of my points?" Andrew shook his head. "And what's your name?"

"Andrew Haas."

"And your name?"

"Clive Baxter."

"And your professions?"

"Photographers."

"And who do you have to thank for that?"

"You."

"I'm sorry? Who do you have to thank for that?"

"You, Pierce. You, Pierce Tallon."

"Don't you ever forget that. Now, I say we put the rest of our equipment in the van and go over to Hugh's place and fuck this chick. I will do the fucking, and you two will do the filming and vice versa." Andrew and Clive nodded, and the two men started putting equipment into crates and walking them out of the house as Pierce looked on.

Judy got up off the floor with the camera still running and ran out the back door to her car and laid down on the seats until the men were in their van and ready to leave. As soon as they pulled out onto the street, she followed them while tears were streaming down her face. She looked into her phone after reading off the plate number of the van and said, "Oh dear God! What have I gotten myself into?"

CHAPTER ELEVEN

"So, who's going to do the whipping?"

John and Chris were sitting in the dark on the opposing side of the two-way mirrored interrogation room at the sheriff's station. Both men had their tablets recording but said nothing.

"You have been accused of drugging and raping your close friend Judy Bench. Do you understand that?" Sam asked.

Sally nodded, and Parker tried to speak, but she interrupted him. "Leave it alone, Parker. I have answered all of these questions already."

Sam asked several more, and Parker pulled a yellow police report from his briefcase, handed it to Sam, and said, "Look it over, Sheriff. Read every question and every answer. Do NOT ask the same question again. My client has been instructed not to answer you. If you have something new to ask, then ask it. If not, release her."

Sam handed the sheet to Jim, who looked at it for two seconds and handed it back. He sat back, stretched, and asked, "Did you murder Mr. Alan Fleece?" John and Chris broke out in light laughter.

"You are asking my client if she murdered someone?"

"Yeah. Well, Ms. Owen. Did you?"

"Don't answer."

"I did not murder Al. I loved Al. He was a close friend of our family. I'm devastated by his death."

"He was a convicted sex offender. A pedophile. Did you know that?"

Carter started to speak, but Sally cut him off, "We all knew his history, Mr. O'Brian. He made some poor choices when he was young, but he paid his debt to society and was working hard to earn back the public trust."

"What public? He wasn't in government."

"You're right, Mr. O'Brian. There are more crooks in government. That was an insult to my friend's memory. I miss Al, and I hope they find the monster who murdered him so brutally."

The conversation went back and forth for almost an hour, and Chris looked at John and asked, "So, is she a killer?"

"No, but she has a secret."

"How do you know?"

"Her body language; her ease at answering questions. She is either a victim of abuse, or she is involved in it."

"Jesus John! You think that girl could be engaged in illegal activity?"

"As either the victim or a recruiter."

"Recruiter? This isn't the damn military."

"No, it's not. I think it is a thousand times more savage. I want you to hack her car's GPS as well as her cellphone. I want to know her every move."

"You want a tap? We need a warrant."

John's eyes glistened from the light emanating off the mirror. "No, I don't. Just get it done." Chris left the room while John texted Jim and Sam. Sam looked at the text then looked at Sally and said, "Thank you for your time, Ms. Owen. We have all we need. You're free to go."

Carter looked concerned. "You have all you need? What does that mean?"

"We have no further questions for Ms. Owen at this time." Jim and Sam stood up and walked out of the room.

Sally sat for a few seconds then looked at Carter and asked, "What just happened?"

"Don't say another word. Let's go."

The van pulled into a gated community in Hidden Hills. Judy knew the enclave well. It was the home of the super rich and the super famous. It was a city within a city and was for the most part self-supporting. Judy waited for the van to enter then drove up to the security gate where she was recognized right away. "Hi Judy! Are you here to see Maggie?"

"Yes. Is she home?"

"You have a free pass. Come on in. I haven't seen her or her entourage leave today, so I'm sure she's home." Judy nodded and drove through the gates. She followed Long Valley Road, looking at the gated houses and high fences. "So many high walls and high gates. Is it to keep people out or in I wonder?" As she approached Maggie's house she slowed but drove past until she reached the end of the cul-de-sac. Two huge mansions sat at the end of the street; one was gated, but she could see through the gating and parked her car and walked up to the gate where a security camera moved from side to side as she peered in. She saw the van parked way off at the end of a circular driveway, and she went back to her car and drove down the street to Maggie's house and pressed the intercom at the gate. A well-dressed young man stepped through the opening electric gate and leaned on Judy's driver's side window.

"So, what brings you to the gates of hell, beautiful?"

"Hi, Josh. Is Mags here?"

"She's here, and she's on a holy tear so be warned."

"What now?"

"You know her new music video just went viral, right?"

"Everything Maggie does these days goes viral."

"Yeah, well, this one has the paparazzi driving her and all of us insane. We tried to sneak out the back gate this morning, and a group of the assholes somehow got onto the adjacent land. Fortunately, we didn't have the gates open."

"Oh, shit! What did you do?"

"You know Mary Owen, right?"

"Of course. Her oldest daughter Sally is one of my best friends."

"Well, she's close friends with the property owner at the end of the street."

"You mean the mega mansion?"

"Yeah. Anyway, he has a private road that he can use to leave his property from one of the emergency exits, and his security people came to the rescue and got us out of there and helped us get home."

"Who's the neighbor?"

"Some big wig in the venture capital industry you've probably never heard of before."

"Try me."

"Hugh Masters."

"Hugh Masters the money man?"

"One and the same. He's a nice guy and helps Maggie and her family out a lot. Hey, sorry for talking your ear off. Go on in. Mags is in the recording studio. If she's pissed that you're here, don't tell her I let you in." Judy laughed and drove in.

Maggie Pulp was sitting on a stool and staring into a mirror when she saw Judy enter the house. She jumped up and ran to her and threw her arms around her neck and cried. Judy patted her back and said, "It's okay, Mags. Josh told me about what happened."

"I hate this shit, Judy. I hate it. I can't go to the bathroom without someone trying to stick a camera in the stall. I'm a prisoner in my own home."

"You are the one in control, honey. You're a pop star. I have read several stories about celebrity and one of the things that has always come up is the more accessible you make yourself the less interest the paparazzi will have in you."

"So, what, should I walk my fifteen-year-old ass down the street without security?"

"No, but instead of being standoffish with the press, hold a news conference once a month, take walks, talk to people, hang out with your friends in public. Of course, you have to have your security, but answer questions, and you will see over time this will fade."

"And that works how?"

"The media will lose interest if you're more accessible. They'll go hound someone else, and you'll get your life back."

Maggie's mother, and manager, was in the room and said, "Judy's right. We'll start off slowly and then just incorporate this into our daily lives, and it will get better."

Maggie smiled and hugged Judy. "How is it that you always make things better?"

Judy laughed. "I don't make them better. I can just see things from the outside. Josh told me that a neighbor helped you with the mob earlier."

"Um… yeah. Mom, who is that guy?"

"Hugh Masters. He's been our neighbor since before you were born. He has several roads on his property that are secret to most. He built them in the event of a fire, so he could get out if other routes were blocked."

"So, you know him well?" Judy said.

"As well as you can know anyone. He's a venture capitalist and loaned us the money to launch Maggie's career a couple of years ago."

"He sounds like a nice man."

"He's a very nice man. Why do you ask?"

"Oh, I overheard some people talking about him."

"Is that why you're here?"

"No. I came by to see Mags, and the subject came up, and since he is such a nice guy I was just curious about him."

Maggie laughed and pulled her cellphone out. "Hi Hugh. This is Maggie. I have a friend who would like to meet you. Can we come over?" There was a pause, and Maggie was nodding her head. "My friend's name is Judy Bench." Maggie hung up the line and said, "Come on. Hugh wants to meet you."

"Why does Judy Bench want to meet me?"

Mary's mouth fell open as she held the phone. "Judy Bench wants to meet you? How the hell would she know who you are?"

"That's my question. Is there something that I need to know?"

"Hell if I know." Mary turned to Sally in the front seat of her car. "Sally, why is Judy meeting Hugh Masters at his home with that little pop star Mags?"

"Judy is doing what?"

"You heard me."

"I have no idea. I know that Judy and Maggie are friends, but how you get from Maggie to Hugh is beyond me."

"She doesn't know, Hugh."

"When are you coming over?" Hugh asked.

"As soon as I drop off Sally. She just got a grilling from the Los Angeles Sheriff Samantha Pritchard and Jim O'Brian."

"Not the rape thing again. I thought you put that to bed with Mark?"

"So did I, but two deputies showed up at my house and took Sally in for questioning."

"Did they arrest her?"

"No, Parker Stone was there to protect her, but the questions were pretty much all the same as what Sally has already answered, so after about an hour they let us leave."

"Watch your back. Someone in law enforcement smells a rat. If you and Sally are not already under surveillance, you will be."

"I don't understand."

"This Judy girl started a wrath of shit with the cops, and given Al's murder and long rap sheet, they might have some nutty idea that you were involved."

"Are you crazy? I don't know who killed Al and neither does Sally."

"Well, I know law enforcement. They must think they have something, so be careful. You might want to lay low and just handle real estate for a few weeks and leave the trafficking and auction off the table. You have the infrastructure in place to oversee all of the operations, and I can monitor things for you. I have the kids for the sale here at my compound, and they are being sent to the stable right now."

"So, who's going to do the whipping?"

"Who do you think?"

"Oh, that's right. If there is one thing you love more than anything else, it's whipping those naked little asses in the stable."

"It sends the point home to these animals that they are to obey their masters, and I get a kick out of it."

Mary shook her head. "I'm still coming over to talk to Lori. Let me know how it goes with Judy."

She hung up the phone, and Sally said, "Judy knows something."

"About Hugh?"

"Yeah."

"How could that be?"

"Someone at the house must've talked about him, and Judy must have gotten wind of it. We ended up hiding her and then leaving with the sheriff. Pierce, Andrew, and Clive were filming at the house. If they said anything in earshot of Judy, she will follow it up."

Mary pulled into the drive and saw that Judy's car wasn't there. "We need to find her and get her over here now."

CHAPTER TWELVE

"Jesus! I'm a killer."

Hugh was sitting in his drawing room when Maggie and Judy arrived. Maggie made introductions, and Hugh smiled and asked Judy, "So, why did you want to meet me?"

"Maggie has been my friend since pretty much birth, and when I learned of your kindness I was curious."

"Okay. What do you do for a living?"

"I'm a senior in high school, but I am starting a job in the next few weeks as I have finished all requirements for graduation."

"You're in high school? May I ask how old you are?"

"I'll be eighteen very soon."

Hugh looked at the sexy outfit she had on and said, "I'm sorry, young lady, but I would have guessed you were in your early twenties."

"I get that a lot."

They talked for a while, then Maggie and her mother excused themselves as they had a commitment, and Judy asked to stay behind. The two chatted over sodas and cookies, and after about a half hour Hugh said, "I hate to break up this great conversation, but I have business to attend to."

"I'm sorry, Mr. Masters. I didn't mean to crash your afternoon."

"No, no. It's quite alright. I have horses, and my stable man is off today, so I need to feed them."

"I love horses. Can I come with you?"

"I'm afraid not. I simply need to feed them and then I have some work to do. I tell you what, though. If you're free tomorrow afternoon, come back by the house, and I will take you horseback riding. I have twenty acres of land here and a lot of great trails. Do you ride?"

"I do, indeed, and would love that." Hugh called for one of his house staff to see Judy out. The servant walked her out then returned inside without noticing Judy sneaking back across the driveway and up to the front door.

Lori had stopped screaming as Pierce and Andrew raped her. Clive had been filming and waiting for his turn. Lori was on her side with both men inside her, and she just stared off into space at the dark wall of her cell as the two men grunted and groaned. "Is the bitch alive?" Andrew asked.

Pierce looked down at her tear-stained face. "Yeah. She's just in shock. My cock is bigger than yours. Let me fuck her ass, and you do her throat."

There was a gardener's shack off the main house, and Judy looked around but didn't see anyone. The side door into the house was open, and she was about to enter it when she saw two men in green coveralls walking toward her. They were speaking Spanish, and she could pick up bits and pieces of what they were saying.

"Have you had a piece of that bitch upstairs?" one asked the other.

"Yes. Really nice. Master let me fuck her the other night after everyone was gone. She's a feisty one. I wish I had money, so I could have a slave like that."

"I heard the master say that she's not going to be sold. He's going to keep her and use her until he's tired of her."

The two men laughed, and one asked, "Have you been to the stable?"

"I fed the horses. Master has quite a few girls and boys down there now. He's having a whipping party. A lot of crying and screaming."

"Well, you've felt the leather of the master's bullwhip. It hurts like hell."

"It does, but when he's finished there won't be anyone that will break a rule."

The other man nodded and unlocked the shed and took out some tools. He asked, "Why do you have three mower blades on the grinder bench? I thought you had sharpened them."

"I did, I did. I just haven't had time to put them back on the mowers. Remind me when we're finishing for the night."

The two men walked on down a path to a lower terraced garden, and Judy slipped into the shed and looked around. She saw the mower blades and picked one up and cut her finger. "Shit! Jesus that's sharp." She grabbed a pair of gloves off a shelf, put them on, then grabbed the blade and a hammer. She walked into the back door, and there was a staircase to her immediate left. She climbed it quietly into a long hall with a lot of high windows. There were doors along the hall, and she slowly opened several to find what looked like guest rooms. "Nice place," she said to herself. She was about to turn when she heard a door open and close quickly. She heard rustling and then the sound of a lighter and someone taking a deep breath. She peeked around the corner and saw Andrew standing nude near a window at the end of the hall smoking a cigarette. He was a little out of breath but smoked quickly then went back into the room. Judy followed his steps and placed her ear to the door. She could hear bedsprings and soft crying, then she heard Pierce's voice.

"You see? My cock is longer and thicker than yours, now her ass is wide open. Want to hear her scream?" There was a pause, and Judy heard a female voice let out a blood curdling scream.

"Oh God! Please, no more."

Pierce had placed a deeply spiked steel cock ring over his penis. It fit almost like a condom, but it was open at the end, and there were dozens of small razor-sharp spikes that protruded through the leather. He had a firm grasp on Lori's pelvis from the side and was all the way inside her anus.

"Won't that kill her?"

"No. It hurts like hell, and she'll bleed, but it's not sharp enough to cause internal bleeding." He thrust in and out of Lori several more times, and her arms jerked against her restraints as she let out high pitched screams for mercy. Neither man paid attention to her pleas, and a small pool of blood had formed on the bed. Pierce wasn't paying attention to anything except the injury he was inflicting on Lori until what appeared to be a closet door opened, and Mary Owen walked in. He was caught off guard as he was orgasming, but Andrew and Clive spotted her right away and pulled away from the girl.

"Get the fuck out of her, Pierce. All of you."

"Mary, what the hell are you doing here?"

"I came to try and reason with the girl." She walked over to Pierce standing nude and erect and grabbed his penis. "That instrument of torture is cruel. Have you ever had one used on you?"

Pierce shook his head, and Mary pulled the unit off his penis and threw it to Andrew. "Put it on and fuck Pierce up the ass."

"I'm not gay."

"I don't give a shit. Put it on and fuck him up the ass. Pierce, bend over the girl's bed and pull your ass cheeks apart." Pierce did as directed, and Andrew came up behind him and put some lube on Pierce and then on his own penis. "What are you waiting for? Jam it up his ass." Pierce let out a shriek as Andrew pounded him. Mary just watched and smiled. Judy had her ear pressed firmly to the door and could hear the whole conversation and the brutality. When Andrew had orgasmed, Mary made the men reverse roles, and when they were finished she said, "Now, you know what it feels like. Do you want to ever feel that again?" Both men shook their heads. "Get out of here, the three of you, and use the back exit that I just came in through." The men grabbed their clothes and left the room.

Judy was still pressed against the door as Mary taunted Lori. "So, you're willing to endure all of this and so much worse because you think that you will be freed?"

"One way or the other, I will be free."

"Tonya told me that you have a death wish. You'll spend your entire life chained and restrained. You will never wear a stitch of clothing again as long as you live. You will be raped with your hands either cuffed, zip tied, or otherwise restrained. You will eat and drink out of a dog bowl while being watched. That will be your life as long as Mr. Masters decides you will live. And when he finally allows you to die… well…you will die in even more agony than you have endured this past year. So, if you think that you will somehow commit suicide and get out of the life of a slave, think again. You will be dehumanized and eventually you will break to the will of your master, but by then you will have been a slave for who knows how many months or years. You'll be nothing short of a human toilet for the pleasure of men and women." Lori looked away. "It doesn't have to be like that, Lori. Just submit, and I will get you into a caring master's hands."

"What is your obsession with me? Why do you people want to destroy me? What the fuck have I done to deserve this? You tricked and baited me into this life, then when I wanted out I ended up here."

"I own you, bitch. You are in demand. Your photos and videos have been on my auction site for months. I have desirable middle-class suburban people who want to purchase you, and I know these buyers. Your lot in life will be very, very comfortable."

"How am I supposed to trust you, Mary? You have lied from day one. How do I trust that I'm not going to go from this nightmare to an even worse one at the hands of another?" Lori paused. "You can't buy and sell human beings, Mary. We have a right to live our lives as we see fit. We have a right to be free and to give consent to relations. I might be beautiful and have a body that men and women want, but it's not what I want."

Mary stood. "Hugh will be taking you to the stable tonight. Have you been out there yet?" Lori got an even more frightened look on her face and shook her head. "Well, with the whipping you are going to receive…if you survive, you will break. And if you don't, then you might just get your wish. Death…after hours and hours of whipping. Not the gentle stuff you have been enjoying so far either. Hugh has a special system of torture out in that stable, and I have yet to see anyone come out of it unbroken and alive."

Judy heard a door close as Lori wept inside. She tried the door handle, but it was locked. She heard Pierce's voice down the hall and saw Mary and Andrew walk down the stairs. She had the mower blade in her hand as well as the hammer and went back down the stairs to the empty shed. She was shaking and crying and had found a large piece of equipment to hide behind. She heard the two gardeners coming back to the shed, and the late afternoon sunlight cast long shadows from the trees and statues in the gardens. Judy bolted out of the shed and hid behind a large green trash bin. The two men walked on by, and Andrew stepped out the door and stood smoking a cigarette. Judy was seething with tears running down her face. She threw the hammer to the other end of the shed, and Andrew perked up. He called out, but there was no reply as he walked to the source of the sound. He never saw Judy or the mower blade that she imbedded in the back of his skull. He hit the ground like a ton of bricks, and Judy grabbed his body and drug it back to the shed. Andrew was gasping for air as she pulled the blade out of his skull and said, "You're a raping sick bastard." She slammed the blade down across Andrew's throat decapitating him. Blood was shooting out of the top of his body into the deep grass. She picked up his head and threw it into the trash bin then hacked him into several pieces and threw the body parts into the dumpster as well as the blade. She looked around and saw Mary, Pierce, and Clive speaking near the front of the house. Pierce called out loudly for Andrew, and Judy took off running for the open gates and Maggie's house. She threw the bloody gloves into the back seat of her car and drove off. As she drove back to Valley Circle, she was crying and talking to herself. "Jesus, what have I done? Who was that poor girl? What if they find the body? Jesus! I'm a killer." She called home and asked Tabitha if their father was home. When her sister said no and asked if she was okay, she said, "I'm fine. I'm alright. I'm on my way home."

Jim was sitting with Sam when they received a text of a 911 call at Hugh Masters' home in the unincorporated suburb of Los Angeles County. The estate actually straddled two counties, Los Angeles and Ventura. He read the text then looked at Sam and said, "We need to hurry!"

"What's going on?"

"A brutal murder in the Hidden Hills estates."

Karen was in her office with a patient when her cellphone rang. She looked down to see that it was Judy and excused herself for a moment and left the room. Judy was hyperventilating when Karen answered and was trying to calm her down. "I need you to slow down, Judy. I can't understand you."

"I need to see you. I'm on Roscoe, heading toward the hospital."

"Okay. I am finishing up with my last patient of the day. Come on in." Karen hung up and finished with her patient then called Mark. She told him about Judy's call and asked if they'd had some type of falling out.

"No. She was fine when I left this morning. Where is she?"

"On her way to my office."

"Do you want me to come up there?"

"No. Let me talk to her first and see what's going on. If it's serious, I'll call you." She hung up just as Judy walked in. She was shaking hysterically with tears streaming down her face. Karen sat her down and said, "You're having a panic attack, Judy."

"I don't know what the fuck it is, Karen, but I'm losing it."

Karen pulled some sample packets from a locked cabinet and gave Judy two low doses of Ativan with some water and had her lie down on the sofa. Karen waited for about fifteen minutes until she could see the medication was starting to work and then asked, "Feeling better?"

"Much. What did you give me?"

"Ativan. An anti-anxiety medication. Now, do you want to tell me what's going on?"

Hugh was standing in his driveway with his two gardeners. Both men were his slaves, and the one that found Andrew's body was a wreck. Jade and Jessica were on scene as were both the Los Angeles County Sheriff and the Ventura County Sheriff. Jessica had been trying to sort through the body parts in the bin while Jade talked to the deputies who were arguing over jurisdiction. Sam arrived, and the deputies and homicide detectives from both departments groaned when they saw Jim step out of the car with her. The Ventura County watch commander faced off with Jim and said, "It's our case."

Jim didn't say anything. He pulled out his tablet and located the property on the assessor's website with the parcel number then reviewed a satellite image that clearly showed the line that divided the property and handed it to the commander who looked at the two images. "Now, do you still want to argue, or do you want to get off our crime scene?" The commander turned and ordered his men off the scene. Hugh was standing next to his men, and Jim asked, "Who found the body?" One of the gardeners raised his hand. "Great. Would you like to tell me about it?"

The man began to ramble a bit in Spanish, and Hugh stepped up and said, "My employees don't speak English, Sheriff."

"I'm not the sheriff." Jim pointed to Sam who was over with Jade. "Samantha Prichard is the Sheriff. I'm her second in command. Tell me where you found the body." The gardener explained that he slipped on the grass near the dumpster. He fell and when he got up his partner realized that he had slipped in blood. They spotted blood on the outside of the container, opened it, saw the body, and called 911. Hugh was not happy, and Jim could see it in his eyes. "Mr. Masters, do you know who the victim is?"

"His name is Andrew Haas. He has done some freelance work for me and my companies."

Jim nodded while lighting a cigarette. He called out to Jade and asked, "What do we have?"

"A man hacked to pieces and thrown into this dumpster."

"Interesting. Do you have any idea what the fatal blow was?"

"He was decapitated and then dismembered. He hasn't been dead an hour."

Jim jerked his head to look over at Jade. "You're fuckin' kidding me?"

"Nope. His body is ninety-two degrees. He bled out due to the blow to the head and neck."

"He has two wounds to the head?" Jim walked over to Jade while asking Hugh and his men to stay put. Jade had Andrew's head propped up on some tree trimmings, and she showed Jim the deep cut on the back of the skull and then where the blade had taken off his head. "So, someone got the drop on him?"

"Oh, yeah. He never saw the first blow coming. The second looks to have been across his throat, so he got a good look at his attacker when he was beheaded."

"What the hell type of blade would be sharp enough to not only take off the guy's fuckin' head but his arms and legs?"

Jessica lifted a large evidence bag with the mower blade in it. "This would be sharp enough."

"Jesus! We have the murder weapon?" Sam exclaimed.

"Yep. This killer wasn't trying to hide a damn thing."

Hugh and the other two men stood stonefaced, and Jim asked, "How would someone have gotten a weapon like this?"

The gardener spoke up. "I had removed the blades from some of the mowers and had sharpened them this morning. I hadn't had time to put them back on the machines."

Sam's CSI team had arrived on site, and she instructed them to seal off the shed and the area and to start processing it for prints and other evidence. Jim took the bag from Jessica and looked at it closely. He kept it in his hand then pulled out his phone and called John and said, "We have a grisly murder scene in Hidden Hills."

"Is there another kind?"

"I think you should come out right now." Jim walked away from the others and back over to his car with the blade in his hand. He was long out of earshot of the others.

"And why would I want to come out there?"

"Because someone just beheaded a guy, who I'm pretty sure is going to be another sex offender, then hacked him to pieces and dumped his head and body parts in a bin while leaving the murder weapon behind."

"So, you processed it?"

"There is blood on both ends of the freshly sharpened blade, John. On one end of the blade there is the flesh and remnants of the victim, and on the other…"

"There's blood because the killer got cut?"

"You got it. We have DNA evidence here. This was one savage killing. Someone had a real ax to grind with this guy."

"Okay. Hold the weapon aside for me. I will get Chris, and we will head out there."

Jim walked back to the scene, and Hugh was still standing with his workers. Jim asked, "Do you know of anyone who would want to see this type of harm come to Mr. Haas?" Hugh and the other two men shook their heads. "Has there been anyone here at your home, Mr. Masters, that you didn't know or who knew the victim?"

"No. Whoever did this would have had to have been very, very strong."

"Not necessarily. We'll know more when we run some tests on the blade, but your employee really sharpened this blade well, and a really sharp blade can cut human flesh and even bone like butter."

Hugh shrugged. "There was no one at my home today that I didn't know or who would do something like this."

Sam laughed. "Well, actually there was, Mr. Masters. You might not have seen them, but someone was lying in wait for Mr. Haas, and perhaps others. Why was he here?"

"A meeting on some upcoming deals."

"When was the last time you saw him alive?"

"I don't know. A few hours ago? I didn't realize that he was missing. I thought perhaps he was walking the property. All of my guests are invited to enjoy the gardens and fountains. I have twenty acres here, and I have people who come out by invitation only to hike my manicured estate."

"I see, so Mr. Haas was not leaving that you knew of?"

"No."

Jim looked around and asked, "How large is your home?"

"Twenty-thousand square feet."

"How the hell can you keep that size home and all of this property secure?"

"I have a private security firm that patrols the property as well as guards on the house twenty-four-seven, and I have a very, very expensive and expansive security system."

"We should do a search of your premises. The killer could still be here."

"Not necessary, Mr. O'Brian. I have already had my men do a complete search of the premises. Only a small portion of the house is open to visitors. The majority of my home is kept in constant lockdown. No one gets in unless they have been approved by me."

"Do you have enemies, Mr. Masters?"

"Everyone has enemies, Mr. O'Brian. Everyone."

CHAPTER THIRTEEN

"What have I done?"

Karen had gotten Judy settled, and the two were talking about her crisis. "I just can't explain it, Karen. I was just driving down the street, and all of a sudden this total and complete feeling of dread and panic came over me."

"What had you been doing?"

"I spent the morning working with Mary and Sally Owen. They were training me for desk work in Mary's headquarters."

"Were you feeling anxious then?"

"No. I was having a good time. We worked together for several hours, then Mary and Sally got dragged off by the sheriff for questioning in my rape."

Karen interrupted. "Sally and Mary?"

"Sally but Mary went with her. I felt so bad, but there was nothing I could do. I kept out of sight, so the police didn't know I was there."

"Why didn't you step up and let them know you were there?"

"I got scared, and Mary told me to stay in her office while they dealt with the police. I heard some yelling, then the two were gone."

"Was anyone else in the office?"

"A couple of her workers were doing some decorating and getting ready to stage some homes."

"Stage?"

"It's a real estate term. When Mary and most realtors are selling homes, especially high-priced homes that are new or empty, they rent all kinds of furniture and artwork. They need to make those homes look like homes for the rich and famous. I'm really getting an education."

"How did you feel when the sheriff showed up?"

"Scared. Bewildered."

"How long ago did this happen?"

"This morning."

"And what happened after they left?"

"I stayed and listened to the men talk and then went out to Hidden Hills to see my friend Maggie Pulp. She's a pop star. You might have heard some of her music. She goes by Mags."

"I've heard of her. I'm not into hip hop music, but I know her name. How long have you two been friends?"

"Our whole lives. She had a crisis this morning with the paparazzi chasing her down and was traumatized, so I stayed with her for a bit before heading for home, that's when the attack came on."

"Do you think there is a connection?"

Judy looked up at the ceiling and then the floor. "Wow! I hadn't even thought about that. Between what happened to Mary and Sally and then Mags, I was in a really, really stressful environment, and when I was finally able to let down I freaked out."

Karen was looking over her tablet as she recorded the session, and while she did that Judy reached into her bag and pulled out hers. The light in the room was dim, but Karen saw something on Judy's right hand. She turned up the lights and when she did she saw that Judy had a gash on her hand. "Judy! Oh my God. What happened?"

Judy looked at her hand and then at Karen and said, "I have no idea. I felt a little stabbing pain on my hand a few hours ago when I was putting papers away. I thought it was a papercut. I never really looked at it."

"You didn't notice a cut like that?"

"No."

"You need stiches and a tetanus booster. Come with me. We're going down to the ER, so I can stich you up and clean that thing." The two women were walking out of the office when Judy pulled a flash drive from her pocket and slipped it under one of the guest chairs in Karen's lobby. Karen locked her office door and said, "I'm calling your father."

"You can't tell him about our conversations."

"No, but you shouldn't be driving with that size cut on your hand, and I know he is still here. He needs to take you home and take care of you." Judy got tears in her eyes as the two got off the elevator in the ER, and when Mark came into the room, she ran to him and threw her arms around his neck and started kissing him and crying. Karen watched from a distance as Mark held Judy tight.

"What happened, honey?"

"I don't know. I cut myself. Karen just noticed it." Mark pulled her away from him to see the cut and then walked her over to the table and allowed Karen to take care of the wound. When she was finished, Mark asked Judy where her car was. "It's here in the structure."

"Okay. I have to finish up a report. Come with me to the lab, and then I will drive you home." Judy nodded, and Mark asked, "Have you talked to Tabitha today?"

"About an hour ago. I wanted to see if you were home and then I came in to speak to Karen."

Mark nodded, and Karen told her to take it easy on her hand for the next few days. She gave her some Vicodin for pain and told her she wanted to see her in two days. She watched Judy clinging to Mark as the two left the room, and she typed a note into her tablet in Judy's file.

"Judy Bench is exhibiting symptoms of a possible Electra complex. Will readvise Mark once again to use caution."

John and Chris had taken the blade back to their own lab. They were running it for DNA and then cross checking it against all databases. Chris was reading news on his tablet when a message came over on the DNA. "Well, we have more information on Andrew Haas."

John looked up from his computer and said, "The guy was a pedophile and rapist. Is that the news you're going to share?"

"Nope. He was a blood relative of Hugh Masters."

"What?"

"According to this report, the DNA of both men is in the national crime registry, and they are a match."

John typed something quickly into his computer and then looked at the report. "I'll be damned. Masters has had two DUI arrests, but I don't see any other offenses."

"Why didn't Masters tell us that?" Chris asked.

"That's a good question and one we need to revisit Masters about. Is there any information on the DNA from the other end of the blade?"

"Nothing. It's not in any database that I can find. The person has no history."

"The person has a history all right. I am beginning to think that Sally Owen may have more going on than a rape accusation."

"You don't think that Owen committed these two murders?"

"Everyone is a suspect until they aren't, Chris."

The screams inside the barn were deafening. Hugh Masters stood nude with a bullwhip in his right hand as Mary and Pierce looked on from a windowed room. Two dozen young women and three men were stripped nude, their hands locked in handcuffs raised above their heads stretching their bodies upwards to the point where they were on their tiptoes. Hugh had beaten several of the victims into unconsciousness, and their bodies hung limp with their knees bent. Blood was running down the backs of all of the victims, and after over an hour of torture Hugh hung up the whip then proceeded to sodomize each of those hanging from the stalls, awake or not. When he was finished, he entered the office where Mary and Pierce were standing. Sweat dripped off his body, and he had feces on his penis and the front of his groin. The smell made both put their hands over their faces.

"They are ready for auction," he announced. He walked into a bathroom off the office, showered, and put on a robe. Pierce and Mary were removing the victims from their restraints, and all crumpled to the ground. Pierce sprayed them with water from a firehose to remove the blood and the dirt. Hugh yelled out, "We don't want infection, and horses are known for carrying tetanus. Make sure they all get shots. There is a gallon bucket of antibiotic salve in the hose pantry. Wipe their wounds with it." Hugh dressed and left the stable for the house, and Mary and Pierce finished cleaning up the victims. They chained them together and walked them back to a large barracks on the other side of the barn where they then chained them to their bunks face down.

Judy was making dinner for herself and Mark. She had fed Tabitha when they first got home and then got her off to bed. Mark was showering, and Judy opened a bottle of wine and poured him a glass as she was finishing the meal. Mark was still upstairs, and Judy looked at her purse on the counter and then the glass of wine and back again. She opened her purse and took out the Ecstasy that Sally had given her earlier in the day. There were a half dozen tablets, and she dropped two into Mark's glass then put the rest into the bottle of wine. Mark came into the kitchen in a robe and asked, "How is your hand?"

"Better. I took one of the pills Karen gave me, so I'm not feeling any pain."

Mark took a sip of his wine and asked, "You really expect me to believe that you cut your hand that badly on a piece of paper and didn't know it?"

"That's what happened, Mark."

He paused after sipping his wine then said, "What happened to Dad?"

"I'm a grown woman. I'm a little old to be calling you daddy or Dad, don't you think? I respect and love you. Don't you respect and love me?"

Mark was quiet for several minutes as Judy prepared their plates and put them on the table. Mark smiled and asked, "You made all of this after the day you had and even took care of Tabitha?"

"Of course. I do it all the time. You're just not always here to see it. You keep a roof over our heads and food in our stomachs. You deserve it." There were two candles on the table, and the two ate and talked, not like father and daughter, but like husband and wife. Judy poured him another glass of wine, and Mark was getting more and more relaxed as well as flirty. "You have grown into a beautiful young woman." His speech was a bit slurred, and Judy smiled and thanked him. The conversation went on into the third glass of wine and as Judy sipped water she watched as Mark became more and more intoxicated and more and more sexual in his conversation. She cleared the table and was washing the dishes when he came up behind her and put his arms around her waist and began to kiss her neck. "You are sexy!" Judy smiled as she rolled her neck along with the kisses. Mark stopped and pulled back and asked, "What was in my wine? I feel so strange."

"Wine was all that was in your glass, Mark. You're tired. You've been working hard and worrying about me and Tabitha. Come on. Let's get you up to bed." Judy dried her hands and took another Vicodin then helped Mark up the stairs to his bedroom. When she removed his robe, he had a raging erection. Judy smiled and said, "We should do something about that, don't you think?"

"And just what can you do about it?"

Judy stripped off her clothes and pushed Mark back on the bed. She kissed him, and he kissed her back, then she pushed herself up on top of him. "There is only one man I want to take my virginity, and it's you." She slid her pelvis forward, allowing Mark's penis to enter her. She gasped as the shaft penetrated deep into her, and Mark rolled his eyes as she began to move up and down on him. In a matter of minutes, the two were engaged in full-on sex, and Mark had flipped her onto her back and was on top of her pumping and moaning. Judy was writhing with her hands on his hips, pulling him deep inside her.

"I'm going to cum."

"Go ahead, baby. Cum inside me." Mark grunted and thrashed a few times before collapsing onto her. She lay underneath him with a smile on her face as he began to snore. Judy rolled him off and then covered him up. She looked at the clock, and it was ten after nine. She went downstairs and poured the last of the wine into Mark's glass and threw away the bottle. She took a sip then returned to the bedroom where Mark had come to and was sitting up. He was bleary-eyed, and Judy handed him the glass then opened his nightstand drawer and moved around some porno magazines and found his lube. She did a little dance in front of him as she put the lubricant on her anus. "I want you to fuck my ass, Mark, then my pussy, and then I want to taste your semen." Mark was excited as he mounted her. The sex went on until after three a.m. with Mark's final climax down her throat. She lifted her head off of his penis, wiping remnants of semen into her mouth, and swallowed loudly. "Now, that is how I always imagined I would lose my virginity. You made it a reality, Daddy."

Mark was barely alert but smiled and said, "I love you, honey. I've missed you so much. You can't imagine how much."

Judy looked over at the wedding photo that her father kept on his nightstand and all of the pictures of her mother in the room. She walked out onto the balcony and began weeping. She put her head in her hands. "Oh God. What have I done? He thinks I'm Mother. What have I done?" She wept for several minutes and then looked up at the starry night sky. "If there is a God, and you can hear me, please don't let him remember what we did tonight. And if he does, let it be like a dream."

CHAPTER FOURTEEN

"She will be broken."

Sam woke up on the balcony with a bottle of scotch in one hand and a photo of her and Maria in the other. Her face was streaked with tears, and she drank the last golden drop in the bottle and threw it off the deck. She was still in full uniform and staggered inside. "Five-thirty. Might as well shower and dress for work." The cold shower jolted her awake. She looked at the mirror in the bathroom and her nude body reflected in it. "I know I'm not any soberer, just shocked, but I do have a hell of a body." Her smile was quickly replaced by agony, and she pressed her back against the shower wall and slid down it, calling out Maria's name.

Judy and Tabitha were in the kitchen eating breakfast when Mark walked in. He had a smile on his face and poured himself a cup of coffee, grabbed the paper, and said, "Is this a great day or what?"

Tabitha looked at Judy and asked, "What's up with Dad?"

"If I didn't know better, I would think he got laid."

Mark heard Judy and smiled and said, "I did get laid last night. What a night."

There was a look of horror on Judy's face, and Tabitha saw it. "Who were you with last night, Daddy?" Tabitha asked.

"Well, in my imagination I was with your mother."

"Mother is dead, Father."

"Yes, Tabitha she is. I think I was with Mary. She must have come over at some point after dinner." Judy let out a deep breath. "Are you okay, honey?"

"I'm fine, Dad."

"What happened to calling me Mark?"

"You remember that?"

"Why would I forget it? You made a wonderful dinner for the two of us and called me Mark. You said you're not a little girl anymore and heaped all kinds of praise on me."

"So, you're okay with me calling you Mark?"

"It's fine with me if it's fine with you."

Judy nodded, and he got up, kissed Tabitha, and then her. He paused, and a strange look came over him. "Are you okay?" Judy asked.

"Yeah. I just had something like déjà vu."

"How much wine did you drink last night?"

"I guess a little too much." Mark told her to get Tabitha to school and to be careful working with Mary today and left the house.

Judy was staring at him with a smile on her face, and Tabitha was staring at her in confusion. "What's wrong?" Judy asked.

"Have you showered this morning?"

"Not yet. Why?"

Tabitha leaned in close then sat back. "You smell like Dad's cologne."

"Well, he did just give me a kiss as well as you."

"No. It's in your skin. Have you been putting on his cologne again?" Judy nodded, and Tabitha laughed. "Judy wants to be a man..." she said in a snarky little girl way. The two got up from the table, grabbed their books, and left the house.

Karen was sitting on a bar stool in the kitchen eating a doughnut and reading the paper. The story of Andrew's murder had made the front page. Chris came in dressed in a suit and tie, grabbed a bottle of water from the fridge, and said, "Brutal killing, huh."

"Who leaked it to the press?"

"Jim of all people."

"Jim? Why would Jim leak this?"

"I have no idea, but he did."

Karen grabbed her phone and called Judy and asked how her hand was feeling. She said it was throbbing a bit but that she was fine. "I want you in my office at three."

"I'll do my best, but I have work, and I have been invited by a friend of Mary's to go horseback riding this afternoon."

"Horseback riding? I didn't know you rode."

"Yes. My mother started me young. I haven't done much since her death, but it was a wonderful invitation, so I accepted it."

"Okay. Call me when you're finished riding."

"I will. Have a nice day."

Karen hung up the line, and Chris asked, "What was that all about?"

"One of my patients. Judy Bench. The girl just started working for Mary Owen and her daughter Sally. She was working with paper and boxes yesterday and got a nasty gash on her hand. She showed up in my office for her appointment and didn't even know she had cut herself."

"What type of cut?"

"A long gash on her hand that required ten stitches."

"And she's working for Mary Owen and her daughter?"

"Yes. It's a long strange story."

"I know part of it. She accused Sally Owen of drugging and raping her."

"Yes, but they have withdrawn the charges from what I've been told."

"It's not that easy. In cases of sexual assault, victims recant all the time, but cases are still investigated." Karen nodded and kissed him then ran to the bathroom to shower. Chris told her he loved her and headed for the office but stopped and called John. When he answered, Chris said, "New twist in this case."

"Go on."

"Karen is treating Judy Bench."

"Okay. What does that have to do with us?"

"Bench has taken a job with Mary Owen working with Sally at her real estate company."

"Interesting."

"You want something even more interesting?" John said yes. "Judy Bench arrived at Karen's office last night for a session and had a large gash on her hand that required stitches. The kid didn't even know she was hurt."

There were a few moments of silence, then John said, "We need to get a DNA sample from Ms. Bench."

"And just how the hell are we going to do that?"

"If there's a rape report, there's a rape kit. Find out where she was treated and then have Jim order the kit."

"You don't think," Chris stopped mid-sentence.

"I don't think that Ms. Bench's injuries are a coincidence if that's what you're about to ask me."

"And you won't stop short of calling her a murder suspect either?"

"No."

Judy walked into Mary's office at her home, and Mary saw the bandages and asked, "What the hell happened to you?"

"I cut my hand on some boxes yesterday."

"Jesus, Judy! When those things happen, you need to tell me right away."

"I'm sorry. I will. Where's Sally?"

"She took her sister to school."

Judy sat down across from Mary. "Your friend Hugh Masters invited me to go horseback riding with him this afternoon. Is that okay with you?"

"Of course. We're not shooting today. There was an accident at Hugh's home last night."

"You mean a murder. It's in all the papers."

"Yes, a murder." Judy asked another question, but Mary's cellphone buzzed with a text message. Mary excused herself for a moment and read the message.

"You will need an alibi for your whereabouts last night. The police are snooping around."

Mary looked up at Judy and asked, "So, tell me about last night?"

Judy's face lost all color. "What about last night?"

"I received a text message from your father at three a.m. He wanted to know where I had gone."

Judy laughed and said, "He did say that the two of you had sex last night."

"Really? He shares those type of intimate details of his love life?"

"Sometimes. He was in an exceptionally good mood this morning and mentioned that you had been over." She paused. "Father had been drinking. Perhaps he imagined it was you with him last night?"

Mary smiled. "I was, but I prefer to keep my trysts to myself. Your father has never been one to kiss and tell."

Judy laughed. "You obviously haven't been with him when he gets drunk."

"Is he abusive?"

"Not at all. He's a happy drunk. He gets maudlin at times when he thinks about our mother. He misses her so."

"I understand. We've shared many a night of tears over our lost spouses."

"So, you were at the house last night?"

"Yes. I came over about ten when you and Tabitha were asleep, and we had some wine and fooled around."

"What time did you leave?"

"Around three." Judy let her shoulders down in a gesture of relief. "What's wrong?"

"Nothing. Dad was just talking up a storm, and since I'm a light sleeper I was sure he was having some kind of issue."

"Issue?"

"You know. A vivid dream. He was sure he had been with our mother last night."

Mary had a puzzled look on her face. "He did call out her name several times while we were making love."

"Well, that explains it."

"It does?"

"You know my father. His room is a shrine to our mother. Her photo is on every wall, his nightstand. Her nightstand has been left undisturbed all these years since her death. He got drunk; you came over. You two had sex, and he was caught up in his imagination and drunken state with, for a fleeting moment, being with her again."

"Does that worry you, Judy?"

"Not at all. It makes me feel better. I was worried, but now I understand. It's great news to me."

Sally had been back working in another part of the office for an hour and didn't want to interrupt the conversation but cleared her throat as she entered the office. "When did you get back?" Mary asked with a surprised tone.

"Just this minute. I heard from a little birdie that Hugh wants to take my best friend horseback riding today." Judy nodded, and Mary told her to get going. After Judy was long out of the house, Sally asked, "Looking for an alibi for last night?" Mary nodded. "You have Mark. I have nothing."

"Why would you need an alibi? You were here in bed."

"Um, no, I wasn't. While you, Hugh, and Pierce were at the stable beating the new slaves into submission, I was having sex with a very combative Lori along with Clive."

"And?"

"And nothing. She's a biter, so Clive put a spider gag in her mouth, then I was able to sit on her face and piss down her throat. She is one nasty bitch, Mom. No one is going to break that cunt."

"Perhaps not for the sale, but she will be broken…even if it's just for the last few moments of her life."

John had sent the rape kit down for processing along with the DNA sample from the weapon. Jim and Sam were in his office as they had picked up the kit and delivered it to John. Chris was reading on his tablet on a couch in John's office as the four sat in silence. Jim looked at Sam and said, "Did you pass out again?" She nodded. "And you have a massive hangover?" She nodded again.

"You won't find solace in the bottom of a liquor bottle, Sam. I've tried," Chris said.

"I will continue to medicate until I can sleep or die."

Chris said, "Drinking fifteen hundred milliliters of rotgut booze will send you to the crematorium long before you get clarity on this," which sent Sam into a yelling fit. John put his tablet down, grabbed Sam firmly in his arms, and pulled her to him. She screamed and cried while beating on his chest fighting to resist. She caught John twice in the lip and once in the nose before he had her wrapped up in his embrace. As she settled and fell into a weeping state, he held her firmly against his huge chest, and Jim and Chris both looked on with tears in their eyes.

The embrace lasted fifteen minutes and was only ended by a call from the laboratory.

John put the call on speaker and asked, "What do you have?"

"We have Ms. Bench's DNA off the rape kit as well as Sally Owen's; however, the sample that you have on the weapon is just too small. I can't make a definitive ruling."

Jim asked, "Can you make a damned guess?"

"We don't guess in this lab, Jim. We either have hard facts, or we need more information. In this case, we need a larger DNA sample from Ms. Bench and Ms. Owen."

"What the fuck difference will a larger sample make if you can't identify what we have given you?"

"We have sequenced Bench's DNA, so we have isolated chains that will only match her with a larger sample. We can run that and then compare it to what we have and know with 99.9% accuracy if the DNA on the weapon is that of Ms. Bench."

John said thanks then looked at the others and said, "You need to interview Ms. Bench and get her DNA." Sam nodded, and Jim shook his head. "Get the kid to drink a coke, coffee, touch something we can secure."

"Do we know where she is now?"

"Working for Mary Owen, so she should be easy to grab. Once you have her, let us know, and we will come to your office."

Jim nodded as Sam sat silent. "Let's go, Sam. We have police work to do."

Sam sat back with tears in her eyes. "And if we're able to match the DNA on the weapon to this seventeen-year-old girl who has been through hell based on what I have read, are you going to torture her, John? Are you going to drag her into your lair and decimate her like the others?"

"That's a question I can't answer right now, Sam. I don't understand the motive for these killings. I don't know what's going on in that kid's mind. I won't know until I meet her face to face."

Sam stood up and walked out, but Jim stayed for a moment and said, "This is unlike any case you have ever dealt with as an agent or the Eagle. Tread lightly here, John. When you're dealing with a traumatized child, you and the Eagle don't have a friend in me if you try to destroy her."

After Jim left the office, Chris asked, "Did that sound like a threat to you?"

"Not so much a threat as a warning."

"Do you agree?"

"Absolutely. Jessica killed in self-defense and for self-preservation when she was on the streets. Everyone close to me has had a motive to kill. Look at Carter. I allowed him to kill his attacker."

"Yeah, but you wiped his memory. You can't do that with this kid." Chris paused. "But what if she's actually a sociopath or psychopathic murderer?"

"These are uncharted waters even for me."

CHAPTER FIFTEEN

"Keep telling yourself that."

H ugh was seated on a black stallion near the front gate of his estate when Judy drove up. The gates opened, and she parked. A smiling teenage girl held the reins of a tan gelding with a white blaze across its nose. Judy approached the horse slowly and petted its nose. "What a beautiful animal! Nine hands?"

"Five. I don't know how well you ride, but this is the gentlest trail horse I have."

"And your stallion is for stud?"

"Good eye. This is Hans, and you have Kendall."

Judy mounted her horse and said, "Well, it's one p.m., and I have an appointment at three that I promised to keep."

"Well, then, let us be off."

The two rode off, and the teen walked back up to the house. Pierce was standing at the side entrance where Andrew had been killed the night before. He called the girl over and asked, "That's Judy Bench?"

"I believe so, sir."

He had her enter the house and a small bedroom off the main level. "Remove your clothing!" The girl did as instructed, and Pierce told her to lift her long blond hair, so he could inspect her whip wounds. "You are healing well."

"For less than twenty-four-hours, I am feeling okay."

"What's your name?"

"Gloria."

"Can you lay on your back?" She nodded. "Then lay down on the bed." She did as she was told, and Pierce raped her then got up and told her to go back to the stable and wait for Hugh and Judy then called Tonya. When she answered the phone, he said, "I want to place a bid on Gloria."

"Ah, Gloria. What a stunner, and so well behaved. She is over eighteen, you know? I didn't send you a packet on her since you don't like the older girls."

"Well, I will make an exception. She seems to have the maturity I need to manage my stable of girls."

"She does have the experience. I was quite displeased with Hugh's beating of her and several others. She has been nothing but obedient since he broke her nearly a year ago. I had to talk her down last night."

"I, too, was disappointed in Hugh's treatment of those for sale, but he needed to take out his frustrations after Andrew's murder. Did you know they were half-brothers?"

"Indeed, and while outwardly they fought, they were close, and his murder really shook Hugh up."

"He's getting over it. He has Clive working in the fields, and I'm here at the house. I raped and beat Lori twice this morning. No change. The spider gag was a great idea. Clive shoved his cock down her throat nearly suffocating her."

"Don't kill her, Pierce. Hugh and I have plans for her."

"What the hell type of plans could you have? She's worthless. She must be restrained twenty-four-seven. She's getting more and more violent. If you ask me, you're creating a monster. If you don't put her down, she's going to find a way to kill one or both of you if not others."

"She's not that dangerous."

"Keep telling yourself that. As for me, I'm staying away from her going forward."

Jim and Sam arrived at the Owen home at one p.m. There was a group of sad faces when they knocked on the door. Mary and Sally weren't home, and Judy was not there either. They asked her whereabouts, but the two office girls didn't know. Jim left his card and asked that Judy contact him when she was back in the office then called John. "The Bench girl isn't at the Owen home."

"Any idea where she is?"

"No one knows, and the mother and daughter weren't there either."

"I don't like it. I think that Ms. Bench might be in danger."

"Well, Professor Dipshit, if indeed she is the killer of these last two pedophiles and has infiltrated a group of them, then yeah; she's in deep danger."

"Have you spoken to Mr. Masters since last night?"

"No. He was pretty distraught. We asked all the usual questions and got the usual answers. Why? What are you thinking?"

"I'm thinking that there's more going on at Mr. Masters' home than venture capital work."

"Oh yeah? Prove it."

"Chris and I are going out there."

"As the FBI?"

"We'll see. I will need you and Sam to go out there first."

"What the fuck for?"

"To let Masters know that the FBI is stepping into this investigation by invitation of the sheriff's department."

"You think you can rattle this guy that easily?"

"I don't know, but let's try."

Hugh and Judy had stopped at a five-acre lake on the property, so the horses could drink. "Mary tells me that you are learning the business."

"What business would that be?"

"Um…real estate?"

"Oh, yes. I am. It's only my third day, but I have already learned a great deal."

"What happened to your hand?"

"I was clumsy with some boxes yesterday and cut it."

"Did you let Mary know?"

"Not until this morning."

"The first rule of business is worker's compensation insurance. If you're injured on the job, report it to your boss immediately."

"I understand. Mary read me the riot act this morning."

Hugh took a deep breath. "Do you have plans for this evening?"

"Just dinner with my father and sister. Why?"

"What does your father do?"

"He's the head of the testing laboratory at Northridge Hospital."

"And how old is your sister?"

"Ten, about to be eleven, and as smart as a whip. She's going to end up being placed in high school next year due to her intelligence. I think she will be out of college before I even start."

"A real smart cookie, huh?"

"Yes, she is. She tries to be a kid, but she is just too smart for that."

"And your mother? What does she do?"

"She was a firefighter. She and Mary's husband were in the same unit of the Los Angeles Fire Department. They were killed fighting the great fire."

"I'm so sorry."

"It's okay. It's been a long time."

"How is your father holding up? Has he remarried?"

"No. He's made me and my sister the center of his world as we have made him the center of ours. He dates once in a while, but I don't know that he will ever love anyone as much as he loved our mother."

"That's understandable. And you want to get into real estate instead of going right into college?"

"I want to take a year off and try my hand in the real estate market."

"I must say that I am quite surprised at your willingness to work with Mary and Sally after you accused Sally of rape. Mary and I are good friends, and she told me about it when it happened. Why the sudden change of heart?"

"Sally and I have been friends our whole lives. I overreacted to some experimentation that was fueled by drugs and alcohol."

"I see, so you went to one of Sally's parties?"

"I did. What do you know of them?"

"Not a lot. Sally is a bit of a free spirit. Always has been. Her father and I were close friends before his death. Sally would come out here a lot to ride and hang out with some of the kids who I take in on occasion."

"You take in children?"

"I have done some foster parenting through the years. I hate to see any child suffer. I want to help any way that I can."

"That's really nice of you."

Hugh grabbed the reins of his horse as well as Judy's. "We all have our crosses to bear, and we all have our secrets, don't we?" Judy didn't respond but mounted her horse. "So, I'm having a small get together at my home tonight, and I would really like it if you would attend."

"I will have to speak with my father."

"Of course, of course. He is welcome to accompany you." The two rode back to the house where Judy was helped off her horse by Gloria, who then took the other horse and walked them back to the stables. Judy was walking the edge of the stables and noticed blood on the ground in front of several stalls.

"Have your horses been injured? There's blood all over the ground in front of several stalls." Gloria had reappeared dressed in leather boots and riding pants and a flowing white blouse.

Hugh shrugged. "I'm sure it's nothing." He turned to lead Judy out of the barn, but Judy paused to watch Gloria hanging up the horse's gear. When she turned her back to Judy, Judy could see that Gloria's shirt was speckled with blood. She didn't say a word as she followed Hugh out of the barn.

Jim and Sam were waiting near Hugh's estate for John and Chris. The two sat smoking in silence while listening to the police radio. Jim took a deep hit off his smoke and asked, "So, you're not sleeping?"

"When I sleep, I see Maria and replay that final night in my mind."

"I understand."

"How could you?"

"I play the night Barbara died over and over in my head even now, hearing her final words to me as I was slipping off to sleep. She was saying goodbye, and I failed to recognize it."

"And you still beat yourself up over it?"

"Not literally. I have Cindy for that." That drew a chuckle from Sam. "But yes, I still have nightmares and a million questions. I wonder what if I had woken up? What if I had stayed awake? Perhaps I would have seen her stop breathing. Perhaps I could have resuscitated her."

"Jade and Jessica did the autopsy on Barbara; even they told you there was nothing that you could have done."

"That's cold comfort, Sam. It hasn't stopped me from asking the questions."

"So, what do you do?"

"Right after Barbara's death, I did what you're doing…drank myself into a stupor every night, so I wouldn't dream. Then I realized that Barbara would kick my ass if she saw the way I was acting. She had also blessed a relationship between me and Cindy but only after her death."

"That's all fine, Jim, but that's not how things ended with me and Maria. There were angry bitter words. She stormed out of the house, then she was dead."

"You can replay it in your mind all you like, Sam, but it's not going to change what happened. Maria made a foolish decision, and that is not your fault. Would she have come to her senses after she sobered up? I only knew Maria on a peripheral level, but I don't think so. I think she would have run straight to the cops with her theory on me or John as the Eagle, and that would have started a world of shit that none of us was prepared for."

"So, you feel her death was a good thing?"

"I didn't say that. Her death, while tragic, though, saved lives."

"So, Maria's death has allowed the Eagle to continue to operate out of the line of sight?"

"We'll see. Even John gets tired of being the Eagle. Even he thinks about hanging it up."

"He can't do that. He's the last bastion of justice when justice fails. Maria didn't see it that way, but she had her own demons. Deep down, I think she approved of what the Eagle does. She just couldn't reconcile it in her own legal mind."

John and Chris pulled up next to them, and Jim spoke to security at the gate of the Masters residence, and they were allowed in. The long driveway that snaked up to Masters' home was two lanes wide, and as the two cars drove up, Judy Bench was driving down. Chris snapped a photo of her license plate and ran it through DMV. "You're never going to believe who was driving that car?"

"Judy Bench."

"That wasn't a guess, was it?"

"No. I recognized her."

Chris looked at the imposing home coming into view and said, "And the plot thickens."

Judy arrived at Karen's office at three, pressed a button on the entrance, and sat down. Karen welcomed her and was happy she had shown up. "So, how was horseback riding?"

"Interesting."

"Interesting? In what way?"

"It's amazing how being with such magnificent creatures changes your attention to detail. I saw and felt things that I have never seen or felt before."

"Talk about that."

"It's a general feeling and impression, not something that I can articulate in words."

"So, how are you feeling? How is your hand?"

"I'm feeling pretty good; the hand isn't bothering me. I was able to ride with no trouble. All in all, I'm feeling pretty good."

"How are things between you and your father?"

"Never better. We had an interesting night last night, and he was in a great mood this morning."

"What was interesting about it?"

"I fixed him his favorite meal after getting my sister to bed. He enjoyed a bottle of wine and then had vigorous sex all night long."

"Vigorous sex? With whom?"

"The best I could gather from him and Mary Owen, each other."

"Did you see Mary last night?"

"No. I was asleep and then a bit surprised by my father's revelation." Karen asked why. "Well, I never woke up, and Mary is not quiet in bed. My father said that Mary left early in the morning, but that it was like a dream. He thought he was making love to our mother."

"Interesting. Do you have a photo of your mother with you?" Judy rummaged through her bag and pulled out a small photo album and handed it to Karen. "You bear a striking resemblance to her."

"Everyone tells me that. She was eighteen when I was born, and I am nearly that age now."

"Has your father ever commented on the resemblance?"

"He always tells me I have my mother's strong will and spirit."

"So, tell me more about this horseback ride."

"Not much to tell. I went out riding with a friend of Mag's and Mary's. He took me around the grounds of his estate, and we chatted about general things."

"He? His estate?"

"His name is Hugh Masters. Nice man in his early forties."

"A nice man who invited an underage girl to ride horses with him?"

Judy laughed. "I'm only underage for a few more weeks, and it's nothing like that. He is a venture capitalist who helped Mary get started, and she introduced us. He runs his business from his home but also travels the world. My friend Maggie made the first introductions and when Mary found out that I had met Hugh, she must have spoken to him. He wanted to speak to me again, and we hit it off, not in a romantic way at all. He has been giving me some sound advice on business."

"I see. I'm familiar with Mr. Masters. He does a great deal of philanthropic work and is on the board of several large charities in Los Angeles."

"So, you've met him?"

"Many times."

"Then you know there is nothing to worry about."

"I do know Hugh Masters well, Judy. He likes to keep company with much younger women."

"That's his business, not mine. I have no interest in a man twice my age, Karen."

"Okay. Did you see Mary and Sally today?"

"I did."

"And did Mary talk about her night with your father?"

"We spoke about it. I'm not a fan of my father being involved with her, though. She can be a stern woman, and while I'm ready to leave the nest, Tabitha will be around for at least eight more years unless she continues her acceleration in school and goes to college young. I'm not saying I don't like Mary. I just don't like her for my father."

"Is there anyone that you would like your father to be with?"

"He's not over the death of Mother. I don't know that he ever will be. While I don't want him to be alone, I don't know of anyone who really deserves the type of man he is."

"That's both a huge compliment and disturbing to me. What are your plans? Where do you see yourself in five years?"

"Hmm. I really haven't thought that far ahead. I am taking a year off before college."

"Are you going to move out of your father's home?"

"Oh, heavens no. Tabitha still needs a mother figure, and I fill that role, and my father needs me to help out with the house. He works long hours and doesn't trust anyone to be a live-in housekeeper, and neither do I. I have no long-term plans to leave home."

"I see. Do you feel an obligation to your father?"

"Of course. I love him. You know how I feel about him and all he has both been through and done for us."

"I'm going to ask you a question that you might be uncomfortable answering." Judy was reclining on the couch and nodded. "Do you have romantic feelings for your father?"

"What kind of question is that? Of course not. He's my father, not a lover. I love and respect him. I might be a little protective of him, but that's only because he is much more sensitive than people know. Do I come across as if I'm romantically infatuated with my father?"

"I have my concerns. Sometimes, when traumas strike, children take on the role of the lost spouse. Love is complicated and sometimes that love is misplaced or confused, especially over a long period of time."

"Are you implying that I have an Oedipus complex?"

"No. I think you might have what is called an Electra complex. It's the opposite of the Oedipus...the female version."

"That's just sick! You think I want to have sex with my father?" Judy shot up off the couch and got right up in Karen's face, which shocked her. Karen put her hand up, and Judy pulled back. "I'm sorry. I'm protective of my father."

"I can see that. Please sit." Judy sat back down on the couch but was still reeling. "Your anger and hostility are out of line, Judy. I can't treat you if you are going to behave like this." Judy started to cry, and Karen pushed some tissues over to her. "The doctor patient relationship is based on mutual trust. Your aggression is concerning to me. Outside of my concerns about the Electra complex, I have seen a more aggressive side to you in this session. What else is going on?"

"I'm just tired, that's all. I'm working, taking care of the house and the family, and I still am confused over my feelings for Sally. I have all of these emotions running through me." She paused then said, "Emotions and feelings that I like but am also afraid of." Karen told her to continue. "Am I gay? Am I straight? Am I bi?"

"Have you had sex with a man?"

"Yes."

"Recently?"

"Yes."

"Protected sex?"

Judy started shaking violently and broke down weeping. "No...no. It wasn't protected sex. There was no condom, and I'm not on birth control."

"When was the sex?" She told Karen it was the previous day, but when she pressed Judy to talk about it, she shut down. "Why don't you want to talk about it? There's a morning after pill I can prescribe. Do you want the pill? I can get you one."

"No."

"Are you trying to get pregnant?"

"Oh, God no. I just had my period. I'm sure I'm fine."

"Your body is changing, and you can conceive a child right after your period. The pill is a last line of defense."

"Not interested. Any more questions?"

"You were a virgin. How was the experience for you?"

"I loved it. It was romantic, hot, sensual, everything I ever imagined it would be. I lost my virginity to my one true love."

"And who might that be?"

"That's none of your business, and I don't want to talk about this anymore."

"Okay, tell me about your horseback riding today."

"It was fine. Hugh Masters has only known me for a day or so, and he has invited me and my father to his house tonight for a get together."

"Have you spoken to your father about it?"

"Not yet. I was going to stop by the lab after our session to talk about it."

Karen ended their session and said she would like to see Judy again before the week was out. She agreed to check her calendar then left. As soon as she closed the door, Karen wasted no time in calling Chris, saying, "I'm sorry to bother you, honey, but I believe that Judy Bench is in trouble. She's exhibiting extremely aggressive behavior."

"John and I want to speak with her anyway. Is she still in your office?"

"She left, but I believe she is still in the hospital. She told me she was going to speak to her father about a dinner invitation for tonight with Hugh Masters, a playboy venture capitalist who likes the company of young women and is rumored to have sexual relations with underaged boys and girls."

"Why are you just telling me this?"

"It's a rumor, Chris. There is no solid evidence for it. I'm not going to point a finger abstractly, but when a very attractive seventeen-year-old patient is asked by him to visit for a gathering that makes me wonder."

"See if you can track down Judy. If you can, get Sara to help keep her there and call me right back." Karen hung up the line and headed for Mark's laboratory.

CHAPTER SIXTEEN

*"You think you might
have been drugged?"*

Mark was talking with one of his techs when Judy entered the lab. "Well, what a nice surprise. Did you have your session?"

"Yes. How's your day going?"

"Good. What's up?"

"Do you have a few minutes to talk?"

"For you? Of course. Let's go to my office." Judy took a seat in front of her father's desk, and he sat down on the edge of it. "What's on your mind, honey?"

"I've been invited to a gathering at a friend of Maggie's tonight, and I would like to go."

"Who is this friend?"

"His name is Hugh Masters, and he is a venture capitalist and friend of Mary's as well as Maggie."

"I know Mr. Masters. Why has he extended an invitation to you, and how do you know him?"

"We met yesterday and hit it off, not in a romantic way, Mark, but in a business way. I went out horseback riding with him today, and we had a nice talk about business and how things get done."

"I've heard rumors that Mr. Masters likes young women."

"I don't know about that, nor do I care. I have no interest. He has extended an invitation to you to chaperone me if you wish."

"Oh. What time?"

"Six p.m."

"I'm on until ten, honey, and I have a backlog of labs that need to be finished for patients before I leave tonight. Will Mary and Sally be there?"

"Yes, and I promise to be home by eleven."

Mark leaned down to kiss her on the cheek, but she turned her cheek and caught his lips, and the two locked lips for several seconds. When Mark pulled away he had a strange look on his face, and Judy said, "I'm sorry, Dad. I thought you were going to give me a peck on the lips."

"Uh…okay." There was a further pause, and Mark sat down in his chair and asked, "Last night when I got home, you had made dinner and poured me a glass of wine."

"Yes."

"And that was at ten thirty, right?"

"I wasn't watching the clock, but it sounds right."

"You don't recall Mary being at the house?"

"I didn't see her, but when we spoke this morning, she told me you two had a fun night."

"Mary told you that?"

"Yeah. She said she arrived, and you had eaten dinner, then you shared a bottle of wine and went to bed. She said she left the house between three and four a.m. The way she tells the story you had a very fun night."

"What I can remember of it."

"So, can I go to Mr. Masters' home this evening?"

Mark still had a strange and confused look on his face but nodded and said, "I want you home by eleven. No later."

"Thanks, Dad." With that, she jumped up and kissed his cheek and left the office. She looked around the lab and saw that everyone was busy. She crept into one of the medication rooms and looked at several different bottles then grabbed three large ones and stuck them in her bag and headed to the elevator.

Mark still looked confused when Karen knocked on the door and asked if Judy had stopped by. He nodded and said, "She just left."

"Are you okay?"

"I'm not sure."

"What's wrong?"

"I'm not sure, but I have a really, really bad feeling." Karen went to sit, but Mark walked back into the lab and brought back a tourniquet, a blood draw needle, and three empty tubes. He handed them to Karen and asked her to draw his blood. She tied off his upper arm and swabbed it with alcohol and drew the blood. She handed them back to him and put the needle on his desk.

"Why are you drawing your own blood?"

"I just have a bad feeling."

"Do you want to expound upon that?"

"No…not yet, but keep your cellphone close. I might need you later tonight."

"Okay. You're not my patient; Judy is, and I can't treat the two of you outside of family therapy."

"I understand. Judy might need you. We might need some therapy."

"Did something happen?"

"It has, or it might be coming. I don't know which, but I'm taking your advice on Judy's behavior much more seriously."

Karen put her hands on his shoulders. "What exactly are you worried about?"

"Drugs."

"Drugs? You think you might have been drugged?"

"I sure as hell hope not."

Hugh was seated across from Jim and the rest and was looking the four over with curiosity. "So, let me see if I understand this. The FBI has been invited in to investigate Andrew's murder?" Jim nodded. "But I thought this was the sheriff's case?"

Sam spoke up. "We often ask for the federal government's assistance in cases, Mr. Masters. This is not unusual."

"What would raise this murder to the federal level?"

"It's not an official federal case, Mr. Masters," John said calmly. "We have been asked to look over evidence and to give advice and guidance in the matter. This gives the sheriff's department access to our labs and other investigative tools that they might not have."

"You're the experts. I want to know who killed Andrew as much as you do, probably more."

"Why more?" Chris asked.

"Andrew was my half-brother."

Jim sat back against the chair. "Yeah, we know that. We found out last night when we were typing and crossing blood for DNA. Why didn't you tell us earlier?"

"I didn't think it was relevant. Andy had his demons, and I have been working hard for years to help him with them."

"You mean his appetite for children?" Sam asked.

"My brother was a pedophile, Sheriff. That is no secret. I know it can't be cured, but I was working really hard to help him."

"So, who would want to see your bother dead?" Jim asked.

"Andrew had a lot of enemies and victims. Too many to count; however, no one had access to my property who would have wanted to harm him." Jim laughed. "Is there something funny about that statement, Mr. O'Brian?"

"Yeah, something really fuckin' funny. Your brother was brutally murdered on your property. That means that an enemy gained access and got to him...or someone on the inside murdered your brother, which means your security really sucks."

"Sara, it's Karen."

"What's up?"

"Something bad. I just did a blood draw for Mark Bench."

"So?"

"The draw was from Bench."

"What the hell for?"

"He's looking for drugs in his blood."

"Go on."

"Well, I had a disturbing session with his daughter Judy this afternoon, and now Mark is really, really upset."

"What are you thinking?"

"I'm thinking about one of the largest epidemics in this nation that no one wants to talk about."

"Incest?"

"Yes. I think that Mark was drugged by Judy."

"You think that Judy drugged her father for sex?"

"Yes." Sara was quiet for a second, and Karen could hear the keys on Sara's keyboard being struck hard. "What are you doing?"

"Blocking the blood sample, so it doesn't get back to Mark."

"Where are you having the results sent?"

"To me."

Hugh was in the barn with Gloria, who he had strapped nude to one of the stalls and was whipping. "You didn't clean up the blood from last night, you little bitch." Gloria was barely conscious and was hanging by her arms as Hugh continued to beat her with a bullwhip.

Tonya had entered the stable and cried out, "Hugh, for Christ's sake! You're going to kill her." It was five-thirty, and Tonya had arrived early for dinner. Hugh drew back for another strike but stopped and checked Gloria for a pulse.

"She's alive."

Tonya got Gloria down, and she collapsed to the ground into a bloody bale of hay she had been standing on. "Jesus, Hugh! What the hell did this child do to deserve a beating like this? She is one of your most trusted slaves."

"She didn't clean up the stalls after last night's beatings before your auction. I had Judy Bench out here for a horseback ride, and she noticed the blood."

"The girl would not connect a little blood with anything we are doing, Hugh. Poor Gloria is going to have scars for life if she survives."

"Who gives a shit? She didn't do her job, and I had to have Pierce come out here along with Clive to clean it up. I have dinner guests coming in a half hour, and I just lost it."

"Well, you might have lost it, but Gloria is going to need medical attention." The bloodied back of the girl was all he could see.

"Tie her to her bunk and put some salve on her. If she dies, she dies. I have guests to greet." Hugh left the stable and walked sternly to the house." Tonya lifted Gloria and carried her to the barracks.

Gloria was in and out but whispered, "Master is right. I let him down and did not do my job." Her head fell back, and she passed out. Tonya put her on her bunk but didn't restrain her. She wiped her down with a cool wet cloth then put salve on her back, buttocks, and legs.

"I will check on you before I leave." There was no response from Gloria, who was breathing deeply and labored.

Sally and Mary were already at Hugh's and were mingling with a few other people in the living room when he appeared. He was dressed in a suit and greeted everyone with a hug and kiss. Pierce had entered the room looking a bit flushed, and Hugh took him by the arm, pulled him aside, and said, "Have you been with Lori again?"

"I can't help myself. There's just something about her."

"Leave her the hell alone, Pierce. I have enough problems. I have invited the Bench girl to the house tonight and before the night is through I plan on drugging and fucking her."

"Do you really think that's wise?"

"It's what I want. She'll be none the worse for it."

"Are you planning on breaking her?"

"Too soon to tell."

"If you touch that girl, we will all be caught."

"How do you figure?"

"Her father's line of work and all the people in law enforcement looking into her rape allegations against Sally. If I were you, I would keep an arm's length from her until things settle down."

"But I want her."

"Think with your head and not your cock. You know damn well I'm right!" Hugh nodded as two other people approached, and he smiled and gave hugs and introductions, all the while scanning the room for Judy.

"Judy has left the hospital, Chris, and I have a bad feeling."

"Talk to me."

"She's been invited to Hugh Masters' home tonight, and I feel that something terrible is going to happen."

"To her or Masters?"

"That's the key question. I know Hugh. He's a smooth talker and can get into just about any woman's pants."

"Do you think she is susceptible to him?"

"I don't know. We had a very strange and somewhat aggressive session this afternoon. I think that you and John need to crash the party."

John was sitting at his desk, and Chris had his phone on speaker. "You think Masters is going to make a move on an underaged kid?"

"Something is going to happen, John. I just don't know what that something is."

"Chris and I will go back out there."

"Thank you. Please call me after you have been there."

Judy arrived at Hugh's home but parked at the end of the street and walked through the open gates. She had a large bag over her shoulder and entered the house from the side entrance near the gardener's shed. She quickly ran up the stairs to where she had been the night before and then quietly checked room after room. She got to the end of the hall and found the room where she had heard the men talking. The door was locked, so she knocked lightly, but there was no response. She opened the door to the room next door and entered. She looked around the small room, but there was only a bed, a bucket, a wash basin, and a closet door. When she turned the knob, the door led to yet another unlocked door, and in a matter of seconds she was standing in front of Lori Fleming.

The room was dark, and Lori was laying still as Judy approached. "Hello?" Judy called quietly.

"Who's there?"

"A friend."

"Unlikely. Who are you?" Judy felt around the walls for a light switch and when she clicked it on, the room came to light. What it lit up was a scene of horror so despicable she almost threw up. Lori was chained to the bed on her stomach. Her rear was raised in the air above a blood-soaked pillow, and her anus was exposed. Judy looked at the deep red and purple flesh of Lori's whipped body with disbelief. Lori had her head turned in Judy's direction, and as Judy stepped into her line of sight, she asked, "Who are you, and how did you get in here?"

"My name is Judy Bench, and I'm a guest of Hugh Masters."

Lori laughed. "You're a hot little number. You might be a friendly guest of his now, but I promise by morning you will be a slave like the rest of us."

"The rest of us? I don't understand."

"You're in a slave house, Judy."

"A slave house?"

"Well, it is a stopping point for most of the domestic slaves that Tonya Hart and Mary Owen trade in."

"How long have you been here?"

"Almost a year. They're going to kill me."

"Don't say that. I'm going to get you out of here."

"If you so much as touch one of those ropes or chains, and they see it before I can get out, we are both dead." Judy opened the large bag and pulled out a pair of bolt cutters. "What the hell are you doing with those?"

"I thought I was going to need them for the barn."

"You've been to the stables?"

"I went riding with Hugh this afternoon."

"And he told you that you were smart and beautiful, and that he heard that Mary had taken you under her wing, and he wants to help you in business?"

"Pretty much."

"Run. Run like hell away from this horror house. Go to the police. If Masters and the others don't know you have been back or been in here, there's a chance you could get the police here before he can hide us again."

Judy shook her head. "No. Monsters like this don't deserve to live."

"How old are you?"

"Almost eighteen."

"And you're going to stop these monsters?"

"I've killed two already."

Lori's eyes went wide. "You did what?"

"I killed Al Fleece, and last night I killed Andrew Haas with a mower blade."

"You killed Al and Andrew?" Judy nodded. "But how?"

"I killed Al with a straight razor to the throat, and I cut Andrew's head off then chopped up his body."

"That's impossible. You're, what, five feet tall?"

"It's all about understanding the laws of physics. If you understand that, you can do anything."

"There is no way you are going to free me in time. Pierce or Clive will be back here any minute, and the second they find you we are both dead."

Judy laughed while reaching into her bag and pulling out her straight razor. "I'm hoping Mr. Tallon comes in. As soon as he moves to mount or hurt you, I will take his head off."

Lori was about to speak when the two heard footsteps coming down the hall. "Get out of here." Judy shut off the lights and went back into the closet but kept the door cracked enough so she could see into the room. The door opened and then closed quickly.

Clive's thick English accent cut the air along with Pierce's. "We don't have a lot of time as your master has guests, but I am going to rape you one more time tonight, and Clive is going to film it," Pierce said as he stripped off his clothes and mounted her. Lori said nothing. Pierce and Clive were so engrossed in the abuse they were inflicting on her that they didn't notice Judy coming out of the closet…or the straight razor glistening in the light. Clive's back was to her and blocking Pierce's view of the closet. Judy grabbed him by the hair, pulled his head straight back, and slit his throat from ear to ear. She grabbed the camera as Clive's body slid down to the floor and blood pooled all around her. She had the bolt cutters in her hands and swung away at Pierce's head, sending him careening to the floor where she struck him once more. He was breathing but unconscious. She then worked quickly to cut Lori's restraints and in a matter of two minutes the girl was freed.

Lori stood staring down at Pierce's nude body then grabbed him by the hair and began kicking him in the face. Judy stood back as blood and teeth began to fly across the room. Lori was speaking softly and deliberately, "You sick fuckin' piece of shit. You raping, murdering monster." Lori stopped and asked Judy, "What's in that bag of yours?" Judy smiled and handed her some duct tape. The two girls were able to get Pierce taped off just as he was starting to come to. They had managed to get him on the bed, and Lori stood over him with the straight razor as Judy stood with Clive's camera. Pierce's mouth was taped shut, and Lori didn't say a word as she slid the razor under his scrotum, slitting it in half. She bared her teeth and took his left testicle into her mouth. Pierce screamed; Judy filmed, and Lori moved her head from side to side violently until she raised up her blood-covered face. Her cheeks puffed out, and she spit the testicle onto Pierce's chest then buried her head back down into his groin going for the next one.

Lori raged on Pierce until his groin had nothing but a hole where his genitals and penis had been. Judy handed her a towel, and she wiped the blood from her face and chest as best she could. Judy asked, "So, how does revenge taste?"

"Absolutely great." Lori put the blade against Pierce's throat and said, "I told you I would kill you, didn't I?" Pierce was barely alert when she slid the razor across his throat slowly, keeping his carotid artery from spraying blood across the room. Instead, she controlled it with part of a sheet and her blood-soaked pillow. As Pierce bled out, she smiled. "No matter what may happen to me, I got the satisfaction of removing two pieces of scum from this planet." Pierce's eyes were open and dilating as Lori stood up.

Judy said, "I doubt anyone is going to come up here for a while as Masters has a large party going on."

"No, that means that he will come for me and the others when they are finished with their meal." Judy pulled out two bottles she had grabbed at her father's lab. "What's that?"

"One's a blood thinner and the other's a strong antibiotic."

"What the hell are you going to do with those?"

"These are commonly used in rat poison, but the dose I will give will just make people really, really sick for a day or two."

"And the purpose?"

"So, I can winnow out the rest of the bad people."

Judy was looking over the large bottles when Lori said, "You don't have to go to those extremes to know who the bad people are."

"Do you know?"

"I know the key players; I don't know who the buyers are. Based on conversations I have overheard, though, the buyers are people in the upper middle-class suburbs of LA County."

"You heard right. They aren't going to the super rich. Mary, Sally, and Tonya cater to the upper middle-class. They're all sexually exploited by the buyers, but as a general rule they are purchased as domestic slaves, maids, butlers, and nannies," Judy said.

"Wait! Nannies? People are going to trust the lives of their children to sexually and physically abused slaves?" Judy nodded. "I wish this were just some kind of nightmare that I have been enduring."

"I'm sorry, Lori, but it's as real as it gets. How are you still lucid and intact?"

"I'm hardly intact. Masters likes to use pretty sophisticated torture on his slaves-to-be. Sensory deprivation tanks, insomnia treatment, keeping people up for days, sometimes weeks on end. Using drugs that make people more susceptible to suggestion. Of course, his favorite is forcing the slaves to watch as others are raped, beaten, and in some cases killed. He even has them partake in the torture. For instance, about six months ago, Hugh had three kids about our age brought to him for the final breaking of their wills before sale. While the girls broke fast, no matter what he did to the boy, he just couldn't break him. He did just about everything he has done to me thus far but worse. The kid wouldn't break, and he kept trying to free his sisters who were so brainwashed that they would report it to Hugh or one of his cronies. One night, the boy got free and made a run for it from the barracks behind the stables. He almost made it, too. He got to a sheriff that was patrolling around three a.m., but the sheriff's deputy knew Hugh and brought the boy back. Hugh locked him in the hot box overnight and for most of the next day."

"Hot box?"

"A black steel box that is kept out behind the barracks. No light, no food, no water, and hundred-degree temperatures. He was stripped and beaten before being placed in it. When the kid was brought out, he was out of it. Hugh then took him to the burial field in the back of the property and made him kneel and then go down to his hands and knees. His ass and head were left accessible, but the rest was covered in dirt and cement. The kid was then raped repeatedly by other kids; boys used their cocks; girls used whatever they could find. Sticks, bottles, pipe. The kid's ass looked like hamburger."

"Did he die?"

"Not right away. It took five days. He begged to be released. Hugh had broken him, but Hugh has a rule. When a slave gets to that point, there is no return, only a cruel end."

"So, how did he die?"

"Screaming. In the middle of the night, a mountain lion picked up his odor and consumed a lot of him, and then the coyotes finished off what they could get to through the dirt and cement. I remember that night. He had to have screamed for a half hour. Cold, blood curdling screams. His sisters were in the barracks with us, and they actually laughed."

Judy was silent, and she and Lori moved into the other room and then down the back stairs. The sounds of conversation and music were coming from the gathering area of the home, and the two girls slipped out the side door to the shed where the door was open. Judy looked at Lori. "I'm going into the house. Don't run. If you run, they will find you."

"What are you going to do?"

"I'm going to arrive like I'm his guest. It's seven thirty, and I will make small talk and try and poison food or drinks. Once people are sick, get out of here."

"What about Mary, Sally, Tonya, and Hugh?"

"Once they are sick enough, I will come back and take them out."

Lori watched as Judy left the shed and shuddered while speaking under her breath, "We are both going to die."

CHAPTER SEVENTEEN

*"Oh...and they never
saw it coming."*

The sun had long set over the Masters' estate. There were bright lights coming from inside and outside the mansion. John and Chris parked on the other side of the security gate and were in full body armor. "With all of the light, getting up to and into the house is going to be difficult." Chris nodded. They looked around the property with their night vision, and John pointed to the stable, and Chris took off with a gym bag over his shoulder. The Eagle looked at the house and saw that one of the shed doors was open. He made his way to the shed, looked inside, and saw Lori huddled in a corner. When he entered, Lori scrambled to find something to fight off who she thought was an attacker.

The Eagle quickly subdued her, and once she was settled, said, "I'm not here to hurt you, young lady. I'm here to help." John could see the torn skin and black and blue markings on her body. "What's your name?"

"Lori."

"What's your full name?"

"Lori Elizabeth Fleming."

The Eagle pulled out his tablet and ran her name, but nothing came back. "What are you doing here?"

"I'm a slave to a group of monsters."

"How long have you been here?"

"Nearly a year."

"Do you have family?"

"YES!"

"Okay, but, they haven't reported you missing."

"That's because they sold me to these slavers nearly two years ago then moved out of state with the money."

"I will get more from you later. Right now, I need to know who the slavers are."

"Hugh Masters is the breaking master." The Eagle nodded, and Lori asked, "You know what that is?"

"Yes. The others, please."

"Tonya Hart, Mary Owen, Sally Owen."

"Anyone else?"

"There are several dead people."

"Dead…dead how?"

"Al Fleece, throat slit. Andrew Haas, head chopped off. Clive Baxter, throat slit. Pierce Tallon, emasculated alive, then I slit his throat."

"You killed all of these men?"

"Just Pierce, the raping monster. The rest were killed by my savior."

"Who is your savior?"

"A girl named Judy…Judy Bench."

"Who else is in the house?"

"Hard to say. It's a Hugh Masters party. It could be something formal and legitimate like a business function, or it could be the start of a rape, torture, and murder party. With Hugh, I never know. Hugh has slaves who work for him. They are in the house as staff. I don't consider them bad. I mean, they do bad things sometimes, but they are just following orders in order to keep from being hurt more."

"How many slaves are here?"

"I think about two dozen. We're all supposed to go up for auction next week."

"If you have been here a year, you're not going up for auction."

"No. Hugh has told Mary and Tonya he is keeping me for as long as I please him. When he is finished with me, he will kill me."

The Eagle shook his head. "No. No, he won't, Ms. Fleming. How did you get out here?"

"I had been tied and chained to beds, walls, and stalls in the stable for whippings and rapes for the better part of the year, but Judy freed me."

"Judy rescued you?"

"Yes. Are you going to hurt her?"

"I don't know. Is she one of these monsters?"

"She has been very kind to me. I don't know any of her back story, but she is intent on helping me and the rest of the slaves in the barracks behind the barn."

The Eagle put his hand against his ear and spoke to Chris. "Chris, do you read me?"

"Roger that, Eagle."

"Go to the other side of the barn. There are people who are injured and enslaved there."

"What do you want me to do with them?"

"Just get me a head count, ages, sex, and what, if any, injuries they have." The Eagle asked Lori, "Are there guards?"

"Two at the entrance. They're slaves, too, but have been slaves so long they don't even act human."

"Are they armed?"

"Only with fear. The people will do as told so long as they are there."

"So, Judy saved you single-handedly?"

"Yes. Pretty damned impressive, huh?"

"You could say that. Where is Ms. Bench now?"

"She's inside pretending to be a part of the party she was invited to. She is also trying to make everyone sick using some type of non-lethal poison that she got from her father's lab."

Judy was chatting with people while being introduced. She knew no one in the crowd outside of Hugh, Mary, and Sally. She didn't know Tonya, but she appeared unnerved that she was there. Hugh was watching Judy work the room with Mary and Sally. He grabbed two glasses of Champagne from a waiter's tray and took them into the kitchen where he slipped a clear liquid into one of the glasses and went looking for Judy.

Judy had seen him slip out, and she took the opportunity to excuse herself and ask where the ladies' room was. Sally walked her around the corner from the kitchen to the bathroom and asked, "Is this great or what?"

"It's fine, but who are all of these people?"

"My mom's real estate clients, for the most part."

"Are they into the porn stuff?"

"Oh, heavens no. They're customers who help my mother sell real estate or run her offices around the state."

"So, they aren't customers for the porn or slaves and the other stuff we are into?"

"No. Hugh has been promising to throw this party for Mother for months. He finally has done it. You have no idea how many sales will be generated due to this. It's astronomical."

Judy smiled and stepped into the bathroom. Hugh was asking around for her, but no one had seen her. Once alone, Judy pulled the medications out of her bag and mixed them into a plastic bag. She smelled soup and headed into the large kitchen where six people were shouting instructions, filling salad plates, and bussing them out to the guests. Two cooks were near the stove, and one was working on some type of soup. The twenty-gallon pot was boiling, and she asked the chef, "Is that pot on the other side of the room supposed to be burning?"

"Burning? Dear God, what's burning?" He left the area, and while the other chefs had their backs to her, she emptied the contents of her baggie into the soup, stirred it in, and was about to leave.

"There you are," Hugh said with a smile. "What the hell are you doing in the kitchen?"

"I just used the bathroom, and I love to cook, so I had to see how the pros do it." Hugh handed her a glass of Champagne and walked her out of the kitchen. The two were standing alone near a grand piano that had several cloths on it with serving trays of food and drinks. She pointed out Mary to Hugh then swapped out the Champagne he had given to her for another on a tray. He proposed a toast, and the two drank. "You do know you are contributing to the delinquency of a minor by serving me alcohol?"

"Are you a cop?" Hugh laughed as he asked the question.

When their glasses were empty, Judy grabbed two more glasses and handed Hugh the one he had originally given her and said, "A toast to the corruption of youth." Hugh smiled as they drank. "So, bring me up to speed. Who are these people?"

Hugh looked around and said in a flat tone, "No one that will fatten my wallet. These are the leaches who prey on the weak. They live off of death and divorce."

"Lawyers?"

Judy's words made Hugh break out into uncontrollable laughter, laughter that got the attention of everyone in the room. When he regained his composure, he said, "Not quite that bad but close. Real estate salespeople."

Judy sipped her Champagne as Hugh slugged his down then grabbed another. He was starting to sweat, and Judy asked, "Are you feeling okay?"

"It's hot in here."

"It is. Would you like to go somewhere cooler? Perhaps step outside?" Hugh nodded, and the two walked out the back door off the kitchen. "You have a huge mansion, Hugh."

"I do, but the bulk of it is off limits."

"And why is that?"

"It's my private residence where my staff caters to my every whim."

"Staff? You mean slaves?"

Hugh looked surprised. "What do you know of it?"

"Everything that Mary and Sally could tell me over the past week. I know you are preparing a group for auction and that you have one or two that you can't break. I mean, that's what you do as a side business is break the will of human slaves, right?" Hugh was wiping sweat from his brow as the two stood alone on a large deck. "At least that's what Mary told me."

"It's a hobby. I don't get paid for it. I make it possible for others to make money." His speech was slurring as he leaned down and whispered, "Do you want to know why I do it?" Judy said yes. "I love hurting people. I love breaking the human spirit and watching them as they pray unto profanity. When I have truly broken a slave, I get the most satisfaction, their unconditional praise, and their willingness to do anything to keep from being beaten and tortured. It's wonderful. When buyers leave here, they know they're getting the crème de la crème of servants. No slave leaves this house that isn't fully broken, and I offer a money back guarantee to Mary and Tonya."

"So, you don't make money?"

"I make a pittance. I don't need money, Judy. I have plenty of it. This is my domain, and here I am master of all I oversee. Does that disturb you?"

"It's business, Hugh. I'm getting into this to make money. Sally has talked about this for years, not the slave aspect but the money making."

"Ah, Sally. She is a hottie. I use her every once in a while if I get bored with my own slaves. She's expensive, but she does everything and anything to please." Hugh paused. "Don't ever tell Mary or mention it to Sally." He was swaying a bit from side to side. "I once had Sally in my stable for four days."

"Why would you have her in the stable for four days?"

Hugh looked around before continuing, "You don't know my secret weapon in the breaking process?"

"No."

Hugh grabbed Judy's hand and said, "Come with me, and I will show you." He pulled her roughly by the arm down a path in the direction of the barn.

The Eagle had made his way around the side of the house and was watching Judy and Hugh on the outer deck. He saw him grab her by the arm and start dragging her in the direction of the barn. "Chris, where are you?"

"In a makeshift barracks. There are two dozen men, women, and children in here. All badly beaten and one young girl is unconscious and in terrible shape. She needs medical attention at once."

"What did you do with the guards?"

"They weren't really guards. A couple of young boys. I knocked them out and zip tied them. The rest of the people are all chained to bunks."

"Film them with your tablet but don't do anything with them. Hugh Masters is dragging Judy Bench in the direction of the barn. I'm following."

"What do you want me to do next?"

"I want you to get to the barn but unless Masters moves to hurt Bench, stay out of sight and don't interfere."

"I don't get it. You want me to just watch Bench and Masters?"

"Yes." The Eagle followed at a distance in the darkness. He watched Hugh release Judy and unlock the doors to the barn. The Eagle was close enough that he was able to slip in unnoticed and hid behind several stacks of hay as Hugh led Judy around.

"Are you familiar with BDSM?" Hugh asked.

"I have read a little about it but have never really been involved. Why? Do you like it?"

"Very much. I'm a top. That means the dominant person in a BDSM relationship, but I have a secret."

"And what's that?"

"I like to role play and be a bottom sometimes. That's what I use Sally for. I can trust her to respect my safe word, and I can be a sub while a top at the same time."

"Interesting. Show me." Hugh stripped nude then told Judy to do the same. Judy did as directed, and Hugh felt her up and kissed her neck then walked her over to a well-lit room. In it were a collection of whips and all manner of torture devices, and he pulled several whips off the wall and then a pair of leg irons and wrist restraints as well as a spreader bar and walked Judy out into the stable.

"Have you ever been whipped?"

"Um, no, and I have no interest in being whipped."

"You will once you have tried it." He was now clearly under the influence of the liquid he had poured into the glass meant for her.

"Well, if it feels so good, Hugh, show me what to do to you. I will be your dom."

Hugh stared at her for several seconds then threw a limp wrist her direction and said, "Oh, what the hell? You're tiny. You can't hurt me. Help me with these restraints."

Judy fumbled with the devices, but Hugh was patient and helped her restrain his ankles between the steel spreader bars. "What does this do?"

"It makes it so I can't move my legs while you are whipping me. The human body instinctively moves to protect itself when being hurt.

It takes years to learn the discipline not to move while being whipped, and if you move while being whipped you can get hurt."

"What could get hurt?"

"Your kidneys, for starters. When you stairstep a whipping on your sub, you must be mindful of their middle section. I'll explain. Grab those handcuffs over on the table." Judy got them and locked his wrists together, then Hugh raised his arms above his head and slid the stainless-steel chain through a carabiner clip.

Judy looked at the clip and asked, "Aren't those things used for mountain climbing and working, like on high rise buildings?"

"Yes, but they have many, many other uses as well. We use them in BDSM as they quickly release but securely hold someone's arms and legs in place. There is a small step ladder in the torture room, grab it as you will need it to remove me from the clip after my whipping." Judy got the ladder and placed it near Hugh's nude body. He was now outstretched at the legs, and his bare body was restrained to the stable. "My safe word is yellow."

"What a surprise. Yellow," Judy said as she walked into the closet and came out with several whips. She dropped two on the ground but held in her right hand a leather whip with pieces of steel and tacks in it.

She walked up to Hugh, who was fading in and out, and he asked, "Why are you so alert?"

"Because I didn't drink the Champagne you made me. I have some experience with being drugged, and I have been watching you like a hawk. You're not very subtle or very bright. I slipped the drugged drink to you on our second glass. I do, however, have a nice buzz." She raised the whip to Hugh's face and asked, "Is this a BDSM device?"

Hugh's eyes went wide. "Yellow, yellow, yellow."

"That's what I thought. It's not. Did you use this on Lori Fleming recently?"

"How the fuck do you know Lori?"

"That's not important now. What is important is that I be perfectly honest with you before I start." She got up close to Hugh's right ear.

"I killed Al Fleece. He threatened to rape and murder my sister. I killed that monster Andrew Haas. I also killed Clive Baxter and Pierce Tallon tonight while saving Lori. Their bodies are laying on the floor that used to be Lori's prison." She paused, "Oh…and they never saw it coming. However, you, Hugh, you are going to feel every lash of the torture that I am going to unfurl on you."

"Oh God, oh God. Yellow, yellow."

"You are yellow."

"Where's Lori?"

"Around. Don't worry. You and Lori are going to have your own face to face, now relax."

The first blow of the whip sent Hugh into convulsive movements. The next five ripped the skin from his back, legs, and buttocks. He was screaming for help. "Your victims scream. Do they get help?"

"There are dozens at my party. Someone will hear."

She struck him several more times, sending blood across the room after landing two blows on his kidneys. "No, they won't. Your guests are most likely throwing up in anything they can find and are leaving your party for the ER in droves."

"What?"

Judy laid a few more strikes on his body then took the whip back to the room then picked up a whip of tack board used for holding carpet in place. "Tack board? Man, you really do like pain." Hugh was screaming as blow after blow struck his body. Judy stood nude, spattered with blood. He had long passed out, and she put the items back in the room, dressed, and left Hugh hanging from the stall as she went back up to the house.

CHAPTER EIGHTEEN

"Because I poisoned it."

As the Eagle looked on, Chris pulled Hugh's head back and said, "You have to be impressed with that young woman."

"Yes, well, she is no match for the whole group."

"So, do you want her in the lair?"

"No. We know who the key players are. The slaves are safe. I want to see what other information this kid can extract."

"She's extracting it, but she's not noting it."

"One of us will be around her at all times and record the proceedings. I recorded these actions."

"And if she doesn't get enough information or is attacked?"

"That's what we're here for. Let's let the girl work. I'm impressed."

Chris nodded and asked, "And what do you want to do with this guy?"

"Leave him. Ms. Bench has more in store for him. Besides, Ms. Bench has promised Ms. Fleming her own special time with Masters."

The two men left the barn and stayed under the cover of darkness as they headed for the house.

Judy walked into the main entrance where people were throwing up; some were even passed out on the floor. Sally, Mary, and Tonya were the only ones that were not ill as they had been meeting and had not eaten the meal. Judy greeted them, and they asked where Hugh was.

"He is out in the stable. He showed me around and then asked to be left alone. What the hell happened in here?"

Sally shook her head. "I don't know, but it's bad." Judy walked over to the spread of food and made herself a plate and put a small amount of soup in a bowl and sat down at the table. The three women watched her eat the food.

Mary said, "You haven't touched your soup."

"It's a bit hot. I have plenty, and the soup is actually a bisque. Lobster. I believe that's best left as a chaser. So, where have you been?"

"Talking about you."

"Interesting, and the conversation was?"

"We don't like this sudden friendship with Hugh."

"And that's my fault how? We met; he likes me. We rode horses, and he has shown me around his estate and invited me to a meal. What have I done wrong?"

Sally grabbed a plate after watching Judy eat for several minutes. "Do you think that's wise, Sally?" Mary asked.

"Judy is eating, and she's fine. Half of the people who were here have left for home or the ER, and those left here are sleeping it off."

"You think this is alcohol related?"

"What else could it be? The chef is a five-star chef as are his staff. We have had them cater events for us before."

Chef Aston appeared from the kitchen with some more warm food, and Mary asked, "Aren't you the least bit concerned about the guests?"

"No. They were all pretty drunk before they ate. That was my fault. I didn't have the food out or enough appetizers to sop up the alcohol. It's most certainly not my food that made them ill."

"Did you eat everything?" Tonya asked.

"Of course. I tasted as my chefs cooked, and it is all incredibly good." The chef ladled some bisque into a bowl and ate. "That is a lobster bisque to die for." He left the room, and the rest of the women grabbed plates and filled them. The conversation over Judy and Hugh dragged as the others had finished their bisque. Mary was the first to show signs of illness followed quickly by Sally and then Tonya. All three were doubled over and trying to get to bathrooms as Judy finished a glass of wine.

Tonya looked at her and asked, "Why the hell aren't you sick?"

"I didn't eat the bisque."

"Why not?"

"Because I poisoned it."

Judy went back to the shed and got Lori, and the two went back into the house. Mary spotted Lori standing nude, bloody, and beaten, and started screaming. "Jesus Christ, Judy! Are you mad? That girl is a killer."

Judy looked at Lori, who was smiling, "Are you a killer?"

"Um…yeah!" Judy handed Lori the straight razor. Lori took it then looked at Sally, Tonya, and Mary and handed it back to her. "No…that's too humane for these three; they must suffer."

Judy put the blade back into her bag and pulled out a roll of duct tape. "Well, we don't want them running, so we need to restrain them." Lori worked with Judy until the three were restrained, and Judy leaned down over Mary and said, "Lori isn't as good a killer as I am…yet. I killed Al Fleece, Andrew Haas, and just about an hour ago I slit Clive Baxter's throat. Lori did the honors on Pierce Tallon, and he died badly."

Lori had finished with Sally's restraints and asked, "Where is Hugh?"

"I have him restrained in the stable. He wanted to role play in BDSM. Little does he know just how that role play is going to end."

"It's going to end at my hand, Judy, and no one else's."

Judy nodded. "We need to get confessions out of all of them. I have one from Hugh, but Mary and Tonya are the key players in the slave trade. We need more information from them before we end them. Now…let's find you some clothing. You should not be nude."

The Eagle had a parabolic microphone and was recording the goings on in the house. He had it all on his tablet as well but made no attempts to stop Judy or Lori. Chris came over the headset, "We have two dozen people here. I have sedated all of them."

"The injured girl? How is she?"

"She needs medical attention. I don't know what to do for her, but she needs help."

"I will get medical help out here."

"What? Are you going to call EMTs?"

"No. The girls are doing a great job of dealing with their attackers. I'm not going to disturb them. I'm going to call Sara."

"I don't like it. I don't like it at all."

"You don't have to like it, Chris. Hugh Masters is hanging from a stall in the barn. Check on him and make sure he's out. If not, sedate him, but mildly." The Eagle signed off then called Sara and said, "I have a most unusual request."

"I have been assisting the Eagle for years. I think I have seen it all."

"Chris and I are on scene of a murder torture situation in Hidden Hills."

"Okay. That's not out of the ordinary."

"There is a young girl who is seriously injured and needs medical attention, but I can't bring anyone out here right now. Chris and I need to keep an eye on two girls administering justice."

"Now you have my attention."

"I need you and Karen to come out here and take care of the girl while this plays out."

"So, you aren't hurting anyone?"

"No."

"You are allowing others to do it?"

"Yes."

"Text me the address."

"The home is in Hidden Hills."

"That's going to be problematic."

"You will need to grab Jade and Jessica. They can bring you two out in one of the coroner's vans as a follow up to the murder last night."

"So, you want all four of us on a crime scene where the Eagle is NOT the one bringing justice and to care for a girl?"

"That's about the size of it."

"Okay, you're right. This is all new. I have your text, and we're on our way."

CHAPTER NINETEEN

*"I don't want to be
tortured to death."*

The house was quiet as the last of those drugged had passed out, and the three women had all been taped up and their mouths taped shut. Lori had found a sundress, and Judy complimented her on it. "You do have a really nice figure."

"Thank you. For the record, I'm straight."

"So am I."

"Oh…so they have only gotten you to 'experiment' in girl on girl porn? You haven't gone through the whole sexual identity crisis yet?"

"I had a moment but thanks to a loving father and great therapist I have passed that."

"And your mother? What's her take?"

"She died years ago in the great fires."

Lori looked down at the dress and then at Judy. "I'm sorry, and I'm sorry for snapping at you about being straight."

"It's fine. I had a sexual identity crisis but realized I'm straight. I was a virgin up until a few nights ago."

"Really? Man or woman?"

"Man, silly. I couldn't lose my virginity to a woman. You can strap on all the sex toys you like, but until a man has penetrated you in a loving way with his penis, you are a virgin."

"So, you made love to your first true love?"

"I did."

"Do you have any siblings?"

"A sister. Tabitha. I'm very protective of her."

"What does your father do that he would have a laboratory?"

"He's the head of pathology at Northridge Hospital."

"Ah…Mark Bench?"

"You know my father?"

"Not really, but I have been fucked by him."

"I'm SORRY?"

"He has been to one of the brothels that Mary runs in Woodland Hills. I was fucked by him two or three times before I was moved here."

Judy shook her head. "No…that's wrong. My father loves me and my sister. He would never hurt a child."

"I doubt he knew I was a child. The room was always dark, and he always used a condom. He never spoke, just grunted when he came then left."

"How do you know his name then?"

"I guess from Tonya. On several occasions, she addressed him as Mark and a few times others led him into my room and addressed him as Mr. Bench."

"That could be a coincidence."

"No, it couldn't. I cleaned out his wallet the last time we had sex. There was no ID really, not much other than some cash and condoms, but I'm sure of the name."

"You're wrong."

"Hey, I said he never hurt me. He was always gentle. Come on. Your father needed to bust a nut; you can't fault him for that. At least he went to hookers and didn't slide into bed with you or your sister." Judy turned her back to Lori, and Lori asked, "Are we going to finish these bitches off, or are we going to stand here and argue? If we don't kill them, this exploitation will go on. We have an opportunity to end this shit right here, right now."

Judy dried tears from her eyes. "Where shall we begin?"

"I want to start with Sally. She's the one who took me in when my family sold me to her mother. She was the first person to drug and rape me, so let's start with her."

"Jesus! That would have made her like eleven or twelve."

"Sadism has no age limit. She used me, confused me, and then her mother took me into the sex trade."

"What do you want to do to her?"

"In a perfect world, I would tie her to the ground nude, cover her in honey, and let the ants and other bugs have at her, but we don't have time for that. So, I say I use your straight razor and open her up."

"Disembowel her?"

"Sure. We can take her out to the burial plot, tie her down, gut her, and let nature take its course."

"That could take all night."

"I have nowhere to be; do you? Besides, it's ten after nine. The coyotes are running amuck in the hills. One whiff of Sally's innards, and they will be on her." The two girls went back downstairs, and Mary and Tonya were looking up at the girls as they grabbed Sally by the hair, and Lori used the straight razor to cut off what little clothes Sally was wearing. Judy shoved all of the food and drinks off the coffee table, and they put Sally on it. Lori looked into Sally's terrified eyes and said, "Tell Judy what you did to me. How you and your mother bought me and how you indoctrinated me."

"I was a kid. I was doing as I was told."

"TELL HER!" Lori screamed so loudly that it stunned even Judy. Sally began to share all she had done to Lori and others at her mother's instruction. "Even now, in the face of certain death, you won't accept responsibility for your actions?"

"I did what I was told."

"I remember your laughter in the stables, the whips tearing my skin, and you and Hugh taking turns beating and raping me. That wasn't at your mother's instruction, was it?"

"I'm sick. I have a mental illness. I'm sorry for all the people I hurt. Please don't kill me."

"As I recall, those were the last words of the boy that you and Hugh murdered in the field. You remember him, right? His sisters laughed and helped in the savageness of his end. You were there with Hugh and Pierce that day. He was broken, but you didn't plead for his release. Your last words to him as he had an eighteen-inch flashlight shoved up his ass were, 'go fuck yourself.'" Sally was begging as the two girls stood over her with the straight blade, and Judy laughed while Lori cut into Sally's abdomen. Mary was crying and screaming against the gag. Tonya stared with a glazed look on her face as Sally screamed. "We need something to move the little cunt in. If we stand her up, her guts will come out before we get her out there." Judy nodded and went back outside to the shed and returned with a wheelbarrow. "Great thinking." They lifted Sally and wheeled her out the door.

There were several steps, and Judy asked, "Do you know your way to the spot in the dark?"

"I have been out there many times. Follow me." The two girls moved as the Eagle watched from a distance. When they were several acres away from the house, the lights lit the area up, and Judy recognized it as the light glistened off the water of the lake.

"This is the burial field?"

"It is. When Hugh's victims are dead, whatever is left goes into the water. Gives new meaning to 'swimming with the fishes,' huh? Do you have your cellphone on you?" Judy pulled it from her bag, and Lori took it and aimed the light at a group of bushes. "Follow me." Lori walked off, and Judy followed. After, a few paces Lori moved the bushes to reveal a horrific scene. There were five mounds; three were covered in cement, and bodies were in the pose that Lori had described earlier. Two other graves had been destroyed, and the remains were scattered about. "This was a kill that Hugh did last weekend. These poor kids were all murdered and then nature got to all of them. Hugh had a group of guys out here clearing away remains and throwing them into the lake, and then the cops showed up."

"The cops showed up? Why?"

"You killed Andrew. The staff called the cops without telling Hugh, and people had to clear out fast to keep the slaves undercover. So, the animals have been picking over the carcasses. When you look out into the darkness, you can see the night shine in the animals' eyes."

Judy looked around and saw several pairs of eyes staring at her and asked, "Are we safe?"

"Sure. They'll smell Sally in a second as soon as her innards spill, so get ready to get the fuck out of here. One of those pairs probably belongs to a local mountain lion. It will wait patiently, but if we move too slowly, we will make for its meal, and I don't want to have endured all I have just to be eaten alive." Lori tipped the wheelbarrow over, and Sally fell onto her face, and the smell made Judy vomit. Sally was pleading through her gag, and Lori ripped off the tape and said, "Let you live? No!" Judy was still hunched over when Lori told her, "You better start walking briskly. Don't run back to the house. Things are going to get violent." As the two girls walked back, they could hear Sally's screams and the fighting and howling of the large cat and coyotes.

"Why are the coyotes howling and making such noise?" Judy asked.

"They must wait their turn to get at Sally. The cat eats first, and the dogs get the scraps."

When they got back to the house, Lori ripped the tape off Mary's mouth, and she cried out, "Where's my daughter?"

Lori just smiled and said, "Listen." While the shrieks of agony were dying down, Mary could make out Sally's fading voice. "She's dead or near dead. Eaten alive, now, Ms. Owen, you and Ms. Hart need to have a come to Jesus moment before we send you on your way."

"Oh my God! You're a monster."

"I'm a monster? You do have a warped sense of reality. I'm the victim; Judy is a victim. You and those who work with and for you are the monsters. Now, tell us all about the auctions you have had and will be having. How many people have fallen victim to you and your ring?"

Mary went silent, and Judy leaned down to her with her cellphone in her hand and showed her the video of Sally being attacked. "This is your fate. The longer you talk and the more information you give, the longer you will live." Mary began to meticulously detail the entire slavery operation. The names and ages of victims, where the records were kept on ALL transactions, and lists of those who had bought from her since she started the operation after her husband's death.

The Eagle was in Masters' security center in the main house where he was able to monitor all aspects of the property as well as rooms in the house and outbuildings. Chris had notified him that Sara had arrived with the others and that she was treating the girl. He also sedated Hugh Masters and was awaiting orders. "Come up to the house. Enter via the main entrance of the circular drive. You are never going to believe what these girls have uncovered."

Sara and Karen were attending to Gloria, who had not made a sound as they worked to stitch up several open wounds on her back, buttocks, and legs. Karen wiped some salve away from Gloria's sides, "The kid's kidneys have been struck." Sara nodded, and Karen rolled Gloria on her side to look at the white bedsheet covered in bloody urine. "At minimum, she has kidney damage. She may be in kidney failure."

Sara set an IV and started pumping fluids into Gloria. "All we can do is try and flush her system and watch her urine output until the Eagle gives us the all clear."

Jade and Jessica were sitting on a bench together looking at all of the sleeping people. Jessica shook her head. "It never ceases to amaze me."

"What?"

"The average American thinks that human slavery happens in other countries. They don't understand that it is in every neighborhood and income class in this country."

Jade nodded. "Think how lucky you were never to have been caught up in this."

"You're right. I went through a lot of shit, but I would rather have died than ended up like these poor souls."

When Sara and Karen finished, Karen said, "I was in a situation like this when I was adopted by Simon Barstow. I remember when he came to my foster home. My foster parents were looking to make money off the kids they were caring for. They took money from Simon and allowed him to rape me and three other children. I was only three and didn't understand what was happening. Then he got me, and I lived in hell for nearly seven years. I do understand the desperation that these people feel, the hopelessness, just waiting for it to be over."

"The sexual abuse?" Jessica asked.

"No…life. Barstow and his men liked to choke me while having sex with me. They would put a rope around my neck and tie it off on the bed I slept on. When they would penetrate me, the rope would tighten around my throat, and the harder they pumped, the tighter the rope got until I passed out. I remember one night, not long before the Eagle saved me, I had been choked out several times, and I saw a bright white light. It was warm and inviting, and I started to move toward it but suddenly it vanished. Barstow was standing over me, resuscitating me. I was so angry. I had died, but he brought me back into the nightmare. From that night on, I hoped for that warm light, then I was saved."

"So, you had an NDE?" Jessica asked.

"Indeed. I had more than one, but that one was the most vivid." Karen paused. "How about you guys? Have you ever had an NDE?"

Jade and Sara both shook their heads, but Jessica nodded. "I have had the same experience you described, and I remember the anger in coming back. I can tell you that the last thing in this world that I fear is death." She looked around the room and then down at Gloria's frail beaten body. "Let me rephrase that. I don't fear death. I do fear how it will come. I don't want to be tortured to death." All heads nodded but nothing more was said.

"When are you going to stop this?" Chris asked the Eagle.

"I don't know that I'm going to. These are evil people, Chris, and who better to kill them than their victims. Lori Fleming has been through hell. The only way I will intervene is if someone tries to hurt these girls, or if Lori is not allowed to take out Masters."

"This is some pretty sadistic stuff."

"No more than is deserved. We have all the information we need to get Jim and Sam involved as well as our offices."

"What? You don't want to kill all of the buyers?"

"There are too many of them. I know where they are, and I might want to 'talk to' a few of them, but the justice system will deal with the bulk of them." Chris was watching as Judy and Lori beat Mary with two twenty-pound sledgehammers. Her cries and pleading fell on deaf ears, and as Mary lay bleeding, all of the bones in her arms and legs broken, the girls turned their attention to Tonya. Chris looked away several times. "What's wrong?"

"I'm used to you dealing justice. I'm not used to seeing children doing it."

"They earned it, Chris. It's quite prophetic that those who prey on the weak become their victims."

"As you always say, turnabout is fair play. Aren't you worried about the long-term trauma that these girls are going to deal with after this is over?"

"Nope. This is very therapeutic. It's the best medicine in my opinion, though most would disagree."

"They're still breathing."

Lori nodded, saying, "Yeah, but they won't hurt anyone again."

"So, what do you want to do with them? Take them out to the burial ground?"

Lori shook her head. "No. There is another method of execution we can use."

"There is more that Masters did to his victims?"

"Yes, but that's not what I'm thinking of for these two. Hugh has had his gardeners working on brush and tree abatement. I have heard the chainsaws as well as the wood chippers."

"Do you know where the equipment is?"

"We'll have to look for it, but based on what I was hearing, it isn't far from the house." The two checked drawers and cabinets looking for flashlights. Judy went into the kitchen while Lori looked in the dining room. Judy came back with two Maglites in hand, and they left the house in search of the wood chippers.

Chris and the Eagle left the office and entered the dining room where Mary and Tonya were moaning on the floor. Mary looked up at the men in body armor and masks and said, "You're with law enforcement. You're here to save us?"

The Eagle shook his head. "No, Ms. Owen, we're here to see that justice is served."

"I don't understand. If justice is to be served, then arrest us and get us medical attention before those two animals come back. They murdered my daughter, and they are going to murder us. How is that justice?"

"Ms. Owen, you and Ms. Hart profited off the enslavement and suffering of others. Mr. Masters, well, he's just a sick sadistic animal that needs to be put down. Prison is too good for you, and while Ms. Bench didn't suffer nearly as much at your hand as Ms. Fleming did, she is helping Lori get some much-needed revenge, and I support that."

Tonya lifted her head and asked in a labored voice, "Who the fuck are you?"

"Ironically," he paused while laughing, "I'm the Iron Eagle. The man next to me helps out from time to time. To be honest, when we were first coming out here tonight, I thought I and my friend were going to be administering your punishment, but in an ironic turn of events, we are merely voyeurs, watching justice unfold. I must admit, it is a strange spot for us, but we have been following you all evening and have recorded your confessions." The Eagle saw the flashlights coming back toward the house and said, "Well, we must go back to our viewing area. Since I doubt the girls would think to send you two into death properly, I will. May God NOT have mercy on your souls." Chris and the Eagle walked away as Lori and Judy came back inside.

Mary and Tonya were trying to scream, but their ribs were broken, and both were starting to spit up blood. Mary got out, "The Iron Eagle."

Lori and Judy looked at each other, and Lori asked, "What about him?"

"He's here."

Judy looked around as did Lori, and the two shrugged. "We found two wood chippers that Hugh's gardeners are using on the property, so how about we grind this out, so Lori can take care of Mr. Masters? We've been neglecting him, and he is just hanging around the stable." Lori grabbed one of Mary's arms, and Judy took the other, and the two drug her out of the house and down a small concrete path and then through dirt and debris and dropped her body near a chipper and went back to get Tonya. When both women were lying next to each other, Judy turned the unit on. The girls lifted Mary up to the feeder and put her legs in. Judy looked at Lori and said, "On three." Lori nodded, and the girls counted in unison then pushed Mary's feet into the chipper, which drew her whole body in so fast that she never made a sound. They did the same with Tonya.

After the chipper was clear, they turned it off, and Lori looked at Judy and said, "Take me to Hugh."

CHAPTER TWENTY

"...grab the girls and hold them.
You'll only have one shot at
keeping them alive."

Hugh Masters was starting to come to when Judy walked into his line of sight. "You fucking cunt! Release me now!"

"All in good time, Mr. Masters, all in good time. There is someone who wants to... deal with you."

Hugh looked around but saw no one. "What's your game, bitch?"

Lori answered from behind him, "Her game? Oh, Hugh. This is now my game."

"Lori? Jesus, Lori."

"I am Lori, not Jesus. You don't believe in that guy anyway. You told me that months ago."

"Lori, come to your master. I love you and care for you. Come to me, and I will make it okay." Lori held the bloody bullwhip in her hand that Hugh had used on Gloria earlier and on her and so many others in his long career as a slave breaker. She sent the first several strikes ripping through Hugh's body, and he shuddered against them, and his eyes rolled up in his head. "Yellow," he said strongly.

"Yes, indeed, you are yellow. I mean, that's your favorite color… the color of cowards." She struck him several more times and, as she did, she recited the things he would say as he worked to break a slave. "You're mine, you asshole. You're not worth the dirt you're standing on. I'm doing this for your own good." Judy stood in stunned silence as Lori worked, and Hugh screamed with each strike of the whip. "You're not human. You deserve nothing. You are the servant, and I'm the master. Your mind is not your own; it belongs to me. You only live because I allow it, and you will serve me and any master who purchases you with love, faith, and admiration." Blood was running down Hugh's back and legs and pooling in the dirt at his feet. His head hung down, and his arms were limp when Lori walked up to him and asked, "Are you my slave, or do I continue?"

Hugh heaved a deep breath as tears ran down his face. "I'm yours. Do with me as you please."

"What pleases me is to beat you more, so you have twenty lashes coming. You will count them out loudly and thank me. Am I clear?"

"Yes, mistress." Lori walked back to her spot and landed the first of twenty on Hugh's back. "One, mistress. Thank you." She continued until Hugh's voice was just a whisper and his legs went out from under him.

Chris followed the Eagle into the stable, and the two men stayed out of sight as Lori finished with Hugh. "So, when are you going to make your presence known?" Chris whispered.

"Soon. Very, very soon."

"Why wait?"

"Just watch, and you will see." The Eagle had his tranquilizer gun in his vest. He also had a long piece of barbed wire in his right hand.

Chris looked on as the two girls walked around Hugh's seemingly unconscious body. The Eagle was watching closely and said, "When I move in, you grab the girls and hold them. You only have one shot at keeping them alive."

Sara, Karen, and the rest had been watching and listening to Lori as she tortured Hugh. Karen had also been watching Judy off to the side with a look of shock on her face. Jade leaned in to Sara and asked, "Are you sure the Eagle's here?"

"He's here, as is Chris."

"Then why are they letting this go on?"

"I don't know."

Jade was looking closely at Hugh's body and his breathing and whispered to Sara, "Masters is playing possum."

"What?"

"He's pretending to be dead. Look at his breathing. He's hurt, but he's just waiting for the opportunity to strike at those girls."

The stall doors were open in front of Hugh, and there were two bales of hay oddly near the stall doors. Judy was looking at Hugh's face; his eyes were wide open but not blinking. "Jesus! I think you killed him."

Lori felt Hugh's neck for a pulse then pulled back. "He's alive." Lori looked above Hugh's head where several bales of hay were hanging from a rope over the stall entrance. She followed the rope with her eyes and saw it was tied off some twenty feet away. Judy got the step ladder and climbed up it while Lori was following the rope. Lori turned just in time to see Judy releasing Hugh's hands from the clip. "NO!" was all Judy heard as Hugh swung his arms around catching her in the chest and throwing her across the barn.

Lori stepped back, and Hugh lunged forward into the stall and came back with a gun between the palms of his tied hands. "You little cunt." He was trying to get his fingers in the trigger when he saw Lori and Judy disappear behind a wall of black. He got his fingers into the trigger but found himself firing the weapon into midair as his entire body was slammed to the dirt floor, knocking the wind out of him and disarming him. The Eagle had Hugh's penis and testicles in his glove-covered hand, squeezing and twisting at the same time. "Oh, dear God! What the fuck is happening?"

"Sara!" The Eagle had pulled Hugh's penis and scrotum out, and Sara appeared with a scalpel and one of the Eagle's battery-operated branding guns. She flicked her wrist and blood shot all over the floor, then she hit the hole with the gun to cauterize the wound then stepped back as the Eagle threw Masters into a wooden wall, knocking him unconscious.

Lori and Judy were screaming as Chris held each in an arm, and the Eagle stepped forward, looked into Lori's eyes, and asked, "Do you remember me?"

"Yes, but you said you weren't here to hurt me."

"I'm still not. I have been watching what the two of you have been doing to your victims."

Judy yelled out, "THEY DESERVED IT!"

"No argument there," the Eagle said in a calm voice. "However, you two aren't trained killers and had we not been here you would be about to endure unbelievable torture at this animal's hands…and, of course, death." Sara stepped out of the shadows as did Karen, Jade, and Jessica. When Judy saw Karen, she went into hysterics. The Eagle looked at Karen and asked, "What the hell?"

Sara handed Karen a syringe, and as she injected Judy she said, "Um…obviously a very shocked patient of mine."

Lori said nothing. She stood in her sundress looking at Hugh on the ground, and the Eagle turned to her. "You want to send him to hell?" Lori nodded. "What means would you like to use?"

Lori had a thoughtful look on her face. "The most painful means I can."

"Well, the wood chipper, while effective, is fast; burial and death by wild animals is cruel and painful but still relatively fast. Mr. Masters has other methods of torture, correct?" She nodded. "Have you been through all of them?" She nodded again. "Okay, so which one was the single most agonizing?"

"The sensory deprivation tank."

"I have used those myself, and I also have a special cocktail of drugs that I administer to make the experience that much more horrific for my victim. Do you know where the tanks are?"

"In the basement where the wine cellar is."

"Does he use cold water?"

"Yes. Ninety-three degrees. Warm enough to keep the victim alive, yet cool enough to drop the core body temperature down to torture."

"Interesting." The Eagle picked up Hugh's body and said, "Lead the way."

Mark Bench was pacing his living room. It was ten after eleven, and he had sent Judy seven text messages, none of which had been responded to. He pulled up an old tracking application that he had on both of the girls' phones when they were younger, so he could see where they were at all times. Tabitha's phone showed up on the application, but Judy's didn't. He remembered that he had not put the app on her new phone, so he had no way to track her. He called Maggie's home, but she was doing a concert downtown. He spoke to her mother but was told that they had not seen Judy today. He called Mary's cellphone, but it was going to voicemail, and in desperation he had even called Sally's. He thought about going to Masters' home but knew if he showed up and embarrassed Judy she would never forgive him. He poured himself a glass of wine and sat down in his easy chair and pulled up the news on his tablet and tried to stay calm.

Hugh awoke in total darkness with his teeth chattering. He was unable to move, and he could feel a slight burn on his right arm. The Eagle had set an IV, and Lori and the Eagle were sitting in a small control room where Hugh had several cameras and microphones set up. The cameras were infrared, and Lori watched as Hugh blinked several times and called out. "Hello? Can anyone hear me?"

"I can hear you." Lori's voice sent Hugh once again into hysterics, and the Eagle laughed as Lori continued speaking to him. "How do you like your tank, Hugh? Fun, isn't it?"

"You listen to me, bitch. I don't know what you're trying to pull, but when Mary and Tonya learn what you're doing they will get me out of here, and then I will get to you."

"Not going to happen!" The Eagle pressed a button next to the IV tube, sending a light greenish blue liquid into the IV. Karen was in the room but remained silent.

"Where the hell are Mary and Tonya?"

"Well, let's just say they got a little 'chippy' with me and Judy, so we dealt with them." Hugh began to scream, and Lori looked at the Eagle and asked, "What's happening?"

"Mr. Masters is receiving his first dose of a powerful medication. As you speak to him, you can suggest all kinds of terrible and horrible things, and, in his mind, he will feel like they are happening to him."

Lori smiled. "Seriously?"

"Oh yes. Feel free to send him down any road you like. The young woman sitting in the chair behind you is a psychiatrist. She will watch over the session and stop you if you push Mr. Masters too far."

"What's too far?"

Karen spoke up, "There is a chance that Mr. Masters could suffer a psychotic break."

"What's that?"

"A break from reality, a loss of awareness of the things that are real around him."

"And why is that bad?"

"If you want him to suffer, he needs to be aware of his surroundings and the reality of his sins. If he breaks with reality, he won't understand it, and you won't get the satisfaction you need."

"You sound like you know what you're talking about."

"Yes, Ms. Fleming, I do. I really do."

Jim and Cindy had Sam over to their house for dinner. The three had finished their meal and were sitting on the deck enjoying a drink when Jim's phone buzzed. He read the text message and took a sip of his scotch and said, "We're needed."

Sam nodded and blew smoke from her lungs as she tapped her cigarette on the ashtray and asked, "Official?"

"Everything is official."

"Where?"

"Hidden Hills."

"We were there last night."

"Yep. There have been some new developments."

Sam took another hit off her cigarette then a drink of her scotch. "I see…so, someone has been busy?"

Jim nodded, flicking his cigarette off the deck, which brought a scolding from Cindy. He apologized, and as he stood Cindy asked, "Is there anything I can do?"

Sam stood as well, and she looked into Cindy's clear eyes and said, "I'm going to give you a tad bit of advice. Don't step into the fray when these calls come in. Police work is hard, Cindy, and it puts demands on everyone in the family. There are some things that are better left alone and unknown when it comes to our work."

Cindy shook her head. "Jim and I have no secrets." Sam looked at them and burst out in laughter. "What's so funny? Jimmy, what's Sam laughing about?"

"Nothing. She'll ride with me. She had a few extra drinks. She will stay with us tonight in the guest room."

He told Sam to follow him, and Cindy asked, "When will you be home?"

"That, my dear, is the million-dollar question. I will call when I know more."

The two left, and Cindy started to clean up the glasses and dishes. "That is the million-dollar question. What the fuck does that mean and just what secret is Jim keeping from me?"

CHAPTER TWENTY-ONE

"Is that the voice?"

Sara was back with Jade and Jessica. "Jim and Sam are on their way." Jade nodded, and Jessica asked, "What the fuck are we going to do with these people?"

"I have no idea, Jess. The Eagle and Karen are dealing with Masters. Judy is off sulking, and we have a shitload of people who need to be moved."

Jim walked into the barn followed by Sam. "Well, isn't this a shit show?" Jessica and Jade nodded, and Jim looked at Gloria who was on an IV and a catheter, "Shouldn't she be in a hospital?"

"We're working on it, Jim. We have women and children here as well as several young men who were to be sold as slaves, and girls ranging in age from ten to twenty-five for domestic work and sex."

"This isn't fuckin' rocket science. All the kids under eighteen go to child protective services, so we should make a call to Anita Bandon, and the older ones should be taken to a shelter until we can debrief them."

The Eagle walked in on the group with Lori in tow. Sara looked on and asked, "So?"

"Mr. Masters is having a pretty wild ride. We will remove him soon and end him. What are we talking about?"

"What the fuck you want to do with these people," Jim said curtly.

"Get Anita Bandon out here for the kids. We don't need to debrief any of them. We need to do a records search and see how many of these people might have missing persons reports, so we can reunite them with family."

Sam nodded, and Jim pulled a cigarette out of his top left pocket, lit it, and said, "Who's the girl behind you?"

"Lori Fleming. She is a victim of Hugh Masters."

"So, out of all of these people, the Eagle isn't taking anyone to the lair?"

"No. Judy Bench did a good job of killing three of these animals, and Lori took out a fourth, then Judy and Lori took out Mary and Sally Owen as well as Tonya Hart."

Karen walked over to where Judy was sitting. "So, this is what you have been doing? Killing wrongdoers?"

"It's all a blur right now, Karen. I never intended for things to go like this. I knew that Mary and Sally were into some bad stuff, but the stuff they were recruiting me for in the porn industry was only the tip of the iceberg. I had no idea the depths of depravity. I also didn't realize just how close I was to ending up like all of these people. Lori went through hell and was destined for death at the hands of Masters."

"So, you decided to take the law into your own hands?"

"I did what was necessary to survive. I had no idea I was going to walk into a nightmare."

Lori spoke up. "I don't know who all of you people are, and to be honest I don't want to know. What I do want is to finish off Hugh and get the hell out of this place." The Eagle nodded and told Chris to retrieve Pierce and Clive's bodies from the house and to take them to the wood chipper.

Sam asked, "And just what are we going to do about all of these people? Jim is right. Anita can take the kids into child protective services; the Eagle can run DNA and finger prints to see how many of these people are reported missing, and we can do an official reuniting. However, we need to come up with one hell of a story as to how this whole situation was uncovered. We have two teenagers that have killed numerous people and would most likely be tried as adults." Judy went to speak but Sam cut her off. "Your justification for the killings doesn't matter. You might be able to plead self-defense for one maybe two killings but not for the bloodbath here. We have one hell of a problem. I don't want to see you two girls go to prison, and I'm not condoning your actions, but I'm not condemning them either. If it were me, I would most likely have done the same thing. But what's done is done." Sam turned to the Eagle. "So, how do you want to handle this? Lay it off on you?"

The Eagle was standing near Gloria, who's breathing was still labored. "Yes. Lori can help me finish off Masters. She has suffered for that right. We have all of the players in this suburban trafficking ring, so I will leave the evidence and the confessions behind, edited, of course, so that Judy and Lori aren't in them. I will make the 911 call, and we are all going to have one long night into morning."

"What about these two?" Sam pointed to Judy and Lori."

"Judy will go home to her father after spending some time with me at the lair as will Lori."

Sara looked on and asked, "Wipe?" The Eagle nodded.

Karen looked around at the carnage and then Judy. "I will take you home." Judy looked at Lori with a sad look on her face, and Karen saw Lori nod. "What?" Judy was silent.

Lori said, "Judy just learned her father had sex with me when I was in one of Mary's brothels a few years ago."

"He introduced himself to you?"

"No. I overheard his name being mentioned several times. The sex was always in the dark, and he never hurt me."

"Rape is a violent act."

"He was never violent."

"Did you see his face?"

"Not well, but I would know his voice in a heartbeat. It was very distinct."

Karen looked at Judy. "Where's your cellphone?"

"In my bag over there."

"I want you to come with me. Lori, you and the Eagle follow. We're going to call Judy's father."

Mark Bench was half asleep when the phone rang. He wiped his eyes and saw that it was ten after one. Judy had him on speaker phone with Karen and Lori next to her. "Daddy, it's me."

"Judy? Judy, honey, where the hell are you?"

"I'm still at Hugh Masters' house."

"What the hell are you still doing there at this hour?"

"I got caught up in a situation. The police are here, and I have been being interviewed."

"Caught up in what?"

"It's hard to explain, and I'm not allowed to say much right now. The police have just started an investigation, but I wanted to call you and let you know that I am safe and that I should be home by three."

"I'm coming to get you."

"No, Dad. You won't even be able to get near here. The whole place is sealed off. I promise I will tell you everything that I am allowed to when I get home."

"Are you in trouble?"

Judy looked at Karen, who shook her head. "No, Dad, nothing like that. There is a lot of stuff that has been going on, and Mr. Masters as well as others were involved."

"Are Mary and Sally with you?"

"They are…here…but not with me."

"Is everyone alright out there?"

"I will explain more when I get home."

"Are you okay to drive?"

"Um… the FBI is on the way out here, and Doctor Karen Mantel's husband is a Special Agent. She's coming out here to assist and is going to drive me home."

"The FBI? What the hell is going on?"

"That's all I can talk about right now, Dad. I just wanted to call you to let you know I am fine and that I will explain more when I get home." Mark was breathing heavily on the line, and Judy said, "I know, Dad. I know. I'm okay. It will all be okay. I love you." Judy hung up the line and looked at Lori, "Is that the voice?"

Lori shook her head. "No. That's not the man who had sex with me. The man had a thick accent. European, I think. I can tell you that is not the man I had sex with."

Judy collapsed in tears, and the Eagle entered the area and called for Lori. "It's time to finish with Mr. Masters."

She nodded and walked over to Judy and gave her a hug and said, "I'm sorry I scared you, but I am really happy that he was not my attacker." Judy nodded with her head in her hands as Lori left with the Eagle.

Hugh Masters was screaming in the tank when the two got back to the room. Lori smiled as the Eagle opened the chamber, revealing Hugh's wet, nude body. The Eagle lifted him out of the water and threw him over his shoulder. "Where did he do his worst to you?"

"The upstairs bedroom." The Eagle had a gym bag on the floor in the security room and asked Lori to grab it and to lead him to the room. The two walked up the stairs and as they did the moaning and groaning of the few people left ill in the house met both of their ears.

"I'm going to have to get the recipe for that cocktail from Ms. Bench," the Eagle said as they entered Lori's holding room. He threw Hugh on the bed, but he bounced off and hit the floor. The Eagle lifted him up and placed him on the bed again then asked Lori to show him where he kept his instruments of torture. She walked the Eagle over to a bureau on a far wall, opened it, and all types of torture implements were laid out neatly in order. Several instruments caught the Eagle's attention: a set of thumbscrews, two pairs of steel pin-laced leg and arm restraints, and a ballpeen hammer and several chisels. "Pick the method of execution." Lori pointed to the hammer and chisels. "How were they used on you?" Lori opened her mouth wide to show the Eagle that all of her teeth had either been removed or had been broken. "He used these on your mouth?" She nodded. "Now I understand why you don't open your mouth when you smile."

"I look like a Halloween pumpkin."

The Eagle grabbed the tools and then Hugh by the hair and drug him from the bed to the floor on his face. "This will not do. We need a more appropriate room, lighting, and a chair." Lori walked into the hallway and pointed to a door at the far end. "Lead the way." Lori walked very hesitantly to the door but would not open it. The Eagle had Hugh by the hair and threw him into the wall while opening the door. Even he wasn't prepared for what was on the other side.

Judy walked Jim and Sam over to the wood chipper and the bodies. Sam looked at Pierce and Clive then Jim and said, "I'm not getting rid of evidence."

Jim had a cigarette hanging out of his mouth but grabbed a pair of nearby work gloves and turned the machine on. He fed Pierce's body into the chipper, then Clive's. When it was done, he shut off the unit, looked at Sam, and said, "There. Happy? One fuckin' guy to go, now let's call Anita and give her a heads up."

Sam shook her head. "Jesus, Jim! What have you become? How will we ever know a cause of death?"

Jim yelled out, "Jade, Jessica, I need you." They came from around the building to where Jim was standing and pointing at the pile of human fragments on the ground.

"Sam wants a cause of death for Pierce Tallon and Clive Baxter. Can you give us one?"

Jade and Jessica looked around the chute of the chipper and at the bone and flesh fragments on the ground, then Jessica spoke up, "The guys stood too close to the wood chipper, got caught in the blades, most likely by loose-fitting clothing. Accidental death." Jim started laughing as did Jade.

Sam stood stoic. "You guys think this is funny?"

Jade shook her head. "No. I think it's monstrous."

"So, you agree what Jim just did to these bodies was monstrous?"

"Hardly. Jim just saved us from having to put those pieces of shit on our table and waste our time on a cause of death. What is monstrous is what's in that barn. What's monstrous is bloody, beaten children who are barely alive. Humans treating humans as chattel. What is monstrous is you feeling that Jim's actions in some way diminish the acts of these animals. You need to grow the fuck up and fast, Sam. Maria is dead. We did the autopsy. Your priorities and compassion have been misplaced since Maria's suicide."

"Suicide?"

"That's what I would have really put down as the cause of death, Sam, because that is what it was. Your girlfriend made all the wrong moves, and she is dead. You are making all the wrong moves, and if you don't get your shit together you, too, will be dead."

Sam stood with her mouth open as Jade and Jessica walked away. "What the fuck?"

Jim lit a cigarette and after snapping his Zippo shut said, "That was the long way of Jade telling you to grow the fuck up!"

CHAPTER TWENTY-TWO

"The first 911 call went out
at just before five a.m."

The Eagle surveyed the large room as Lori stood just outside the entrance. She dropped the Eagle's gym bag as he looked around. There were several modern racks, each covered with flesh and blood. There was an old electric chair in the corner with a bucket of water and several sponges. The execution unit was mounted on the wall nearby. He walked over and rolled three switches, and the power came on to each of them. When he pulled the lever, the chair began to make a sparking noise. After turning it off, the Eagle placed Hugh in it, strapping him in.

Hugh started to mumble. "This isn't happening; this isn't happening."

"Oh, it's happening, Mr. Masters." Lori still had not entered the room, and the Eagle looked at her and asked, "How many times have you been in here?"

"Only once."

"And?"

"And you don't see me entering, do you?"

"You will not be harmed in here."

"I already have been. I can't come in there."

"This is the end of the line for Mr. Masters."

"If it is all the same, I have done enough to him. I will leave the end to you."

"Do you want to leave?"

"No. I just don't want to come into that room, sir. That room has ghosts in it, hundreds of ghosts. I heard screams of agony from this room for nearly a year."

"What did he do to you in here."

"Sterilized me after performing a makeshift abortion. He didn't want children out of his slaves. Those going to market never entered this room. Many slaves are used for procreation. That's why they are all white males and females. That's what Mary and Tonya's customers in the suburbs want for surrogates…or worse. But when Hugh was keeping a prisoner, everyone was sterilized, and his methods were barbaric."

"I can see that. If you're comfortable being at the edge of the room, that's fine. Let's appease the ghosts by making Mr. Masters suffer by joining them." The Eagle grabbed his gym bag and pulled out several pairs of pliers as well as barbed wire. He wasted no time restraining Hugh's head to the chair with the wire and caging his mouth, exposing Hugh's teeth and gums. He wired Hugh's eyes open, so he couldn't blink, and he began extracting teeth one at a time. The Eagle removed the bulk of Hugh's teeth with pliers then started knocking out his wisdom teeth with a hammer and chisel. Lori watched from the doorway as the Eagle worked. He put drops in Hugh's eyes every few seconds as he worked, and Lori watched as Hugh's body jolted with each extraction and strike of the hammer against the chisel. When the Eagle had finished, he filled the bucket with water and wet one of the sponges and put the electrode on Hugh's skull and made sure all of the contacts were in place. "Hugh Masters, you are guilty of cruelty of the highest measure. While I can only administer as much pain as is possible in this life, if there is an afterlife and a God, may God NOT have mercy on your soul." With that the Eagle pulled the lever. Hugh's eyes popped open wide, and his body jolted against the wooden chair. The jolts of electricity were violent, and the Eagle would bring Hugh to the edge of death then shut off the power and allow him to revive. He did this three times before turning on the juice and walking Lori out of the room.

"Are you going to leave the power on?"

"Just until we get the last of the stuff we need out of here. Do you have anything that you need from up here?" Lori shook her head. The smell of Hugh's burning flesh and the smoke from his body were beginning to fill the hall, and she was getting sick. The Eagle took her down the stairs to the back door and called for Jim, who was standing near the shed. "Would you please take Ms. Fleming back to the barn and ask Chris to join me?"

Jim took Lori by the hand. As they walked, she said, "I'm confused as to just who the real monster is."

Jim laughed as they walked. "You just witnessed an Eagle killing?"

"Savageness that even Hugh didn't have."

"Oh, Hugh had it. You're just too close to things right now. You're starting to sympathize with your captor. Don't worry. It's normal and will go away quickly."

"I've watched a lot of people being brutalized. I, myself, was one of them. I just never thought I would see this day come."

Jim smiled and said, "We all have our day of reckoning, Lori. The day we pay for our sins."

"How will the Eagle's day be?"

Jim shrugged. "I hope he dies as peacefully as possible when his time comes. He makes the worst of the worst pay for their crimes."

"I just saw that, but at what cost to himself?"

"Oh, child, the Eagle is a trained killing machine. He doesn't feel pain and things the way we do. He is a cold, calculating killer, and he metes out justice based on the crimes and then compounds them tenfold."

"I suppose I'm feeling guilty about how Hugh died."

"Again, that will pass. What you are really feeling is displaced relief. The monster is gone. He can't hurt you or anyone else anymore. You are adapting to freedom and that will take time."

"Freedom? I don't think that such exists. We're all slaves to something."

"We are only slaves to ourselves. We have the freedom to do what we choose when we choose, but that's not how it worked in the world you just came out of, right?" She said no. "Give it time, kid. Give it time. It will all come into focus."

Hugh's legs, arms, and skull were burned beyond recognition. The Eagle had turned off the power and pulled his branding iron from the gym bag and pressed it into Hugh's chest. When the steel shaft was removed, the seal of the Iron Eagle was perfectly emblazoned. The Eagle pulled out two tablets as Chris entered the room.

"Jesus Christ! Did you burn the guy alive?"

"Electrocuted him."

Chris looked around at the blood and teeth on the floor around the body. "I see you removed a few teeth."

"Yes, well, look at Lori Fleming's smile when we are back with her. The girl was so afraid of this room that she couldn't enter."

Chris looked around. "I can hear echoes of torture based on the room's contents."

"The whole property screams with the blood of the innocent."

"Are you going to move Masters?"

"No. I'm leaving him on his throne of agony, and that's where we will all find him."

"So, calling cards?"

"Of course, but first we need to mix the evidence and confessions. Masters has a sophisticated security room with some high value video equipment."

"Well? What are we waiting for? Let's get this done. I would like to get a few hours' sleep."

"Not tonight, Chris. The Eagle will bring us out here." The two men worked on the mix until it was finished. They walked around the house leaving calling cards and checking on the few people who were still alive, sedating them to make sure they remained unconscious.

Chris stood at the back entrance to the house when all was done and said, "You only killed one person. He was the worst of them to me, but you allowed those two young women to extract justice. How does that sit with you?"

"It sits fine with me. We can wipe most of Lori's memory, but we can't remove the nightmare she lived or her physical scars. She is a strong-willed young woman. This monster couldn't break her. I don't think anyone can."

"Let's hope that theory never has to be tested."

The first 911 call went to the sheriff's department just before five a.m., and by five-thirty, the estate was crawling with deputies. Anita Bandon arrived with several case workers as Jade and Jessica worked near the chipper bagging evidence. Jim and Sam were in the barn when Anita came in, and she looked at the children and adults then at Jim and asked, "Who discovered this operation?"

"The Eagle."

Anita nodded. "We've heard rumors of an operation in the suburbs of Los Angeles, but no one was ever able to prove it."

"Oh, you and I know that's bullshit, Anita. There are as many pedophiles and rapists working in your department as any other. There are many who knew these things were happening, and I have a feeling when this all shakes out a good number of these kids are going to be in your foster care system."

Anita didn't say anything. She had her people attending to the children when John and Chris arrived. She looked at John and said, "So, the Eagle saves again?"

"I don't know. I just got here, but Jim called and told me it's an Eagle scene."

"How are you, Chris? I'm sorry to hear of the loss you and Karen suffered."

"Thank you. We are dealing with it. Seeing this savagery puts our own suffering into perspective, though."

Sam was barking orders to her people as Jim leaned against a bale of hay smoking a cigarette. Anita shook her head. "Doesn't that dumbass realize he could set this whole place ablaze?" Sam must have heard Anita because she walked over to Jim, took the cigarette out of his hand, and put it out. Jim walked off toward the house, and Anita began processing the children. John and Chris were getting ready to walk away when Anita asked, "Have you run these people through the missing and exploited databases?"

"It's being done as we speak."

"Any hits so far?"

"Five children and one man."

"What do you want me to do with them?"

"Take them to a shelter until we can get you the information to reunite them with their loved ones." Anita nodded, and John and Chris walked up to the house.

CHAPTER TWENTY-THREE

"Justice...."

It was ten after five when Karen pulled into Mark Bench's driveway with Judy and Lori in her car. Mark ran out of the house and grabbed Judy in his arms and held her and kissed her as Karen and Lori looked on. "Oh, thank God. I have never prayed so hard in my life."

"Me either, Dad."

He released Judy and grabbed Karen and hugged her. "Thank you for bringing Judy home."

"It's only for a few minutes, so she can get a change of clothes. She still needs to be debriefed. I was given permission to stop by before taking her downtown."

He kissed Judy's face, and she hugged him hard. Lori stood back almost out of sight, and Mark looked over at her and asked, "And who might you be?"

Lori stepped into the halo of the porch light, the yellow sundress and her pale bruised arms and legs came into view. Lori looked at the ground, and Karen said, "This is Lori Fleming. She's one of the victims of what is being called the Owen Trade."

"Owen Trade? I don't understand."

"You will before the day is out. Judy, go get some clothes."

Judy nodded and released Mark and asked, "Dad, Lori and I are almost the same size. Can I bring her with me to get some clean clothes? We could both use a shower as well."

"If it's okay with Karen." She nodded, and the two girls went into the house. Karen followed Mark in, and he offered her some coffee and tried to probe, but she could tell him nothing.

Judy and Lori entered her bedroom to find Tabitha sleeping in her bed. "Who's that?"

"My kid sister. She must have missed me and came in here and fell asleep."

"Does she sleep with you a lot?"

"Yeah." The two girls went into the bathroom, and Lori removed the sundress, and Judy started to cry as she looked at her wounds and scars. Lori started the shower, and Judy watched her wince in pain under the water. She was stiff and couldn't wash herself well, so Judy undressed and got in the shower with her and helped to clean her wounds and body. Lori didn't speak, neither did Judy. They helped each other bathe and when they were finished Judy dried off and then gently patted Lori's body dry. "Do you think you can wear a bra and panties?"

"Haven't been in clothing in nearly a year. I don't know." Judy looked Lori up and down. You're a thirty-six C?"

"Thirty-four D."

"Wow. Okay. I have a bra that will fit you." The two tried on bras and panties and started giggling like kids swapping them back and forth until they had undergarments that fit. Judy took Lori to her closet, and she picked out a loose-fitting dress and was about to try it on but stopped. Judy asked, "Are you okay?"

"Yeah. Can you help me cover some of my open wounds? I don't want to bleed on your dress." Judy got teary-eyed again, and Lori smiled and said, "It's okay. You saved me. If it weren't for you, I would most likely be being raped right now...or worse. Instead, I feel not only like a human being again but a girl." Judy took her into the bathroom, and she spent ten minutes putting bandages on Lori's body. When they were finished, they dressed, and Lori asked, "Do you have any makeup?"

"Am I a girl? Of course! Sit down at my makeup mirror." The two helped each other with makeup, and after about a half hour of showering and dressing the girls appeared in the kitchen, and Mark and Karen's jaws dropped.

"Oh my God! You two look gorgeous," Karen said. "Don't they look stunning, Mark?"

Mark was looking at the two girls, teary-eyed, "Yes, yes, they do. Do you live around here, Lori?"

"Um...no sir."

Karen chimed in, "Lori is an orphan."

Mark's face grew grave. "How did you end up meeting Judy?"

"That's a story for another time, Dad. We really need to go, don't we Karen?" She nodded and finished her coffee while Judy grabbed two bottles of water for herself and Lori. She kissed her father on the lips and said, "I will call you when I am released." Karen and Lori both saw the kiss but neither commented. Karen excused herself and took Lori with her to give Mark and Judy some privacy.

As Karen sat down, Lori looked at her and said, "They're father and daughter?"

"Yes."

"Related by blood or stepfather?"

"Blood."

Karen didn't say anything more, but Lori spoke up, "I hate to break it to you, but there is more going on between those two than just being father and daughter." Karen remained silent. "I know you're Judy's shrink. I heard you two talking in the barn. Now, I have seen her father and heard him on the phone, and I can say without a doubt that he never had sex with me. That being said, I think those two have had sex. I don't know if it was consensual, based on their behavior I think it was. I don't know if it was alcohol and drug induced, but those two are way closer than a father and daughter should be." Karen remained silent as Judy walked out of the house holding Mark's hand. They embraced once more then Judy got into the car. Karen started for the lair, and as they entered the 405 Freeway Lori looked back at Judy and asked, "So, how long have you been sleeping with your father?"

It was noon when the scene was cleared, and the slaves and guests had been interviewed and either released or sent to shelters. In all, John and Chris found all but two of the families of the enslaved, and reunions were being set up for those to be released back after making sure they had not been sold to Mary Owen. Anita had two teens that were unaccounted for. At least, no one was missing them, and the story that they all got from the girls was that they were on the streets and had no family. Anita told John she would deal with them and get them into foster care.

Jade and Jessica had their CSI teams putting bags of remains from the chipper into the van along with the body of Hugh Masters. The black body bag was surrounded by smaller black bags, and Jessica looked at John and said, "Masters died from electrocution?" John nodded. "Based on his burns, I bet it hurt." John nodded again, and Jessica smiled. "Well, the rest of the people we found on that property are going to be like putting a puzzle together. The burial area had a few intact corpses, but a lot of them are in the same condition of the serial killer that preyed on the U.S. Marshals a few months back…and word is that many bodies and parts are in the lake. It's going to be hell identifying them."

"I know you two will do your best." Jade nodded, and the two got in the van and left. The CSI teams all but cleared the scene outside, and a half dozen were working in Masters' mansion. Jim and Sam were leaning on their car smoking cigarettes and talking when John and Chris walked up.

Jim looked at Sam and asked, "So, what do you think?"

She looked at John and said, "I think the Eagle saved a shitload of lives last night and not just the ones here."

Chris nodded. "Indeed. We already have search and arrest warrants for fifty people and entities. This is going to be one of the largest human trafficking busts in recent history."

"John," Sam asked, "why did you let those two girls do so much of the killing?"

"Karma. Sometimes, you let the victims destroy the monsters. In this case, I had two living victims who had seen and survived nightmares, and I allowed them to turn on their abusers."

"And all of this under the watchful eye of the Eagle?"

"Yes. I would never have allowed them to be hurt more than they had been. The Fleming girl reminded me a lot of Jessica when I saved her, and Jim took her under his wing, and she grew to an intelligent and now well-educated woman."

"But Fleming doesn't have that option here. She's a fifteen-year-old girl who is going to be cast into the foster care system, and you and I know she won't last."

"She and the Bench girl are at the lair. I'm going to give her my amnesia medication, which will erase some of the trauma."

"That's not going to wipe the slate clean, and you know it. Fleming and Bench have a taste for blood, and you're supporting them in getting away with murder."

"Not murder, justified revenge."

"What's the difference?"

"Justice…without serving twenty-five to life."

Sara was sipping a cup of coffee on the deck of the lair when Karen walked in with Judy and Lori. Judy was crying, and Lori was stone faced. Karen was sheet white, and Sara invited them for a cup of coffee, which all accepted. Sara poured each a cup and asked, "Have you been having a session in your car, Karen?"

Judy looked at Karen, who looked at Lori and then said, "Something like that. Do you have any pregnancy tests?"

"Yes. Who needs it?"

"I would rather not say."

"Well, it's not for you, so it has to be for either Judy or Lori."

"Do you have two tests?" Sara nodded and left the deck, and Karen looked at Judy and said, "You drugged your father and raped him?"

Lori started laughing, and Karen asked, "What's so funny?"

"I don't know, either this Electra complex you've been talking about or that Judy could get her father so drunk and drugged that he would fuck her. I mean, come on. You can't write this shit."

"Incest is nothing to laugh about."

"I'm not laughing at the incest aspect. I'm just trying to figure out how Judy's father didn't know he was fucking his own kid."

"As I explained in the car, my father thought I was my mother. He was so out of it and so lonely he thought I was my dead mother. His bedroom is practically a shrine to her. Her photos are on every surface. I bear a striking resemblance to her, so I gave him so much Ecstasy and wine that he had no idea who I was. Hell, he thought that Mary had been over and that he had dreamed the whole thing. I even got Mary to lie to me and say she was with my father when I was with him."

Karen asked, "So your father has no idea what you two did?"

"Not a clue."

Sara reappeared with the tests and sent both girls off to the bathroom to take them. "Do you think that Lori got pregnant?"

"No."

"You think Judy is pregnant?"

"I hope the hell not."

"Okay, help me out here. Just what the hell is going on?"

"Electra complex!"

Sam was sitting on the smoker's bench outside her office building in Los Angeles. Jim had been watching her from his window several stories above but wasn't moving. There was a knock on his door, and Cindy came in smiling and asked, "So, early dinner or late lunch?"

"Early dinner."

"Where's Sam?" Jim pointed out the window, and Cindy walked up next to him and asked, "How is she doing?"

"Better. We had a hell of a night. One of those nights that most people only experience in a nightmare."

Cindy didn't look away from Sam sitting on the bench as she asked Jim, "How long have you been involved with the Iron Eagle?"

Jim just shrugged. "Years and years. I knew him when he was just a fledgling killer trying to get his legs."

"Yet you help him and don't arrest him?"

"That's right."

"You feel he does that much good?"

"Cindy, if you knew half the shit that I have seen and experienced since I started helping the Eagle, if you could even imagine the number of lives saved by the actions of that single man, you wouldn't even be asking the question."

"I have no doubt about all of that. I'm just trying to understand how a man who took an oath to uphold the law supports a man who breaks it."

He looked into her eyes and said, "Let me make something perfectly clear. I have upheld the rule of law my entire career. I have seen more monsters escape adjudication on technicalities in law only to see them back in custody after wreaking more havoc and destroying more lives because they were squeezed through the hole of reasonable doubt, or a technicality or defect in the law that allowed them to walk free only to do worse. The Iron Eagle is a serious, diligent, and impartial adjudicator. No innocent person has ever suffered at his hand, and many, many monsters have been removed from society and paid the ultimate and legitimate price for their crimes."

"And the rights of criminals?"

"The rights of criminals?" Jim pulled a cigarette from his top left pocket, lit it, and snapped his Zippo closed loudly for effect. "My dear, there are people whose crimes are so heinous, so outside the box, that they waved their constitutional rights when they started their cruelty. Enter the Eagle. He has no mercy for these monsters. He has proven their guilt far beyond a reasonable doubt, and he has thoroughly interrogated them. The Eagle takes his job as judge, jury, and executioner seriously. And while you and some of the world might see his punishments as barbaric, the world rarely knows the whole truth behind what these people have done. Do you remember the Joling Farms situation? Humans farming humans and selling them as organic meat?" Cindy nodded slowly. "You only know what you read in the paper or saw on the news about that case. I was on that scene firsthand. I was working with the Eagle directly to figure out what the hell was happening to these seemingly young healthy people, and the Eagle uncovered a murder spree so grotesque even the most seasoned horror writer couldn't have invented such a tragedy. Then there was the thwarted high school rampage. You read about that in the papers, right?"

"Yes."

"I was there with the Eagle, helping him save hundreds of kids' lives while almost losing my own. I have seen the Eagle shot, stabbed, and beaten, but he moves on protecting people from monsters. Ninety-nine percent of the time the world doesn't know the half of it, and last night was no exception. The world will never know the full extent of what happened at the Masters mansion. They won't know about the background story. This will be the headline and the story, *'FBI and Sheriff's Department Break Up Human Trafficking Ring; Film at Eleven.'* And what you will see is a bunch of FBI agents and sheriff's department deputies walking around with brown paper bags, maybe a black body bag, but that's it. What you won't see, what the world won't see or ever know is what we saw, what the Eagle saw, what the victims endured, the ones lucky enough to have survived, and, hell, they might not be lucky at that." Cindy was quiet, and Jim turned to the window to see that Sam was gone. There was a light tap on his office door, and she was standing there. "How long have you been there?"

"Long enough. What Jim is telling you, Cindy, is what I will tell you. I know who the Eagle is as well, and I would protect him with my life. Rarely does the world have an unselfish hero, a man who puts his life on the line every day in the service of protecting the people of Los Angeles, the state, even the nation. He asks for no accolades; he seeks no attention for his deeds. The man behind the mask is a sweet, caring, loving, humble man who risks his life to save others while asking nothing in return."

Cindy had tears in her eyes. "You speak of him as if you love him."

Sam laughed. "Oh shit, Cindy. I have loved him, hated him, even despised him through the time I have known him, but even through all my emotional ups and downs he has stood firmly by me. What I witnessed last night was horrific yet humbling, and in the end, he saved countless lives directly and indirectly, and in the process saved two children and took them under his wing for safety."

"He sounds like an incredible man."

"He is Cindy. He truly is."

John had texted Sara to let her know he would be coming home and to make sure to inject both girls before he got in. Judy and Lori came back together, and Judy was leaning on Lori with a shocked look on her face. Karen shook her head, "No... no!"

"Yes."

"Jesus Christ."

Lori looked at Sara and Karen and said, "Well, I have one, too, and I'm supposed to be sterilized."

Both women looked on in stunned silence. Karen leaned over to Sara and whispered, "Can your memory wash get rid of fetuses?"

"No, but it will cause serious birth defects, and I have been instructed to give them the drug now." Karen sat back, and the two girls sat down.

Lori wasted no time. "You're a doctor, right Sara?" She paused. "I don't know your last name."

"It's not important. I'm a doctor."

"Then you can remove this parasite from my body, right?"

"Yes, I can do it right now."

Karen looked at Judy, "You need to rid yourself of yours."

"I can't without talking to its father first."

Karen shook her head. "Its father is your father."

Sara was sipping her coffee as Karen spoke and started choking on her beverage while spitting it out. "WHAT? Judy is pregnant by Mark?"

"Yes. She raped her father."

"She did WHAT?"

"She drugged and raped her father; fortunately, it has only been a few days, so a simple D&C will resolve it."

"I can't abort a child that Mark and I conceived."

"You told me that your father is unaware that you two had sex."

"He is unaware; at least, I think so."

Sara spoke up. "Judy, do you have any idea of the legal implications for you and your father, mostly your father, if you are found to be carrying his child?" Judy shook her head. "It's called incest, Judy, and it is illegal. Your father could go to prison, and you could be forced to give up the child even if you carry it to term. The risks of genetic abnormalities are huge; it is also a first-degree relative. You do know it's wrong, right?"

"I just feel that I should at least tell Mark that I'm pregnant with his child."

Lori asked, "Why do you want to hurt your father?"

"I don't want to hurt him. I love him."

"No. If you loved him, you would never have done what you did. Karen explained the Electra complex on the way here. You obviously have it, and you have already broken every taboo known to man except giving birth to your own brother or sister. You do get that not only would you and your father be the parents of the child, that even if the kid is perfectly normal your father will be both your father and the kid's father and grandfather, and you will be both mother and sister to it. That's some twisted shit. You will get over your complex as Karen has pointed out, but if you get over that complex and you are the mother of your father's child, it will fuck up your life even more than it already is." Judy was seated firmly in a chair, and Lori stood up and asked Sara to help her with the pregnancy.

Sara walked Lori to operating room one and started an IV. There were several syringes on a small steel table and one had a pale greenish blue liquid and the other a pale yellow. Lori stripped and got on the operating table, put her feet in the stirrups, and asked, "Which one of those needles has the mind drug?"

"The light yellow one. Are you scared?"

"A little. I don't want to lose myself or what I have been through."

"That won't happen."

"Then what will it do?"

"It will wipe out your short-term memory about the last thirty-six hours. You will, unfortunately, retain all of what you went through. I can't take that away." Sara rubbed some gel on Lori's abdomen and then ran an ultrasound unit over it and looked at the screen until the fetus came into view. She turned the monitor, so Lori could see it, and she laid her head back on the gurney and said in a sad voice, "It's so sad. I have to kill a life because I was raped, but I'm not ready to be a parent." She paused and looked at Sara with tears in her eyes, "This won't keep me from having children in the future, will it?"

"The procedure? No; however, you have a lot of damage in there. Only half a uterus. I'm amazed that you are pregnant at all. Given the size of the fetus, you are about four months along, and while the uterus is remarkably flexible, I doubt that you would carry this baby to term." Lori nodded as Sara went to work. It only took fifteen minutes, and Sara talked to Lori the whole time. When she was finished, Sara looked at her and asked, "Are you ready?"

"Will I fall asleep?"

"Yes."

"Who will watch over me?"

"I will."

"What happens after that?"

"You're a damn smart young woman, and I know a couple who are doctors who love children and who I think would love to adopt you."

"How well do you know them?"

"They were Doctor Mantel's adopted parents, so…very well."

"You mean I would become Karen's sister?"

"If they agree to adopt you and you agree to be theirs, then yes. You two would be stepsisters."

Lori smiled and let her head rest. "I'm ready." Sara gave her the first injection, and Lori went right to sleep. She gave her the second as John walked into the operating room.

"How did it go?"

"It's been one hell of a morning. I just did a D&C on Lori. She was pregnant, and I gave her the medications. She was a little stressed out, but I think she will be okay. I'm going to call Liz Faber and tell her about Lori to see if they are interested in adopting her. I want to handle it between us."

"So, you want to keep child protective services out of it?"

"She's been through enough."

"And if Liz and Nick don't want to adopt her?" John was standing tall over Sara.

"They will. They have to."

"And if they don't?"

"We can't let her end up back in the system, John."

"Sara, we have talked about this. No kids."

"She's fifteen, almost sixteen. She's as smart as hell and with the right environment and education we could have another Jessica."

"We don't have the life for this." Sara walked out of the operating room with her cellphone in her hand. John watched her leave then looked down at Lori sleeping peacefully and ran his hand over her forehead and hair. "Jesus, kid! How the hell did you endure such torture?"

Karen was sitting with Judy when Sara appeared and asked to speak to her. Karen nodded and told Judy to stay off the phone. Karen followed Sara into the main house, and Sara asked her to sit. "What's up?"

"I'm going to call your mother."

"What did I do wrong?"

The two laughed. "I'm going to ask your mother and father to adopt Lori." Karen looked on. "Do you think they will adopt her?"

"My mom and dad are getting old. My father wants to retire in two years."

"And Lori will be eighteen in two years. This is not a long-term gig."

Karen shook her head. "Parenting is not a gig. It's a life changing commitment, and that child is yours for the rest of your life. My mother is much younger than my father, so she is working and taking care of the last foster child they took in after me. They haven't been active on the registry other than as short-term emergency parents for several years."

Sara started crying. "I can't let her go back into the system, Karen. She has so much promise. She's so intelligent and composed. She reminds me so much of Jessica when Jim got her off the streets. The way she matured. Look at her today."

"What about you and John?"

"There is no way we can do it, Karen. Look at this life we have. For Christ's sake, John's the Iron Eagle. He kills people in the lair. He metes out justice, and neither one of us are ever home. There's no way."

"Have you asked him?"

"Yes…and he reminded me of everything I just told you." Karen sat back in her chair and asked if there was coffee. Sara got up and made a pot, and Karen went and got Judy and brought her into the kitchen with them. Sara's face was streaked with tears, and Judy asked what was going on. Sara poured three cups of coffee and sat down. "We're talking about Lori," said Sara.

"What about her?"

"She needs a home, Judy, and we are trying to find her one."

"I see, well, you both know that Sally's sister Casey is an orphan now, right?" All heads nodded, "And I have made a damn mess of everything."

Karen shook her head. "You didn't make a mess of everything. You were protecting yourself and your sister, and, in a twisted way, your father."

"I'm a murderer." The words had just come out of her mouth when John entered the kitchen. Judy shuddered at his huge frame and the muscles protruding through the T-shirt he was wearing. "Are you a body builder, Agent Swenson?"

"Yes, I am, Ms. Bench. You are correct. You have made a mess of things. I don't know the details of this conversation, but I have a feeling that I'm not going to like it. Lori is out and will be until tomorrow."

Judy looked at John. "The drug lasts that long in the system?"

"Yes, it does, now you need your dose, and you don't have it, so does someone want to tell me why?" The conversation went on for nearly an hour. John listened carefully to every word from Judy as well as Sara and Karen.

When they were finished talking, Judy asked, "Why is this drug needed and how do you know about it, Agent Swenson? It was the Iron Eagle who ordered it."

"I am friends with the Eagle. I help him out, but that isn't important. You need to abort the baby, and you and I need to have a conversation with your father."

Karen spoke up, "Not one of those conversations, John."

"The drugs you gave your father with the wine might have impaired his judgment. He might have even had the type of experience that you speak of, but somewhere deep inside he knew it was you. Now, I have a responsibility as an FBI agent to report incest and the fact that you have been impregnated by your father raises the stakes of your safety and the safety of your sister."

Karen spoke up. "John, have you ever heard of an Electra complex?"

"Yes."

"That's what this is. I'm the expert in this area, not you. You're not going to do anything. Judy is going to abort. She is not going to tell her father anything, and she is going to take the medication that Sara is going to give her that will wipe out nearly three days of memory, then she will remain under my care." Karen was firm and unbending in her tone.

"It's the law, Karen."

"Do you really want to go there, John?" John's face softened, and he shook his head.

"Now, as to a bigger issue at the moment, Lori needs a family. She is also going to need therapy, and it won't be short-term. Sara wants to ask my parents to adopt her, but that is unlikely given my father's age and my mother's desire to work. Neither me nor Sara want her placed in the child welfare and foster system, and I agree she would not do well. I think we need to make her care a communal approach."

"It takes a village to raise a child?" John asked.

"Why not? There are four groups of people who could parent and assist Lori. You and Sara, me and Chris, Jim and Cindy, and Jade and Jessica."

"And where will she live?"

"You two have four or five guest houses just sitting empty. You have a staff that you don't really use. She can live here. We'll all take turns spending weekends with her, and she will be home schooled, and we will have a nanny-type person to assist her. You have maids, a chef, and the rest of the house staff, right?" Sara nodded. "So you really don't have to be hands on. Plus, Lori is a strong, smart independent young woman. I want to test her IQ, and I want to have some other academic testing done to see where she is at in the education process. I think she is very advanced. With the right guidance, she could be through the university system before she's twenty."

John shook his head. "We don't have the time or the right environment for a child."

"She's not a damn child; she's practically an adult. She isn't going to need to be bottle fed, for God's sake. You two can give the girl a place to live and food to eat while Chris and I and the others work with her."

Sara was nodding. John was silent, and Judy asked, "What if Lori comes to live with me and my family?"

Karen shook her head. "Bad idea. You have enough shit going on, and your father doesn't need another gorgeous teenager under his roof, especially one that's not blood. That's a recipe for disaster."

"Well, Lori and I really connected. I think that we should at least talk to my father about it. I mean, we are nearly the same age. We will both be out of the house before my little sister starts high school, and we both need therapy that you are going to provide."

John was still shaking his head. Karen looked at him and asked, "Do you want to be a parent?"

"No, but you're asking to put a young teen into a home where incest has already taken place. Mark is a handsome and successful man, the perfect target for sexual deviance. You have to deal with Judy and her complex. You're not putting Lori into that environment."

Sara stood up and told Judy to follow her. Karen stood and said, "Why don't we all meet at Santiago's tonight and talk it over? Both of these girls are going to be out for twenty-four hours. I think we can work it out in that time." They agreed, and Karen followed Judy and Sara into operating room number two.

"So, I'm giving up this baby?"

"Yes, Judy, you are."

CHAPTER TWENTY-FOUR

"Life's not fair, Sara."

Mark Bench was in his office at Northridge when he received a call from Sara that she wanted to meet with him later in the afternoon. He called his assistant and told her that he was going to be out of the office and to manage the affairs of the lab. He called Judy's cellphone only to get voicemail, and he also called the sheriff's department as well as the FBI only to be stonewalled. His office phone rang, and Tabitha was on the other end of the line. "Hi, Dad. Have you heard from Judy?"

"I did early this morning but not so far today."

"Is she okay?"

"Of course, she is honey. Don't worry."

"I was asleep in her bed last night, and she and another girl were in the bathroom showering and getting clothes out of the closet and talking quietly."

"What were they talking about?"

"I only caught bits and pieces, but you were part of the conversation."

"Really? What was said about me?"

"I'm not sure. Something to do with sex."

Lori and Judy had been placed in one of the Eagle's visitor rooms, and both were asleep. John walked in to check on the two girls, and Sara was sitting between them as they both rested. "How much drug did you give them?"

"They won't remember much from at least the past three to four days."

"Dream state?"

"Of sorts, not as vivid and not explainable. I know you were in with Lori after I sedated her." John nodded. "Having second thoughts?"

"I never had first thoughts, Sara. Our agreement is our agreement. No children."

"That's not fair, John."

"Life's not fair, Sara."

Karen was on a conference call with her mother and father, "I know it is a lot to ask, but she needs a family."

Emily spoke up, "You know that we won't say no to you, Karen. If you feel we are the best fit for Lori, we will take her in and love her as we loved all of our kids."

Nicolas chimed in next, "We can take a few more years to help this child out. Is she as brilliant as you?"

"I think even more so. I haven't tested her, but if you consider all I went through from age three to eleven when I was saved by the Eagle, what Lori has endured makes my time seem like I was in preschool."

Emily laughed, "You were in your own nightmare. You're just many years removed from it. When can we meet Lori?"

"Sara is caring for her right now, but I would say tomorrow afternoon."

"Okay, your father is heading out for a conference in a few days, so I would like us to meet her together. If it looks good, then we will give her your old room, and you can come over to the house and walk her through the house rules."

"Sounds good, thank you both. You're really doing something extraordinary for a wonderful young woman."

Karen hung up and texted Sara. *"My mother and father will take Lori. She has a permanent home."*

Sara was still sitting between the girls as she read the message. She looked up at John and said, "You're right. Life's not fair, but the Fabers are going to take Lori."

"That's good. She deserves a good home."

Jim was sitting back in his chair with a cigarette in one hand and a bottle of beer in the other. Sam was smoking and drinking a beer as well, and Jim asked, "So, what the fuck are you going to do now?"

"Work. It's been my life. The condo is Maria's, so I will put it up for sale and move back to my apartment."

"Oh, now you can't do that. You've had enough of a shit show over the past month."

"Well, what the fuck do you suggest?"

"Look, I own three acres in Malibu. Before Barbara died we had talked about building a guest house on part of it. I mean, shit, I didn't want neighbors, so Barb and I built our house in the middle of the goddamn property, and I subdivided the lots. The plans are finished for the house. We just never got around to building it. When Barbara got sick, all of our attention went to that."

"Okay, but I don't understand."

Jim cracked open another beer and yelled out to Javier to bring him another bucket. "You don't have to be an asshole, Jim," Cindy's voice was clear behind him.

"How the fuck long have you been here?"

"Long enough to hear you speak rudely to Javier." Cindy took the bucket from the old man and kissed him on the cheek.

Javier smiled. "You ever mistreat Cindy, she mine," the old man said laughing as he walked away.

Sam had finished off her beer, and Cindy handed her another as Jim lit a cigarette and handed it to her. "I didn't know you smoked," Sam said.

"I gave it up decades ago, but as soon as Jim came back into my life after Kevin's murder I started up again."

"Jim, you're a goddamned bad influence on everyone you come in contact with."

"No, he isn't. I don't smoke like him; now and then is all. So, what are we talking about?"

"The guesthouse," said Jim. Cindy nodded taking a hit off her cigarette and taking the open beer that Jim had handed to her.

Sam was leaning on the table as she responded, "It's a kind gesture, Jim, but I don't think it is a good idea."

"Why not?" Cindy asked.

"We work together; we see each other practically twenty-four-seven. But being neighbors? Besides, I don't have the type of cash it would take to build a house on the beach."

Jim laughed. "You're not going to pay for it. I'm going to have it built, and you will live in it for tax purposes."

"So, do I pay you rent? I do need write offs, Jim. I make money, too."

"I'm aware. I'm not that nice of a guy. We will work out a land contract, so you can buy the home from me. The property taxes will be high, so we will have to work out an impound agreement, and you will pay your mortgage to me each month and get a write off and a hell of a view."

"Do I get to look at the plans and make changes before you break ground?"

Cindy laughed, saying, "Of course, you do. It's your home, and you won't be really close as a neighbor. I have seen the plans, and the house will be over an acre away from Jim's home, so we won't see each other unless we want to." Jim said nothing. He was just sitting back in his chair looking out at the sun as it was beginning to set.

Sam got a little misty. "I don't know what to say."

"Jesus Christ, woman. Say yes. Come back to the house and look at the plans, so I can get a crew going on building the goddamned thing."

Sam looked at Cindy then Jim. "Yes."

John and Sara were sitting in their living room when Mark Bench was announced. Mark was shown in, and Sara greeted him as John offered him a drink. "Water would be great." John grabbed two bottles and handed one to Mark and invited him to sit. "So, why am I at your home, Sara?"

"John and I wanted to speak to you in a private environment."

"Okay. Where's Judy?"

"Sleeping. She had a very traumatic night."

"What happened?"

"She got caught up in a human slave ring, Mr. Bench," John said flatly.

"I'm sorry? A what?"

"Human slave ring that was being run by your friend Mary Owen."

"Mary Owen ran a human slave ring? I don't think so."

"We call them human trafficking rings, and she, indeed, ran one along with several other people."

"And my daughter was a victim?"

"Close. She was being indoctrinated but figured it out."

"Figured it out? Would you care to elaborate on that?"

"No."

Sara was still, and Mark looked at her. "What do you know of this?"

"Enough to tell you that it is all true and is hitting the media as we speak, and that Judy saved many lives."

"How did she do that?"

"She got on the radar of the Iron Eagle," John said.

"The Iron Eagle? The serial killer?" John nodded. "The Eagle was trying to kill my daughter?"

"From what we understand based on the evidence he left, she was a target but led him to the true perpetrators of the crimes."

"The Eagle kills people."

"Yes."

"What happened to Mary?"

"Dead."

"Dead?"

"I don't like to repeat myself. She's dead along with several of those close to her and involved in the ring."

"So, Sally and Candice are orphans?"

"Sally is dead as well."

"What? The Eagle murdered a seventeen-year-old girl?"

"We don't know who killed her. All we know is she is dead."

"Where's Candice?"

"With child protective services."

"Well, that can't be. She will come and live with me and my daughters. She is not going to be left in the hands of strangers."

"Judy has told us about a situation that occurred in your home a few nights ago. A sexual situation," John said.

Mark got more animated. "I'm sorry. Just what are you implying?"

"I'm not implying anything. Did you have a sexual relationship with a woman at your home in the past three days?"

"Yes."

"Tell me about it."

"It's none of your damned business, John."

"Well, I don't know that yet, Mark, and believe me you want to have this conversation informally with me here in my home and not in an interrogation room at my office."

"I had sex with Mary Owen at my home."

"Were you and Mary a couple?"

"No. Our spouses worked and died together. We were close."

"I see. Have you ever had romantic feelings toward your daughters?"

"What the hell kind of question is that?"

"A valid one. Answer, please."

"Of course not! They're my children."

Sara asked calmly, "Judy has told us that you had a bit too much wine a few nights ago and that the next morning you seemed confused about the sex and that you thought you had made love to your late wife."

"I did have wine, and I did have a strange experience, but it was Mary I was with."

"Judy tells us that you keep the memory of your late wife alive and well in your bedroom."

"I loved my wife, and I miss her every day. I keep many items of hers where they were the last time she touched them. Is that a crime?"

"No, no," John said. "But sometimes feelings get misplaced and things get confusing, and if you compound that with drugs or alcohol, it can be a problem."

"I don't do drugs."

Sara was sitting on the edge of a small loveseat. John was sitting in a straight back chair. He looked at Sara and said, "We have to tell him everything we know." Sara shook her head, and Mark looked at the two of them.

"Look, if there is something that has happened I need to know about it. I can't deal with something if I don't know about it."

Sara took a deep breath. "Judy drugged and raped you." Mark sat with his mouth open then shook his head a few times. "Judy suffers from a relatively common syndrome called the Electra complex. Are you familiar with it?"

"It's the female version of the Oedipus complex."

John leaned in and asked, "And you know about this complex how?"

"After my wife's death, the three of us went to counseling for nearly a year. We had family and individual sessions. In private sessions, my therapist brought it up based on some of the behavior that Judy was exhibiting. I saw it as merely being protective of me, and I have no sexual feelings toward my daughter. The therapist told me she would grow out of it. I mean, Judy was seven, and her sister was not even a year old. It seemed to ease over time, and I really never saw issues. But Karen started seeing Judy a few weeks ago, and she also told me that she felt that Judy might be suffering from the complex and that I should be careful." John nodded. Mark continued, "But how careful could I be? I mean, I was watchful of her behavior. She did have a few strange nights this week."

"Strange how?" John asked.

"Well, a couple of nights ago she had been out for ice cream at a local parlor in our neighborhood. She came home late and ran straight into the shower in my bedroom and when she came out of the bathroom she came out nude and got into bed with me and fell straight to sleep."

"Were you nude?"

"No. I was wearing pajamas."

"Is this something that Judy has done in the past?" John asked.

"We are an open house. We talk about everything, and nudity is not taboo. It never has been. Both of my daughters sleep with me. Sometimes, it is a bad dream that brings them into my room. Other times they are just scared or sad. Tabitha, that's my youngest, doesn't remember anything about her mother, but she sleeps with me all the time. Judy off and on but I will admit that that night was strange."

"How so?"

"She was scared. She was trembling under the covers. She wasn't cold; she was afraid. I didn't understand it, but I knew she was going through a lot of things after the issues with Sally. I just chalked it up to that and nothing more was said about it."

Sara had been listening and finally spoke up, "Judy drugged you, Mark." There was dead silence. "Judy has admitted to drugging you with a high dose of Ecstasy in your wine then seducing you. I saw that you pulled samples of your own blood and sent it through the lab at Mayo. I intercepted the results. So that tells me that even you knew something was wrong." Mark didn't respond. "Judy was pregnant, Mark, by you."

"Was?"

"Was. The fetus was aborted by me with her permission, and to be honest I didn't want this brought up, but John being an FBI agent and learning of the situation felt that he had to move to protect not just your children but you. Judy has been through a lot, a lot of things that neither John nor I can discuss. However, I have the aborted fetus, and I can DNA match it to you and Judy. You can hire a lawyer if you wish, but that is only going to make this whole situation worse."

"But...Mary, even Judy told me it was Mary."

"Judy manipulated both you and Mary. Mary needed an alibi, and Judy unwittingly provided it. Mary was nowhere near your home or her own on that night. She was dealing in human cruelty, even Judy didn't know that at the time. Judy handed Mary an alibi, which she grabbed, and had it not been for me insisting on a pregnancy test from Judy you could very well have become the father in incest."

Mark's face lost all color, and he began to heave. John opened the French doors to the deck. "Head that way, please. We don't want your vomit on our floor." Mark ran out and as he threw up Sara turned to John and asked, "So, do you think Mark is a threat to his children?" John shook his head and said no.

CHAPTER TWENTY-FIVE

*"So, people are getting
away with murder?"*

"What happens now?" Jim asked of all at John and Sara's home. Cindy was in the hot tub with Jessica, Jade, and Sam. Sara had stripped and was getting ready to enter after opening two bottles of wine as Karen was walking a tray of glasses over to the tub nude as well. John and Chris were seated on the deck drinking glasses of wine poured by Sara.

John looked at Jim, who was in his boxer shorts, and said "We wait."

"We fuckin' wait? Wait for what? A murder, another incest, some kid going off their nut because of their childhood trauma? What exactly is it that we are waiting for?"

Sara had slid down into the water along with Karen and all of the women were sharing bottles of wine and chatting. John was stretched out on a chaise lounge as was Chris. Both men were nude and had steam rising off their warm bodies against the cool night air. The surf was crashing loudly on the beach below, and John spoke loudly, "We wait for the next shoe to drop."

Jim shook his head and poured himself another glass of scotch and sat down in a lounge chair across from the whole group. "You act like you're all on spring break. The Bench kid is home with her father; the Fleming girl is with the Fabers. I just learned this afternoon from Anita that she has approved the temporary placement of the Owen girl with Mark Bench. Have you all lost your minds?"

Karen spoke up. "I don't think so, Jim, but outside of what has been done what would you do differently?"

"I don't fuckin' know, but shit, Judy Bench and Lori Fleming are killers. Killing to the general public is like what happens when a wild animal bites a human. They now have the taste for human flesh, so they get put down."

John sat up on his lounge. "Are you suggesting that those two girls need to be killed?"

"No, no. Fuck. I don't know. You're the goddamned murder expert. You're the fuckin' Iron Eagle. You tell me. Do they have the taste for killing, and do you think that they will repeat their offenses?"

"I have no answer to that question, Jim. I understand human nature well. I understand killers and their patterns. These two girls did not seek out victims. They did not look to harm innocent people. They went after their abusers. That's human nature. Who the hell can understand the mind of a teenager?"

"You, of all people, or did you forget the thwarted rampage of not so many years ago?"

"Those kids had an ax to grind, and if you remember, they basically took each other out. We did our job and stopped an attack. I don't see that behavior in Bench or Fleming. If anything, I see bright futures for the both of them. Karen and Cindy are going to be monitoring and treating both with therapy. They know what they are doing. The Owen child is in a better place with Mark Bench than being thrown into the system, which to spite the best efforts of Anita Bandon is a broken system that allows too many children to be used and exploited. I can't fix the whole system, Jim. I wish I could. I can only treat the symptoms. I have no control over the disease."

Cindy stood up and stepped out of the hot tub, walked over to John, and extended her hand. John took it, and she shook it firmly. "So, we meet at last, Mr. Eagle." Cindy got back into the tub as all sat silent. Cindy continued, "Jim told me he knew the Eagle, and here I am in his presence." There was silence. "I know of your exploits and according to Jim I don't know even the remotest part of the people you have saved and the savageness that you have stopped. I do, however, know that those closest to you, John, are so goddamned loyal it is incredible. Sam speaks of you passionately as do Jim and Karen. You have the best in medical staff for friends and loved ones. I feel comfortable that you're no psychopath."

"How do you feel about being let in on my secret?"

"Relieved."

"Really?"

"Yes. I suspected you were the Eagle for some time after meeting you. Jimmy has been so cryptic since we came together. Secret texts, late night meetings and calls, but I had a feeling you were the Eagle after Kevin's murder. Your passion to protect Jim and your tenacity at finding his killers. And knowing how they…met their ends…now knowing for certain that it is you, I can sleep better at night."

Karen laughed. "Knowing John is the Iron Eagle is going to allow you to sleep better?"

"Yes. I know that if Jim is working with the Eagle, he will do everything in his power to keep him safe." There was a pregnant pause, and then the whole group burst out in laughter. Jim was bent over a railing laughing so hard he threw up. John and Chris were sitting over the sides of their chairs laughing, and the girls were all doubled over and standing in the hot tub. "Did I say something funny?" Jim couldn't get his breath to speak.

Chris pulled it together long enough to say, "Don't worry, Cindy, when we are working with the Eagle, we are all safe!" That just brought even more laughter that lasted for a good fifteen minutes.

MASQUERADE

The Iron Eagle Series: Book Twenty-Three

PROLOGUE

Saul Olsen was sitting on a bench on the Santa Monica pier watching the people on the fairway near the Ferris wheel. Several children were trying to make the large umbrella covered gondolas swing, and he smiled at the sight. Young families were walking the pier, and a father was trying to corral two boys under five while the mother pushed a double stroller with two newborns in it. One of the boys ended up falling right at Saul's feet, and he helped the boy up as his father came running over.

"I'm so sorry," the man said.

"It's not a problem. Don't you wish you could bottle that energy and sell it? You would make a fortune."

The young man smiled as his wife approached. "Joey and Phillip, stop it right now." The young woman was pleasant and attractive, and she smiled at Saul, and he smiled back.

"You seem to have your hands full."

"Indeed, we do." It was mid-afternoon, and Saul had staked out a spot on a bench that had shade over it. "May I sit for a moment?"

"Of course, of course. How rude of me." Saul remained seated, and the young woman sat down and looked at her husband and asked, "Phillip, we could all use a cold drink and a bite to eat."

Saul laughed. "Phillip senior?"

The young father laughed. "Yes, this is Phillip junior and his brother Joey. The little ones are Tyler and Stephanie. We're the Simmons family."

"Well, it is nice to meet you all."

The young woman sat for a moment and then put out her hand. "I'm Beatrice; they call me B for short."

"Well, it's nice to meet you."

Phillip looked down next to Saul and saw a four-pronged cane. "Did you injure yourself…Mr.…"

"Oh, I'm sorry. Saul, Saul Olsen. No, no, I didn't. I have been having a bit of trouble getting around."

B looked down at the cane then at Philip and said, "Mr. Olsen has been quite patient. We should ask him to join us for lunch."

Saul smiled, and Phillip asked, "Would you care to join us?"

"That would be nice. Thank you. What are you planning to eat?"

"Our budget is a bit tight. Perhaps we will split some burgers and fries."

Saul stood up with the help of his cane. "Oh, now, don't be silly. I will buy anything that you like. There are two tables over there. B, why don't you grab those, and Phillip and I will go get some food. Just let us know what you would like. My treat."

The boys were jumping all over as Phillip and Saul went to one of the larger vendors and bought food and drinks. Once everyone was seated, the boys fell silent as they ate their meal, and Phillip said, "Thank you for the food, Saul. It is appreciated."

"You are most welcome. So, what do you do for a living?"

"I'm a youth pastor at a church here in Santa Monica. B teaches Sunday School, but as you can see, she has her hands full with the children."

"Oh really. What denomination?"

"We have a non-denominational church on Santa Monica Boulevard."

"Does it have a name?"

"We are working on that. The senior pastor just opened it two weeks ago. I took the job on faith after a lot of prayer."

Saul took a bite of his burger and said, "I see."

"Are you a man of faith, Mr. Olsen?"

"Saul, please call me Saul. No…no. I'm not, Phillip. I'm a man of logic and science."

"I see. What do you do for a living?"

"I'm an astrophysicist at JPL in Pasadena."

"I do enjoy the study of the heavens," said B as Phillip nodded.

"So, you took a break from work to spend some time with the family?"

"You would think that being together as much as we are we would see a lot of each other, but we don't. The pastor is undecided on the direction of this new church. We receive only low wages as we have a small flock that is just as confused as others in our small congregation about not only our name but the core source of our mission. It takes a toll. On top of that, our parsonage is a small one-bedroom apartment in a less than desirable part of Santa Monica. As you can imagine, it's just a wee bit crowded."

Saul laughed. "I would think overly crowded."

The boys had finished their meals and spotted a group of clowns dancing and making balloon animals and asked if they could go watch. B was breast feeding one of the babies as the other began to fuss, and Phillip looked at her longingly, and she smiled and said, "Take the boys to see the entertainers. We will be fine. Besides, I have Saul to help me." Phillip took off after the boys, who were already in the mix with the clowns. B was trying to be discreet as she changed breasts, but her triple D breast fell out of her nursing bra as she tried to switch sides, and she blushed as Saul tried not to look at it but couldn't resist. "I'm sorry, Saul. I'm a bit clumsy today. It must be the heat."

"No problem. It's not the first breast that I have seen." B worked to put it back in the bra and asked Saul for help with the child, who he put back in the stroller as she reached for the other who latched on to the breast for dear life.

"May I ask why you have the cane?"

Saul's eyes looked down at the pavement then to the sky. He was tearing up and said, "Um…it is helping me deal with the unacceptable."

"I see. You look quite young."

"I will be thirty-five in two weeks."

"So, if you don't mind me asking, what is unacceptable?"

"A diagnosis." He took a deep breath and said, "I was recently diagnosed with Amyotrophic Lateral Sclerosis, also known as ALS or Lou Gehrig's disease."

B fell silent as did the baby in the stroller. There were several seconds of awkward silence when a clown suddenly appeared in front of the two of them. B smiled as the character leaned down into the stroller and mimed some baby faces and blew up two balloon animals and handed them to her and Saul. She stopped for just a moment and then realized she had lost sight of Phillip. "Saul, do you see Phillip and the boys?"

Saul looked around as the clown kept dancing in front of them, obstructing their view. Saul asked politely for the clown to stop, but it persisted, and he tried to move the large person out of his line of sight and said, "I don't see them, B." He stood, and the clown stepped back, and B called out to Phillip and the boys, but there was no response. "You sit here. I will go see if I can find them." The clown continued dancing and making noises with a small horn and a bell. Saul tried to push his way through the throngs of people throwing money on the ground at the entertainers while calling out Phillip's name, but there was no response or sign of them. He turned back to the bench to see the stroller in its spot, but B was gone. He walked back over to find the empty stroller and no sign of the family. He called out and asked around as people walked by, but no one had seen anything. He had shaded his eyes looking around the pier when he caught sight of the clown that had been pestering them walking down the stairs holding B's hand. She had one child in her arms, and the clown had another in its arms. Saul watched for several seconds and then started to follow the four. The stairs slowed him down, but he kept an eye on them until they disappeared under the pier.

Saul tried to make his way through the sand to the spot he last saw B and the children, but he fell in the sand and laid on his stomach for a few moments in the late afternoon sun. His face was in the sand when he heard a voice, "It's low tide. Don't you want to come under the pier. It's much cooler under there." The voice was calm yet annoying.

"I have ALS." He felt someone grab his shoulders, and he was being pulled face down under the pier. "Who are you? Where's the Simmons family?"

"There is only one way to find out."

"I don't understand."

"You will, Mr. Olsen. You will."

It was late afternoon, and people were gathering around the pier for their evening photo shoots after high tide. There were several models in swimsuits dotting the sand, and photographers calling out instructions as they waited for the waters to recede, so they could get their subjects near the pylons of the pier. There were nearly a half dozen people dotting the landscape. A surfer had gotten caught in a small rip current that ended up taking him under the pier, and a nearby life guard who saw the event had come running across the sand. The lifeguard was at least a hundred yards from the surfer who was sitting on his board clinging to one of the pylons and waving. The lifeguard slowed from a run to a walk and waved back, putting both hands on his shoulders, a sign used by scuba divers and others to signal they were okay from a distance. The surfer didn't signal back; he kept waving his arms wildly, releasing his grip on the pylon and putting his hands over his mouth. The guard began to run again and as he got closer one of the women on the beach approached the guard and said, "There's a man on a surf board screaming to call 911."

"I am 911," said the lifeguard.

The young woman shook her head. "I don't think you're the 911 he's talking about." The lifeguard hit the water and began swimming out to where the surfer was. The water was only three feet deep, and he stood and started walking in the direction of the surfer.

"What the fuck is your problem, dude. It's low fuckin' tide. You can walk your board out from under there."

The surfer was screaming at the lifeguard, "For God's sake, call 911! There are dead people under there!"

Jade and Jessica were in wetsuits under the pier in about two feet of water. Five pylons had bodies strapped to them: four children and three adults. Jade was barking out orders when Jim and Sam arrived on scene. Jim was standing in the sand near the crime scene tape. "Why are Sam and I here, Jade? This is Santa Monica PD's jurisdiction."

Jade waded out of the water to where he and Sam were standing. "Jesus, Jim. We have two newborns, two toddlers, a female, and two males tied to the wooden pillars under the pier."

"Again, what does that have to do with us?"

"One of the dead is Saul Olsen."

Sam spoke up, "Saul Olsen? The astrophysicist from JPL? The guy who wrote that new bestseller on quantum dynamics?"

"Yes, and the people who are dead with him are a family from Santa Monica."

Jim took a cigarette out of his top left pocket, lit it, and asked, "And what makes that so strange?"

"The man and woman are husband and wife; they're pastors."

Jim's expression changed as did Sam's. "An atheist has been murdered with a religious family?"

"Uh, yeah."

Sam walked down to the water's edge and then in to where Jessica was. Jim watched as the two went deeper under the pier, and he looked at Jade and asked, "Wasn't that Olsen guy working on a federal project?"

"Yes. He's been working on a government project related to his book."

"So...was he being paid by JPL or was he working for the government?"

Jade shrugged. "I don't know. What difference does that make?"

"It's the difference between this being an interjurisdictional case between the sheriff's department and Santa Monica PD or a case that should be handled by the FBI."

Jade shook her head and said, "All I know is that whoever murdered this family and Olsen wasn't worried about their identities being discovered."

"Any visual trauma to the bodies?"

"No. All are clothed and tied to the beams with steel fishing line from their throats to the wrists and ankles wrapped around the pylons."

"There is no way that a single person could have done all of that to seven people without a fight."

"I agree, Jim, but there appears to be no sign of struggle at first glance nor does there appear to be trauma to their heads. I have never seen anything like it. I won't know more until I get them back to my lab, but right now this is one freaky ass case."

"Do we have any witnesses?"

"I don't know. SMPD has been talking to several dozen people, but the bodies are my area; the witnesses are yours." Jade handed Jim an evidence bag with the IDs of the dead. He opened it and pulled out Saul's and ran the strip on the back of the license through a card reader on his tablet. The screen on his tablet lit up with one simple flashing message on a black background in flashing red letters, *"Federal employee; access denied."* Jim pulled out his cellphone and called John, saying, "I have a murder case for you."

"How do you know it's mine?"

"I just scanned one of the victims' state issued drivers' licenses on my tablet, and it came back, 'Federal employee; access denied.'"

"Someone has locked the ID of a murder victim?"

"A federal employee, it would appear."

"Where is the body?"

"Attached to a pylon under the Santa Monica pier with a family of six."

"Who's the victim with the sealed ID?"

"A guy named Saul Olsen."

"Saul Olsen?"

"Yeah, you heard me."

"Shit, Jim. Who's on scene?"

"SMPD, Jade and her CSI team, and oddly enough Sam and me."

There were a few moments of silence, and John came back on the line, "I'm on my way. Get Jade, Jessica, and Sam, and get out of there."

"You want us to leave the scene of a crime?" Jim had gotten the last of the words out when black SUVs and vans were rolling up on the beach as well as the pier above him. Several black watercraft also came racing down the water's edge with people sitting on the edge of the boats dressed in black. The vans pulled down to the water's edge, and people in dive gear with regulators and tanks were entering the water and approaching the bodies. Jim could see Sam, Jade, Jessica, and all of the others being led out from under the pier, and the lights that had the crime scene lit up were all extinguished, leaving Jim in darkness. "What the fuck is going on, John?"

"Just get the hell out of there, Jim. All of you. Get the hell out of there."

About the Author

Roy A Teel Jr. is the author of several books, both nonfiction and fiction. He became disabled due to Progressive Multiple Sclerosis in 2011 and lives in Lake Arrowhead, CA with his wife, Tracy, their tabby cat, Oscar, and their Springer Spaniel, Sandy.